GRACE
in WINTER

Deirdre
Purcell

First published in 2019 by
HACHETTE BOOKS IRELAND
1

A CIP catalogue record for this title is available from the British Library

ISBN 978 1 47369 991 5

Cover design and typeset by www.redrattledesign.com

Printed and bound in Great Britain by Clays Ltd, Elcograf S.p.A.

Hachette Books Ireland policy is to use papers that are natural, renewable and recyclable products and made from wood grown in sustainable forests. The logging and manufacturing processes are expected to conform to the environmental regulations of the country of origin.

Hachette Books Ireland
8 Castlecourt Centre
Castleknock
Dublin 15, Ireland

A division of Hachette UK Ltd
Carmelite House
50 Victoria Embankment
London EC4Y 0DZ

www.hachettebooksireland.ie

For Declan and Mary
with gratitude and love

I

'What the hell?'

At half past two on Thursday, 1 November 2018, Grace McGee stood on the threshold of her kitchen, the contents of her bags-for-life spilling on to the floor and over her feet. She was staring at what her twenty-two-year-old daughter had visited on the room.

The intervals between these episodes were growing shorter.

She was sick of them.

In front of her, cupboard doors and drawers hung open. Their contents – cutlery, crockery, glasses, condiments, sauces – showed under a patchy rug of cornflakes, porridge oats, pasta and rice. Given the context, the primary colours of their boxes and bags seemed inappropriately merry.

In addition, the toaster dangled into empty air at the end of its cord, while the handle of the electric kettle protruded from a sinkful of water, its plug, like that of the toaster, still attached to a socket. On the floor, much of the crockery and glassware was in bits.

Struggling to find her mobile, she upended her handbag over the mess at her feet, retrieved it, then attempted to call her middle daughter, Jacqueline. Her fingers were shaking, though, making contact with the wrong buttons.

She knew better than to call her eldest, Adeline, unless it was a matter of life and death. What had happened here, although troubling, was hardly an emergency, merely a classic Leonie episode.

That her youngest's outbursts, while not insurmountable – so far – were increasing in frequency, was a worry. She herself was also, to use her daughters' vernacular, more and more pissed off that she'd been left alone to manage not just Leonie's episodes but Leonie. Very little help anywhere. To say she felt trapped was a serious understatement: she had forgotten what freedom might feel like.

With her daughter temporarily absent at a 'lunch with Dad' in town, Grace had been looking forward to a couple of hours' peace with the crossword, a cup of coffee – and even a clandestine doughnut.

Off the agenda now. Peace? What was that?

She gave up on the call and crunched across the kitchen floor to rescue the toaster. But what to do about the kettle? Wasn't it dangerous to touch an electrical appliance in water? Should she pull out its plug? Or was that dangerous too – hadn't people been killed that way? A thought struck her: had that been the plan?

Of course not. Nobody wants to murder you – you've been watching too much television, Grace . . .

She contemplated calling Harry, her ex-husband, nested cosily for the past seven and a half years with his second wife, Charlotte, known as Cherry, and their seven-year-old daughter, Jasmine, in a nice red-brick Victorian in Ranelagh (a far more fashionable address than that enjoyed by his former marital home here in Baldoyle). Having had lunch with Leonie, he could maybe shine a light on their youngest daughter's current mood.

But she gave up on the idea as quickly as it had occurred to her. This was just a clean-up job and she saved her Leonie-calls to Harry for situations she felt were beyond her. Her ex, though, while never overtly dismissive, usually made her feel that, in venting, she was interrupting something crucial to his life.

Skirting the worst of the mess, she fetched a dustpan and brush. Before she set to work, she picked up her phone again and managed to punch in the correct information.

The call went immediately to voicemail.

Fed up, holding the dustpan in one hand and the phone in the other, Leonie's mother flopped onto a kitchen chair, squinting myopically at the little screen as though willing it to light up.

Leonie had never before perpetrated anything quite on this scale in their home. There had been no shortage of explosive behaviour but that was par for the course. In the nearest equivalent to today's incident she'd taken a large number of empty glass bottles from the recycling box, spaced them carefully over the tiled floor in the cloakroom and closed the door so that whoever next opened it – Grace – would scatter them, shattering most. Luckily, the only damage had been to the glass.

In many ways, these days she and her daughter played a sort of silent cat-and-mouse game around these incidents. Exhausted by years of rows, Grace now confronted Leonie very rarely. She told herself that this was for her own sanity. Rather than fight, it was easier to deal with behavioural blowouts by turning the other cheek. To issue a challenge meant that for the days – or weeks – following, communication between them was non-existent. Confrontation normally released the dogs of war.

In any event, she had gradually come to recognise the other side of the story, that these explosions, intended to cause her grief, were simply outlets for Leonie's constant frustration.

She knew what many others – including their GP – thought of her own passivity: the prevailing attitude was that bad behaviour shouldn't be tolerated. Period.

She would respond with a rueful smile and leave the stage as quickly as possible, outwardly as Grace the Serene, inwardly spitting fire, rehearsing the retorts she *should* have employed.

In truth, her overwhelming desire for herself and her daughter was both the simplest and most difficult thing to achieve: a quiet life. She was now resigned to the fact that this might never happen, but her own frustration at being trapped in a prison of stress and watchfulness was hard to bear.

Meanwhile, one drama of recent months was potentially far more serious than a few bits of broken crockery: her daughter's upcoming court appearance in February 2019 to face a first charge of shoplifting two lipsticks and a lash curler from a discount outlet and a second of resisting arrest. But Grace had mastered the art of compartmentalising. This was only November and, for now, that particular worry resided as far back in her brain as she could place it.

The phone in her hand tinkled – Jacqueline. 'Hi, Mum, saw a missed call. Everything okay?'

'Hi, Jack.' Grace pitched her voice high and bright. 'Yes, everything's under control here but I need a bit of advice. Is Mick still at work?'

'He is, yeah. Why?'

'I was rushing earlier, filled the kettle while it was still plugged in – stupid I know! Anyway, I dropped the bloody thing into the sink, full of water, and now I'm kind of afraid to touch it. Would you mind ringing him to see if it's safe to pull out the plug? Electricity and water and all that!' Her 'careless' laugh failed horribly.

'Sure.' Jackie's tone, resigned, patient, signified no surprise at this news. 'Okay, Mum, why don't you simply turn off the electricity at the mains? Then you can take the kettle out of the sink. You know how to do it? That little trip switch at the end of the row at the top of the fuse board in the utility room? Remember we showed you that time when you thought you'd smelt gas?'

'Of course.' Grace swallowed hard. 'I should have thought of it. Sorry to make a fuss. Thanks, Jackie. How's Tommy?'

'Great.' Her daughter's voice lightened. 'It's nap time, thank God. I'll be putting him down now. Today's his seventeen-month birthday, can you believe it, Mum? I don't know where the time goes. We're going to have a cupcake later . . .' she turned away from the phone '. . . when *Daddy* gets *home*, aren't we, darling? Aren't we going to have a cupcake? Yeah! *Cupcake!*

'You should see his little face, Mum,' she was back, 'he's actually doing clap-handies! Such a *clever* little dude – aren't you?

'So, anyway,' she added briskly, 'do remember not to stand on a stool or a chair to reach that fuse board, okay? Use the stepladder I bought you. And this is *very* important. Don't use that kettle again until you've dried it out completely – put it in the hot press for a day or two.'

'You're a genius, Jackie,' Grace said. 'I'm clearly losing the plot. Don't worry, I'll be careful.'

'Stop it, Mum, you're far from losing the plot. You're brilliant, the way you cope. I've said it before, I don't think I could do it.'

'Well, thanks again, sweetheart. Talk soon. Cheerio for now.' Grace pressed End Call.

Although she accepted that both of her older daughters had their own lives to live, she was increasingly irritated by what she saw as pointless paeans of praise about her management and tolerance of Leonie. They came not just from Jackie and Adeline, but from Harry too – and even from some of the neighbours. The admiration, almost universal and, she knew, very well meant, was nevertheless in danger of driving her over the edge.

2

Grace had never voiced it but privately had acknowledged that she would prefer a little less flattery and a little more 'How can I help?' Or 'Here's a thought, something I *can* help with, so why don't I . . .?'

But she'd end up berating herself for being an ungrateful whinge. In general, people were disposed to be sympathetic and helpful, but were as flummoxed as she was.

She had learned to choose her battles with Leonie. A few of her friends, with well-balanced 'normal' offspring, had repeatedly advised that Leonie, whatever her problems, should be turfed out of the house and left, sink or swim, to fend for herself. In not 'allowing' her to grow up and take responsibility for herself, Grace had become part of Leonie's problem.

She carried a supply of quiet, well-worn responses to these well-meant exhortations. Such as 'It's hard to describe what it's like unless you've been through it'; or the more challenging 'Have you had any experience of this yourself?'

For who among her friends and acquaintances had lived with someone like Leonie without at least one other person available – family member, partner, psychiatrist – to offer practical relief, a week's respite, useful advice or, at the very least, to act as a witness to Leonie's behaviour so that she, Grace, would be believed when she reported it? She had been abandoned to manage someone like her daughter when even some of the medics were throwing up their hands about a specific diagnosis. The MRI Grace had insisted on putting Leonie through had shown no brain damage or lesions (although the process had terrified the girl). Heavy anti-anxiety medication hadn't helped, by turns either sedating her excessively or seeming to increase the verbal aggression.

There were two exceptions to this shortfall in empathic support: two women with whom she had made friends during a Carers' Workshop. She had found the sessions of little use: the tutors had been excellent but had concentrated largely on depression, a serious condition but in no way comparable to the daily conflagration she confronted.

Jennifer and Harriet had each faced the ultimate tragedy when their offspring, unable to deal with the 'real' world, had died by suicide.

Each had striven to change her child's future, had fought

the system, had written to politicians, had been fobbed off with the we-haven't-the-resources excuse, had borne a reluctant daughter to suicide-prevention charities. On advice, Jenny had practised 'tough love', now the deepest source of her grief because, despite universal reassurance that she'd been in no way to blame for the eighteen-year-old's death, she believed she had failed as a mother.

Although society agreed that the two girls' decisions had been theirs alone, both mothers were afflicted with guilt: they could have done more, they felt, or had misinterpreted the advice offered.

At the end of the workshop the three of them had formed a WhatsApp group, and for Grace, now, it was only to the other two that she felt free to speak of her sense of entrapment; neither ever tried to contradict her, judge her or to foist on her the psychiatric mantra of 'no expressed emotion'.

All three had found this particular advice impossible to follow when dealing with their daughters. They accepted that anger and frustration had to find expression or cause worse damage.

And neither ever said: 'At least your daughter is still alive.'

As yet, as far as Grace could tell, Leonie had manifested no sign of taking her life. Still, Grace lived in fear of it.

Throwing Leonie out would leave her at the mercy of the inadequate state apparatus or, more likely, sleeping rough, with all its dangers. Anyhow, whatever they thought privately, family, friends, even neighbours knew that Grace McGee would never render her daughter officially homeless.

The standout was Maxine Smith. Grace and Max had been best friends since they'd met at their County Mayo boarding school and, as best friends do, had followed the ups and downs of their lives ever since.

Outspoken in the 'You know me, I call a spade a spade' way, Maxine frequently expressed outrage at how her friend had been forced into too close a 'minding' relationship with her youngest daughter. She also believed that, soon after Harry had left her, Grace herself had made that choice: 'Everyone has a choice to make, Grace, however difficult it is. In your case, evicting Leonie will be hard but that choice is available. You're far too lenient and accommodating. Your personality is vanishing before my eyes. Leonie is consuming you!'

For the sake of their friendship, Maxine had eventually accepted that her pal, caught in an intractable situation, wouldn't throw out her daughter. Ever. She didn't like it, though, and kept trying to force Grace into action: 'I don't approve of the way you manage her, but it's your choice. I love you to bits and I'll try to live with it.' Then, at the end of each such conversation, the ominous: 'We'll talk again.'

During the last call between them, Maxine had made another try: 'Not even as a temporary device to wake her up to reality, Grace? Wouldn't it give her a shock? Show her how lucky she is? Nice home, good food – you at her beck and call? For God's sake, she's in her twenties, not five!'

Grace had hung up. It hadn't been the first time she had done so – Maxine was used to it and always called back after a few days, not mentioning it, cheerily imparting gossip from her local Galway neighbourhood. But this time she hadn't. And the longer the mutual telephone silence dragged on, the more difficult breaking it became. Grace missed her pal, but she had decided she couldn't stand any more of Maxine's advice, even though, deep down, she knew there was more than a grain of sense in it. She was not (yet) prepared to go there.

As for Leonie's father, Harry, where was he in all of this?

Nowhere, apart from springing for his monthly lunches with his daughter, spotting her a generous allowance and making sure that Grace, too, wasn't short of money. When he called to discuss something, he nearly always ended the conversation with a cursory 'And how's Leonie, by the way?' But, in Grace's opinion, Harry didn't actually want to be given the details of how Leonie was.

By contrast to her life, Harry's, regularly exhibited on Cherry's Facebook and Instagram postings – Jasmine in her First Communion outfit, himself grinning on golf courses, with Cherry in south Dublin restaurants – rankled: she wondered why she had been abandoned like this, not just by Harry but essentially by Jackie and Adeline, who were always, it seemed, too busy with their own lives to offer their mother a little respite by taking Leonie into their own homes from time to time.

Jackie feared, she had explained, that Leonie's antics would scare little Tommy. As for Adeline, in the school holidays she was always either on a professional development course or bound for, perhaps already in, somewhere like Zimbabwe or Brazil, having volunteered with a charity as a tutor.

Frequently, Grace fantasised about moving to one of those places. Or maybe Hawaii?

She accepted her own part in their seeming abandonment of her: not ten minutes ago, she had instinctively lied to Jackie about the kettle fiasco. Why the hell couldn't she just demand family help?

She groaned. She hated giving house room to such resentful thoughts but had found lately that each time their mean little heads poked out, it was more difficult to shove them back where they'd come from. She reminded herself of the lifetime pledge she'd made to all three newborn children, when cradling each for the first time in the crook of her arm. She would love them as fiercely as she had not been loved by her own mother, she told them: there would be no abandonment. Ever.

Leonie, of course, was the one most in need of the pledge's fulfilment. Grace had regularly to remind herself that *she* was not the victim of this circumstance, Leonie was, and that acceptance of her daughter's humanity was key.

'Shit!' she cried to the ceiling. Then, realising she still had her coat on, she jumped up and took it off. No more of this navel-gazing – it never resulted in any positive outcome. Her newspaper was unopened, her coffee unmade. She'd already wasted too much of today's 'free' time: Leonie would be home soon and everything would tick back to Ground Zero.

Among the mess, she found the bottle of floor-cleaner, then turned on the radio to listen to Joe Duffy's *Liveline*.

There was always someone, many someones, worse off than Grace McGee.

3

In the TV room, crossword almost completed, Grace stiffened, then consciously lowered her shoulders: she'd heard Leonie put her key into the lock. Bringing her newspaper, she went quickly into the kitchen, sat into a chair at the table and opened it at random, looking up as her daughter came in. 'Hi, Leonie. How did it go?'

'You always ask that after I meet Dad. How do you think it went?'

'It must have gone well because it went on for so long. I was just wondering if there was any news, that's all. I haven't spoken to a soul today . . .'

'Well, actually . . .' to Grace's surprise, her daughter crossed the room and sat in the chair opposite '. . . there is news, as it happens. They were both in great form. They had Jazzy with them – she's a fantastic kid, Mum, bright as a button and very nearly top of her class at school.'

'They were there too? Cherry and Jasmine?'

'Does that still bother you? Yes, they were. Get over it!'

Before this could develop, Grace smiled, folding the newspaper to signify her full attention. 'I am over it. It's been a good few years now – so tell us, what's the news?'

'Big. Dad's in line to be captain of his golf club – he thinks it's in the bag.'

'That's great, and well deserved.'

'Are you being sarcastic?'

'Of course not. It's a big honour in the golf world, I know that. A big responsibility too.'

'I hope you mean that, Mother – but anyway that's not all! The *really* big story is that Cherry is to get an award, a really major one, Mum. She's been given "Lifetime Professional PR Person of the Year" and she's getting it at a big gala event in the Shelbourne Hotel and, Mum, I'm invited! And Adeline, Jackie! We're all going – Jackie's even allowed to bring Mick. It's black tie. I can't wait!'

'I'm delighted to see you so happy – when is it?'

'In four days' time and I've nothing to wear. Can we shop?'

'Of course. Tomorrow if you like – listen, on another subject, while we're talking, has something upset you lately? Something recent.'

Leonie's mood changed instantly. 'What? What do you mean?'

'I honestly think you know what I mean, darling.'

'Well, if you know, why are you asking me?' Her daughter jumped to her feet. 'This is typical. You ruin everything – I come in happy and you just have to destroy it, don't you? We all know I shouldn't be living here! I should be with my dad and Cherry – she's *fun*, Mother. Remember *fun*? No wonder my dad left you – I pity you, I really do. It must be terrible to be a failed wife.'

'I'm talking about the mess I found in the kitchen when I came home from the shops at lunchtime.' Grace kept her tone steady.

'What mess? The kitchen? The kitchen was fine when I left.'

'Leonie.' Grace felt her blood pressure rise. *Remember: no expressed emotion!* 'You know what I'm talking about. You do these things when something's bothering you. You can tell me. I'm not angry, just concerned – I do know how hard life can be, and now that Sharon—'

'Jesus! You're evil. You're a head-wrecker – you love messing with my head, don't you? It's your hobby. You have to bring Sharon into it, don't you? You *want* me to be miserable and lonely so you drive away everyone from me. You're in Dad's ear, I know you are, talking about me, telling lies. He told me you were – but you know what, Mother? You're crazy in the head. I'm going up to my room. Don't come near me. You stink, by the way, do you know that?' She flew.

Grace, sighing, folded the newspaper, stood up and, in a saucepan, boiled some water to make instant coffee.

Within the past few years there had been several genuine crises surrounding Leonie, many with repercussions far more serious than the weekly or even daily spats and bad behaviour, such as what had happened in the kitchen that morning.

The impact of some episodes was still playing out – in particular, one from the previous Christmas, which had resulted not just in Leonie going missing but in the permanent loss of her friend, Sharon, who had been loyal to her since their earliest days at primary school. In recent years, she had been not just a true friend to Leonie but the only one.

The split had occurred because of Leonie's obvious and disastrous play for Sharon's boyfriend at a family dinner in a restaurant to celebrate Adeline's birthday. All of the family, including Cherry, had been there and Leonie had asked if Sharon could come with her new boyfriend, originally from Arizona.

With Harry presiding at the top of the table between Leonie on his left and Cherry on his right, Jaden had been seated between Leonie and Sharon. For the first hour or so, Leonie had behaved herself, reacting delightedly to flattery about her off-the-shoulder dress and a new pixie haircut emphasising her eyes. Jaden had enthusiastically joined in, remarking that she was the reincarnation of Audrey Hepburn.

All seemed to be going well and Grace had felt she could relax. For quite a while, she had chatted with Sharon, who talked excitedly about her plans to change job.

Two years previously, she confided, Jaden had sold his fledgling IT company to one of the giants and since then had been living on the proceeds (now, he'd confessed, much depleted). He had put his time to good use, though, and was planning a new venture.

Sharon wanted to leave her own well-paid job to work with him, although they hadn't yet sorted out the terms of her employment.

The conversation continued as the main courses were served. Each woman turned to the guest on her other side, and it was then that Grace, alarmed, saw her youngest daughter was in full-on flirt mode with Jaden.

Sharon had seen what was going on (it could hardly be missed) and even Harry and Cherry had noticed, he transfixed, she stony-faced. Intervention, Grace feared, was already too late: Leonie had worked her strange magic and was at that moment engaged in touching the guy's hand, teasing him about his collar-length hair, even taking a forkful of food from his plate and, eyes fixed on his mouth, popping it meaningfully into her own.

Despite Grace's warning look, twinned with Sharon's dagger-like glare at Jaden, both had carried on regardless.

Sharon had left the dinner early and alone; a few minutes later, Jaden followed, but not before he'd written his telephone number on Leonie's hand. Immediately afterwards, defying even her father's pleas, Leonie had grabbed her handbag and coat, leaving the rest of them speechless, except for Adeline, who called, 'Good riddance to bad rubbish, the pair of ye!'

After that no one had had the heart to continue eating, especially as they were attracting smirks from other diners in the restaurant, and the party broke up.

Early the next morning, Sharon had rung Grace. She had spoken quietly, apologising for what she was about to say. (*She* was apologising? Grace was incredulous.)

While she would not for very long mourn the loss of the boyfriend whom she'd known only a few weeks, she'd said, Leonie had gone too far this time and they could no longer be friends. 'I couldn't bear even to ring her, Grace. I'd be afraid I'd go ballistic and I know only too well how vulnerable she is. I'm sorry to lay this on you, but I think it's best she hears it from you. The bottom line is, though, that what she did, betraying me in front of your whole family, was beyond the pale. I may ring her eventually, but it won't be as her close friend. Any friendship should be one of equals but ours has been wide of that mark for years. I'd felt I owed it to her to stick with it because she'd nobody else, and I've done the best I can, but I can't do it any more.'

'I'm so sad,' Grace had known instantly what this would mean for her daughter, 'but I do understand. The way she behaved was appalling. I'm so sorry.'

'Grace, you have nothing to apologise for, and I do know that she can't help what she does. I have the greatest respect for you and how you cope – I can barely imagine what you have to put up with – but there's no point, really, in saying that we can stay friends. It just wouldn't work – you and I both know that.'

Grace had reassured Sharon that she understood: it

had been a miracle that the friendship had lasted for so long. 'All these years, you've been true and loyal to her.' But she was devastated, having frequently taken comfort in thinking, *Well, at least she has Sharon.*

She held off from telling Leonie about the phone call and, as time went by, realised that her daughter must have noticed her friend's absence, although she had never mentioned even Sharon's name until today.

She'd been surprised that Cherry and Jasmine had come along to the restaurant that day because, only a few weeks ago, Leonie had blotted her copybook with her stepmother.

Harry had persuaded his wife, against her better judgement, to let him bring his daughter to one of her professional lunch events, promising he'd take responsibility for minding her.

The event was being held to celebrate her firm's acquisition of a contract to market the services of a large German company opening in Ireland. Everything was fine until after the meal, when Harry went to the Gents. Then Leonie had decided to make her relationship with their hostess known and to welcome the newcomers to Ireland. She had walked up to the top table beside which the company's managing director stood chatting to Cherry. Leonie had introduced herself to the woman and had asked her pleasantly how soon her baby was due.

The woman, large but not pregnant, had not been amused.

So Grace had her doubts as to whether Cherry had indeed invited her daughter to next week's awards dinner, but it wasn't her place to voice them. She had agreed to shop for it and that was what she would do. Tomorrow Leonie would have a new outfit.

4

The next day it was noon before Leonie emerged from her bedroom. Grace concentrated on scrubbing the kitchen sink. Experience dictated that if her daughter was in a good mood, it wouldn't last, and if she was defensive or hostile, Grace would be the loser if she said the wrong thing. So in most cases, it was lose-lose to the mother.

Eventually she said, 'I'm going into town, Leonie. Arnotts is having a pre-season sale, and we need new sheets for your bed and the spare room. Here's an idea, though,' she added, as though it had just occurred to her. 'Why don't you come with me? They're advertising bargains all over the store, including women's wear. We could find you a nice outfit for that awards do you told me Cherry had invited you to.'

Leonie was staring at her, clearly puzzled. She must have been expecting some kind of pushback from yesterday's row, Grace thought.

'Have a think, Leonie,' she went on cheerily, 'while I'm putting on my coat – but I'm going anyway.'

She fetched the coat from its hook in the hall and called, 'I'll probably eat when I'm out. So if you don't come, you'll have to look after yourself for dinner this evening. That all right with you?' She went into the kitchen and put on her leather gloves.

Surprisingly, Leonie was nodding. 'Okay, I'll come. I haven't got much in the formal line and it's black tie, as I told you.'

'Grand.' (*Result!* Leonie loved shopping.) Grace kept the tone light: 'I'm sure we'll find something. They're open until eight this evening, but we need to leave now, so we can get back on the Dart before the rush-hour crush.'

*

It was early afternoon when they got to the station so the city-bound Dart was half empty. And as they sat together quietly, Grace imagined that to others they would appear to be just an average mother and daughter travelling into the Big Smoke on a shopping spree.

5

As expected, Arnotts was crowded and they headed straight for the first floor, where they had to queue for a fitting room. When they finally secured one, Leonie installed herself while Grace acted as a spotter, pushing through the melee to select dresses and separates glamorous enough to fit the bill, sized to fit her daughter's slight frame. To the limit of the number allowed by the store, she brought them in batches into the fitting room, taking back the discards, leaving Leonie excitedly getting into and out of each garment, even, astonishingly, asking her for an opinion. Grace's task, the choosing and handling of sumptuous, sinuous silks, satins and form-fitting jerseys, was enjoyable and, for a while, she could park her unease about the reality of Cherry's invitation, instead concentrating on finding the best outfit.

She was bringing a fresh armful of CC Petite dresses to Leonie when, buried in her coat pocket, her mobile rang. She took it out. Harry. Did she really want, right now, to talk to him? If she did, she'd have to ask him point blank about the veracity of this invitation.

She took the call. 'Hang on, Harry,' she said. 'I need to finish something here. Thirty seconds?' Back in Leonie's cubicle, she dumped her cargo. 'There's a few here. I won't be long but I have to take a call. I'll be back as quickly as I can but try this one first.' She offered a shimmering, ankle-length sheath in gold lamé. 'It's lovely, isn't it? When I was young we used to call this Cloth of Gold, and I'm willing to bet this is the dress for you. And the size is perfect.

'Sorry about that, Harry,' she said. 'What's up?'

'Of all the stupid questions you've ever asked, Grace,' he sputtered, 'that has to take the biscuit. What could it be about but our daughter? Is she around at the moment?'

'Yes, Harry,' she said steadily, 'she is. We're clothes-shopping. For her attendance at your wife's awards ceremony next week. It's black tie, she tells me, and she doesn't have anything appropriate.'

There was silence at the other end.

'Are you still there?'

'Yes, I am,' he said, and her heart sank. *Please, God, please! I don't pray but I'm begging now, not for me but for her.*

'Bear in mind,' Harry had always sounded pompous when he was nervous, 'that I know what I'm going to say will be difficult for both of you.' He hesitated, then, in a rush: 'Cherry refuses to have Leonie at the awards. There was no argument about it, Grace. I want you to know I did try but it's a point-blank no.'

'But they're all going – Jackie, Adeline, even Mick.' Her instincts about that invitation had been proven right. She felt nauseous.

'She's adamant,' he said. 'The German thing was the last straw and this awards do is huge for her. Try to understand, Gracie, she's getting the biggest award in her business, a lifetime award for services to PR, and she's absolutely determined she's not having it ruined – and, before you ask, yes, I agree with her decision.

'Leonie got hold of the wrong end of the stick. Cherry was on a high and, as far as I remember, she said something along the lines of "It'll be great to have the family there." She meant her own family, Grace. Her brother is even flying in for the occasion with his wife.'

'Will Jackie and Adeline be going?'

'I guess so, but I don't actually know. Even if they are, Leonie has to wake up and smell the coffee. She has to realise, sooner rather than later, that bad behaviour has consequences. I'll make it up to her. I'll bring her somewhere nice for dinner. Listen, Grace, Cherry deserves to have a fantastic night and I want that for her. She's worked hard for it for years and should enjoy every minute without worrying about— Ah, for Chrissakes!' He lost patience. 'You know what I mean.'

'But Cherry has frequently invited Leonie to her big

things. I'm grateful for that, Harry, and almost all of them went fine. If she's still annoyed about that German thing, it was a blip. Is your wife that insecure? Leonie had meant well, I certainly believe her about that, and from her account the woman *was* huge.'

'It's not just that, it's an accumulation of – dammit, I'm not going through everything. You know what I'm talking about, we all do, and Cherry's adamant about this.'

Grace said nothing for about ten seconds, then: 'So when were you going to tell Leonie? She came home yesterday full of it. All right, I accept she might have got the wrong end of the stick, as you called it. But why didn't Cherry make things clear? She's in PR — she could have thought up some reason to keep Leonie away if she didn't want to tell the truth.'

'She felt yesterday's venue wasn't appropriate, and in any event, to our surprise, she was behaving perfectly – I think it was because Jazzy was there . . .' He trailed off.

'You're unbelievable.' Grace was close to boiling point. 'That lunch was a set-up, the two of you there all the while waiting for her to kick off and then there'd have been an excuse!'

'Whatever you think, Grace, she can't come to the Shelbourne that night. The beginning, middle and end of it is that Cherry is entitled to ensure that her big night isn't ruined. Remember last year? The Trocadero? Vegas? What we – what *I* – had to do to extricate her from that bastard, Jaden? How much it cost me?'

'Let's not go there again, please, Harry. It was nearly a

year ago and she's suffered for it – still is suffering. She's largely isolated now that Sharon's out of her life. Bear that in mind before you go on about the money – it's not as though you don't have it.'

'You're right.' Harry was using his resigned voice – *the ex attacking me, believing she's been hard done by . . .*

Grace was having no more of it. 'Get to the real point of this call, Harry.' She knew what was coming but she was determined to make him say it.

'Well, she'd take it better from you,' he said. 'She'd never speak to me again.'

'And it's all right with you, Harry, if she doesn't speak to me? Anyhow, it's Cherry pulling the plug, not you, so let Cherry deliver her own bad news. Why should I be the one to do it?' Her raised voice was attracting attention from those around her. 'I don't want to do this, Harry, and I won't,' she said quietly. 'You owe a bit of loyalty here to your daughter. She'll be shattered. She's this minute trying on the dress we're buying for the event.'

'I'm sorry, Gracie, but what can I do? Cherry's made up her mind. It's her big night, as I keep saying, and that's the way it is. I'll think of something to make it up to Leonie, I promise.'

Grace cemented her decision. 'You do what you like, but I'm not going to tell her. Is that clear? She'll be distraught and furious, no matter who tells her, and for once I choose not to be the one to deal with her reaction although she'll blame me anyway.'

'Gracie, c'mon . . .' he wheedled. 'Yes, you're right, you

are taking most of the burden and it's not as though we don't appreciate it, but that's life, isn't it? That's what you sign up for when you have children.'

How dare you? Grace thought. Then: 'Not going to happen, Harry!'

There was another pause. 'Thanks for nothing, Grace.' He ended the call.

6

It had felt good to stand up to her ex, Grace thought, as she walked back to the fitting room, but the victory had been Pyrrhic. She knew in her bones that Cherry's dis-invitation would hold and that she'd be the one to break the news.

In her cubicle, her daughter had taken her advice and had put on the lamé sheath before trying anything else. It fitted like a glowing second skin. On seeing her pirouette happily in front of the mirror, Grace's heart broke. At the very least, her daughter should have this dress.

'You look wonderful,' she said, fighting tears. 'We'll take it.'

Grace had never got her own kicks from shopping, and

as the two of them pushed their way to the till, the crowd seemed to have grown, creating a sense of claustrophobia. Having finished the transaction, she asked Leonie if she'd mind going straight home and, for once, her daughter agreed without arguing.

At the last moment, however, as their train was arriving into Connolly station, Leonie's phone pinged with a message. She smiled widely on reading it. 'You go on, Mum, I'll see you later – that was Arnotts again.' She clicked off. 'I signed up for notifications and this is the latest one. They're pushing shoes in their sale now – I should have looked when we were there but I'll hop back now. They're sure to have something to go with my dress.'

'Good idea!' Grace smiled, relieved that her daughter's brief taste of joy had been extended. 'It's lovely to see you so happy, Leonie! Do you want me to take the bag for you?'

'Not at all. I need it to match up. It's as light as a feather anyhow – you get on that train or you won't get a seat!'

Miraculously, Grace did get a seat. Even at sale price that dress had cost a fortune, she thought, but it had been worth it: it had given Leonie those few hours of happiness. Ringing in her ears, though, she could already hear the bitter recriminations: *You knew all along and you said it was lovely to see me happy. You're a two-faced bitch, Mother, a fucking hypocrite, you're sick actually, do you know that? You're sick, sick, sick. All you want is to have power over me . . .'* Grace knew the routine, knew that in her own mind Leonie was always the tragic victim targeted by an army of enemies.

As the Dart squealed out of the station she knew that, for Leonie's sake, she would have to tell her she was no longer invited to Cherry's event. If she left it to Harry, Leonie would be dressed and getting into the taxi by the time he finally found the nerve to call.

Briefly, she wondered if she could persuade Jackie and Adeline not to go in solidarity with their sister.

Maybe, but why spoil their pleasure too?

It was no comfort to recognise that, as always, Leonie was largely the architect of her own misfortune. Isolated and lonely, Grace and Harry's third daughter was frantically over-eager for love and acceptance but didn't understand how to achieve it.

The play for her best friend's boyfriend in the Troc that night, and the consequent flight to Las Vegas for an ill-fated marriage, had been a perfect example. He'd turned out to be a con man.

When eventually Leonie had revealed some details about what had happened, it transpired that she and Jaden had been married by a guy dressed as a Navajo, complete with war bonnet (the impulse to tie the knot had come from Leonie, apparently) but Jaden had vanished the next day, after asking her for money, claiming that while she'd been sleeping, he'd gone down to the hotel's casino, but the result of his visit hadn't been great.

She'd shown him what she had, a few euro and a hundred dollars she'd obtained at Dublin Airport. She'd told him that her modest monthly income was from a trust fund set up by her father, next payment due in four weeks' time.

She had no savings.

'But your dad has money, hasn't he?' he'd said, scribbling on a pad the numbers Harry would need to make a transfer into his checking account, and details of how to set up a Western Union app for the task. He'd told her to ask for 'ten Gs' – ten thousand dollars: it should see them through for a few weeks, he'd said, because he was due a hundred Gs from a debtor in the next month or so. This, he informed her, would be a short-term loan to be paid back.

Harry was no fool and, in response to a tearful call from his daughter, had been on the first flight he could get. He found her still in the Bellagio, quite disoriented. Luckily, she'd had enough sense not to tell her new husband about her bank debit card, which was how she had extended her stay in the hotel. By that time, her 'husband', was, presumably, far, far away.

While paying the hotel bill, Harry had discussed with the concierge whether or not he should involve the authorities, but Leonie had overheard and begged him not to. She just wanted to get home.

The most amazing thing for Grace was that Sharon, clever, and who had lived with Jaden for more than two months, had been convinced by his cover story of selling his IT company and, it turned out, had even invested some of her savings in his supposed new venture. Poor Leonie hadn't stood a chance. 'She actually did me a favour, I think, Grace.'

'Harry says there's a lot of these guys around,' she'd told Sharon, during their final phone call, 'so don't beat yourself up.' She was sad that Sharon hadn't offered even to have a cup of coffee with Leonie.

She didn't blame her, though: that betrayal, however much it had saved Sharon from worse, had been unforgivable.

*

Grace's first heartbreak on Leonie's account had happened when her daughter, aged eight, had come home from school crying her eyes out because the little circle of friends to which she'd belonged had expelled her. 'They don't want to play with me any more. They hate me now. They say I'm weird . . . A nutcase. And I don't even know what that is. What is it, Mum?'

All her mother could do was to hold her close and try to convince her that the rift was temporary. As for 'nutcase', it was someone, she explained, who enjoyed playing conkers – 'And that isn't you, is it, pet? They've got that all wrong. They're just silly-billies. They don't know what they're talking about.' But the little group never did let her in again.

For years in primary school, Grace's daughter had had to hang around with those generally known by her fellow pupils as the 'rejects'. She had developed attention-seeking strategies, such as being the bold girl, exasperating teachers but entertaining the pupils, and was tolerated as the class clown because she could distract the more boring teachers.

But she'd never been invited to the popular girls' birthday parties.

Her mother had been helpless to fix this for her – she couldn't make other girls like her daughter. All she could do was to stay steadfast and 'be there'. Entirely unappreciated.

But when Sharon had arrived into the school in fifth class she had intuited that this one girl needed support, and had decided to take her on. When they'd graduated to the same secondary school she had remained loyal – and had kept it up in adulthood until that last disastrous night in the Trocadero. Her loss was immeasurable.

Right now, what words could Grace use in revealing Cherry's new rejection? Bubbling with anticipation and pleasure, Leonie would arrive home this evening with her dress, showing off how her new shoes went with it. She was so rarely happy, Grace knew she couldn't puncture that bubble straight away.

Standing up to Harry and his new wife had felt good but hadn't lasted long. This time, though, rather than plunge into self-castigation, Grace reminded herself of an epigram uttered frequently by her friend, Jenny, who had lost her daughter to suicide: *I am only one and I will not let what I cannot do interfere with what I can do.*

She'd looked it up online. It had originated with Edward Hale, a nineteenth-century American cleric.

Neither Jenny nor Harriet could wind back the clock, but they could try to forgive themselves, making the most of their own lives in honour of their daughters'. Grace's child was still living so she had the opportunity to make the most of that. She couldn't live Leonie's life or relieve her loneliness, though, couldn't ameliorate her humiliation and sense of abandonment following the Las Vegas wedding, and it was too late to repair her daughter's friendship with Sharon. But while she couldn't change Cherry's fixed mind, she was in a position to buy Leonie a magnificent dress. She could prolong her daughter's happiness for a few hours by not immediately telling her that Cherry didn't want her and that her father was too weak to stand up for her.

With the heads of almost everyone in her carriage bent to their electronic devices, she took out her phone.

Earlier, when they'd still been at home, she'd said she'd eat out. It had been a long time since she had treated herself. *Hi Leonie,* she texted, *as I told you before we left home, I'm going to eat out this evening but there's plenty of food in the fridge. That dress is gorgeous – well chosen! You are a very beautiful young woman and in that dress this afternoon, you looked like an angel. Love, Mum.*

7

Next morning, Grace was still in her nightwear, having breakfast in the kitchen, when the doorbell rang. Believing it to be the postman with a package she'd ordered from Amazon, she went to the door and found Harry outside, wearing golf gear and looking somewhat sheepish. 'Sorry if I've woken you, Gracie, but I'm due for a foursome at ten and it'll take me a while to get back across the city at this hour. We need to talk.'

'About what?' But Grace knew what he wanted. 'Come in,' she said, 'but you've had a wasted journey. My mind is made up.'

'Hear me out, please.'

'I'm telling you, Harry, you're wasting your time.' She

stood back and let him in. 'I'm having my breakfast so whatever you want to say it'll have to be in the kitchen. There's still tea in the pot if you want to help yourself.'

'Thanks, but I'm good. I got a breakfast roll in the Spar and ate it on the way here.'

Classy, Grace thought, as he sat at the table opposite her and her half-eaten toast. 'What's so important that you've come all the way over through the rush-hour?'

'It's about the awards do.' He gazed at her. She recognised his trepidation and felt good about that. At least he didn't see her as a walkover or a patsy. In his mind the cancellation had probably been relatively trivial, to be dealt with like every other difficulty in Leonie's life: far from the groves of Ranelagh.

'What about it?' she asked. 'We've had this conversation, Harry. You made this decision, you and Cherry, I didn't, and I'm certainly not going to take the flak for it. End of story. She has the dress and the shoes and she's really looking forward to the evening.

'God knows what she'll do if you take all this away from her, especially as the other two are going. Now,' she added briskly, 'I'm making myself fresh tea. Do you want a cup or not?'

'No, thanks.' His expression had changed. Could he be developing respect?

'Suit yourself.' She crossed to the sink and noisily refilled the new kettle.

'Gracie,' he had to raise his voice, 'please listen to me.'

'Of course I'll listen. I always do. That's been my downfall for years. Go ahead! Tell me again that I have to be the one to shatter Leonie's expectations. I'll listen, but my mind is made up. I'm not going to do it. If you and Cherry are determined to go through with this, one of you will have to tell her. I believe it should be Cherry – and if one of you doesn't tell her in time, you can deal with her when she turns up at the Shelbourne. As she most likely will.'

'Well, actually . . .'

'Actually what?' Water only half boiled, Grace angrily switched off the kettle. 'Actually what?' she repeated into the sudden silence, and saw him take a deep breath.

He told her then that, through one of her tourism and travel contacts, Cherry had suggested booking a last-minute cruise for Leonie and herself, departing a couple of days hence, so that Leonie would be away, 'enjoying herself', on the date of the event.

Grace was appalled. Because they could, these two would splash their money around to shunt Leonie out of sight. As her father, Harry would be happy with this. 'You mean so she wouldn't intrude? Might cause a stir? Might even—'

'You said you'd listen,' he cut in. 'There's logic here . . .' He launched into a rigmarole about how when Leonie was difficult as a child, he and Grace used to distract her from a strop by offering her a biscuit or an ice cream or, when that didn't work, would fish out a new toy from a stash under the stairs, kept specifically for such an event. 'And that usually worked, remember?'

'You're being ridiculous, Harry. I do remember, probably

better than you do, because you were off conquering the financial world. She was a baby.'

'I'll ignore that little barb but, yes, she was a baby. And in some ways,' he said levelly, watching her, 'you have to agree that she still is.'

'Well, I don't!'

'Don't you?'

Grace refused to admit – to him at least – that what he'd pointed out was at least partially valid. 'Let me be clear. I'm not going there, Harry. I find your attitude, yours and Cherry's, not just patronising – offer us a new toy and we'll go along with anything – but disgusting. This is a fucking bribe!' While Leonie sprayed such words around like snuff at a wake, Grace rarely used that kind of language and it gave her satisfaction to see shock register on his face. At least he was listening now. 'She won't go along with this,' she added furiously, 'and neither will I. The cheek of that woman thinking we might. Anyway, sequestered together on a ship, with no means of escape, Leonie and I would probably kill each other.'

'Cherry's thought of that,' he said, addressing this not to her but to the table. 'She's reserved two separate cabins.' Quickly, looking up again, he added, 'If I know you're on board with this, Grace, it makes it easier for me to talk to Leonie. I'd say she'll grab it. We can present it to her as a birthday present—'

'What's this "we"? You can forget about that. Her birthday isn't until the eighteenth of December, which is nearly seven weeks away. We're barely into November yet.'

Grace was stunned that he could be so crass. *Their* birthday present. She was to be used now?

Leonie, she felt, wouldn't buy this phoney offer for a second. 'Stay there,' she ordered. 'I'll wake her and bring her down so you can put this to her directly. You can explain why you and your wife don't want her. I'll be in another room.' Without waiting for a response, she left the kitchen.

It took Leonie a while to comprehend that her father wanted to speak to her in the kitchen, but eventually she got out of bed and went ahead of Grace down the stairs.

'Dad!' she exclaimed. 'What are you doing here? What's going on? Is Jazzy okay?' Worried, she looked from one of her parents to the other.

'She's fine.' Harry was using his reassuring-the-client voice. 'Everything's fine, but I came to tell you that we have a birthday present for you.'

'But my birthday's not—'

'We know that, and it's an early present. Cherry and I were talking about what you might like and, well, we've found something you might really enjoy.'

'I'll leave you to it,' Grace said. 'I've stuff to do upstairs.' Then she sat at the bottom of the stairs where she could hear what was going on.

As Harry talked, she realised, incredulous, that her daughter seemed to be listening, making few interventions as he outlined what was on offer. At the end, sounding a little puzzled, she said, 'But if it's that soon, Dad, doesn't it mean I'd be away on the night of Cherry's awards gig?'

'That's unfortunately the case, honey. Cherry's upset

about that, of course, but when she discovered this offer she thought it was too good to miss. She reminded me you hadn't had a real holiday for ages.

'And, by the way, you and your mum would be getting the last two cabins on the ship. They were cancellations and there's a waiting list for them so we can't delay our decision. It's *ten days*, Leonie. Your very first cruise – to the Arctic! Bet you didn't expect that – or that you'd be able to see the Northern Lights.'

'But won't it be very cold up there? And I have this amazing dress for Cherry's gig.'

'So your mum has told me,' Harry said brightly, 'and, yes, it will be cold, but ships are heated, these days, and you'll have the right clothes – you'll need to do quite a bit of shopping. *Shopping*, Leonie. As for the dress, there'd be formal nights where you can wear it to stun your fellow passengers. Pity about Cherry's thing but there'll be others, and you can wear your dress again then. This, though, is a once-off, the chance of a lifetime, Leonie . . .'

'I dunno, Dad. Thanks, but amn't I a bit old to be going on holidays with my mother?'

'She mentioned that too, funny enough. She thought you wouldn't like it – in fact, right now she's saying she won't go, but there'll be plenty of other people there too, from all over the world, eight hundred of them, I understand. You'd be in separate cabins, as I said, and if you do decide you'd like to go, your mother has assured me that she'll let you do your own thing!'

Grace couldn't stand any more of this. His stress on

'shopping' had been low, given Leonie's recent history. She had forgotten that before he'd ascended to the heights of corporate banking directorships, Harry's role as a bank manager had included high-powered salesmanship, at which he had excelled. Their family had benefited from his generous bonuses.

It had been quite a spiel – she got up quietly from her stair and went back into the kitchen. 'How are we doing here? What do you think of Cherry's offer, Leonie? It's probably too soon, just a couple of days before we'd have to leave – and, anyhow, you'd miss Cherry's big night, wouldn't you?' But then – although she deplored Harry's deviousness – she realised the positive side of all this. If her daughter bought into it, she would avoid being humiliated – and Grace, who hadn't had a proper holiday in years, could make the most of this one.

She smiled at her daughter. 'Of course, Leonie, your dad could be right about one thing. There would probably be other events to warrant wearing that dress, wouldn't there? And I've heard that a lot of ships run formal dinners with dancing – you could wear it there too, as he suggested.'

'I've a few bob here in an envelope.' Harry handed it to Leonie, whose eyes opened wide on seeing its contents. Grace could read her thoughts: *Arnotts has a huge sports department. Fancy ski-type stuff!* 'I'll go and get dressed,' she said. 'We don't have much time to get kitted out.'

Although she couldn't show it, Grace, entirely outmanoeuvred, was again furious. *He'd been so sure he'd get his way that he'd come with the money already in the envelope...*

She was also disgusted with herself for colluding with him, but the die was cast. She, who believed she knew her daughter intimately (better than he did), had been proven wrong. 'You'll be late for your golf date, Harry.' To make sure he knew he was dismissed, she turned her back to dispose of her cold toast and put her crockery into the dishwasher.

'It's for the best,' he said from behind her. 'For you, for her, the other two girls, for Cherry and me – not to mention all the other guests at the awards do. There'll be a lot of celebrities, media types and high-powered business people. I can't emphasise enough how important this thing is for Cherry. It has to go smoothly.'

If she hadn't been rearranging the top level of the dishwasher, Grace would have spat.

Unfortunately, she'd have to agree with Cherry's logic, self-serving though it was. The risk of having Leonie at that celebration was high. 'The Arctic, Harry? In the cold? You'll owe me a favour for this, a big one, and don't think I won't claim it.'

'Whatever you want!'

'You know the way out.' She went into the utility room, rooted out the vacuum cleaner, ancient and very loud, turned it on and, almost rejoicing in its discordant whine, took out her anger on the kitchen floor.

From Leonie, she knew that Cherry had a cleaner, two in fact on two separate days, one for the tough stuff, floors, toilets, polishing the silver, the other for organising the dry cleaning, sorting drawers, light dusting and tending the plants, both indoors and outside.

When Harry had left her, Maxine had been livid on her behalf but Grace had recognised that, although he had tried hard for many years, Harry had eventually run out of tolerance for the situation in his home and could no longer handle it. Grace had understood this only too well because she frequently felt that way herself. But while he could escape, she'd had no other choice but to cope.

For a time she had resented Harry's cowardice in the way he had left her: he hadn't had the guts simply to walk away honestly. Instead, he had seized on the escape hatch offered by Ms Charlotte Burns, diminutive, blonde, red lipstick, with an eighteen-inch waist. The description had come from Leonie, who had used it as yet another tool with which to flay her mother, a clodhopping six-footer (almost!), who took size sixteen, even eighteen, if she wanted to be comfortable, and wore size eight shoes.

Grace's first glimpse of her replacement – and chance to check out her reported waist measurement – had happened while she and Jackie, shopping in Arnotts, had come across Cherry in the shoe department. Wearing a beautifully tailored coat of fine black wool with a flared skirt, that little waist tightly cinched with a wide red belt, she was trying on a pair of silvery shoes with six-inch heels.

She had jumped up immediately on seeing one of her stepdaughters. And as she did so, Grace saw that, yes, under the belt the waist was indeed Barbie-sized. It occurred to her that Cherry clearly used Barbie's hairdresser too.

Their encounter had been brief but civil, Grace quickly excusing herself and Jackie, saying they had to run because rush-hour on the northside Dart now started earlier and earlier. 'Tell me about it,' Cherry trilled. 'It's the same for us. Isn't it *awful,* Grace? May I call you "Grace", or would that be a little awkward for you?'

'Not at all, Cherry!' Grace had forced a smile. 'I have to run. They're beautiful shoes, by the way.'

When she'd got home that day, it had taken Grace less than three minutes to bin everything in the treats cupboard, along with a full box of Kellogg's Honey Nuts, two half-bags of sugar, an unopened pack of Brennan's white sliced pan, a jar of raspberry jam and three cans of beer, followed by a half-eaten chocolate cake from the Tesco Finest range.

Then, unusually for her – she had a deserved reputation for stoicism – she had burst into tears.

8

On the afternoon before she and Leonie were to leave for Hamburg, where they would join the ship, Grace, returning from their second shopping trip in as many days, heard the hall phone ringing behind the front door. She dropped her bags on the step and pushed open the door to get to it.

Maxine's husband, Dieter, had rung, he said, because Maxine had asked him to. 'She tells me things are not right between you two at present,' he said, in his very correct English, 'and she asks me to emphasise on her behalf that she is very, very sorry for that.'

'Thank you, Dieter. I'm sorry too. It wasn't all her doing.'

In the background at his end, she heard a dog bark. 'Just

one moment, please.' She heard his footsteps recede, then a heavy squeak as he opened a door.

He was back within seconds. 'I am sorry about that. But there is something we need to tell you and she has asked me to let you know that, unfortunately, she has been diagnosed with cancer. We are shocked, of course, but she thought that you, too, might be upset in spite of your differences and that I should make the call so you should have a few moments before you spoke to each other.'

'My God! I'm so sorry, Dieter.' Grace was aghast. 'When did this happen?'

'She has not been well for some weeks. We had tests and we received the diagnosis last evening.'

'She must be devastated. You too, Dieter.'

'Yes, but she is determined to fight this. We have more tests next Monday and, depending on what they show, we will be starting treatment as quickly as possible.' His voice, normally so steady – monotonous, she'd always thought – had begun to shake.

'Are you all right, Dieter?'

'I'm fine.' He cleared his throat. 'Don't worry, we are both fine, we are not the only ones who face this, and the cancer services here in Galway are excellent.' He stopped and, in the ensuing silence, she could hear the dog again, claws tapping on Maxine's kitchen tiles. Their kitchen was enormous, its surfaces gleaming, its appliances oversized. Maxine loved cooking . . .

Had loved cooking. 'What type of cancer? I'm sure it's very raw for you right now so don't go into detail if you don't want to.'

'Of the stomach—' But he couldn't continue.

'Thank you for letting me know, Dieter,' she said quickly. Despite her mixed feelings about Maxine, her eyes were filling and her voice cracking as she reassured him that of course she and Maxine would talk. Right now, though, she wouldn't be able to keep it together during a telephone call – the last thing poor Maxine needed was to have someone sobbing into the phone at her.

In other circumstances, she would have been on the road to Galway tonight. Now she said: 'Unfortunately, Leonie and I have an appointment in Dublin later this evening and we're leaving for Germany tomorrow. Would it be okay if I called Max tonight? Or tomorrow morning? We don't have to leave for the airport until about noon. I wouldn't want to rush her when we do get together – it's been almost a year and we have a lot to talk about. Far more than I would have thought an hour ago.' Her voice had vanished deep into her throat and she couldn't get it to sound. She coughed a couple of times.

'As I say,' he came in, 'the care is and will be excellent. We are staying hopeful. Depending on Monday's results we will start the treatments as soon as practicable. I'll give her your message. She's already on some medication and may be sleeping tonight, so tomorrow morning would suit very well. She'll look forward to that. She'll be happy.'

'Until tomorrow, then. Please give her all my love – to you too, Dieter. You're both strong, you'll get through this.'

'We will. Hopefully.'

She could tell he was again on the verge of breaking

down so she said, 'Bye-bye,' and put down the receiver. They were hopeful, he'd said, but he hadn't sounded it. Stomach cancer?

Grace read newspapers. She knew that stomach was one of the bad ones.

What was she going to do without Maxine? Mouthy, pushy, bossy, control-freak Maxine – angry when Grace wouldn't agree with her views on Leonie.

Behind it all, though, she was utterly loyal, which was what had made the silence between them these past months so awful. What made it worse for Grace now was that she'd been the one who had severed the ties when, by her pal's own lights, all Max had been doing was looking out for her. Now that lost year might turn out to have been her last on earth.

She turned away from the phone table to see that Leonie was still in the hall, watching. She had obviously heard the whole thing. 'What appointment do we have in the evening, Mother?' she asked. 'Quite the liar, aren't you? Who knew?'

'Would you, for once in your life, shut up!' Grace snatched up her shopping and fled upstairs to her bedroom where she dropped the bags, lay face down on the bed beside her suitcase and wept. Maxine was going to die, no matter how much hope Dieter, she or anyone else held out, no matter how many novenas people made or how many rounds of chemo and radiotherapy Maxine endured.

Selfishly, she entertained the thought that once again, she was to be abandoned and, again, she was at fault. Reason dictated that she was being ridiculous – cancer was an equal-opportunity illness – but reason didn't apply here. The news had cut deep, drawing the blood of past trauma.

9

The father Grace had adored had been killed when rushing home on his bicycle and this, too, had been due to her actions.

On one of the dying days of fourth class in primary school, she'd been sent home early with a note for her mother to say she was being suspended for a week: she'd punched another girl in the playground, knocking her down. A lump the size of a duck egg had risen on the side of the other girl's forehead so she had had to be taken to hospital for assessment.

From Grace's point of view, that girl, ringleader of a group who had taunted and bullied her since she'd grown to be six inches taller than the next tallest in the class, had deserved what she'd got. That afternoon their taunting had driven her beyond endurance as, not for the first time, the girl and her group had joined hands to surround her, closing in on her while chanting: 'Giraffe, giraffe, give us a laugh . . .' Others in the yard, jeering and giggling, enjoyed the show from the sidelines.

Grace, humiliated and angrier than she'd ever thought possible, had leaped on their leader, hitting her as hard as she could.

After the ambulance had departed, with the class teacher in attendance, the principal had telephoned her mother to tell her what had happened, to expect Grace home shortly, and not to send her to school for the next week, pending further investigations.

Grace had always felt that her mother, a chilly woman, had never wanted her or any child. All those feelings came again to the fore as she trudged home dejectedly, knowing that her mother would be furious, because, given all the witnesses to her onslaught on the other girl, within hours her transgression would be a source of gossip and scandal all over the parish.

Her mother had always prided herself on the Christian rectitude and respectability of her small household – they'd been dubbed locally 'the Holy Family'. She had always been the first to volunteer when flowers for the chapel or repairs to Mass vestments were needed. That her daughter could put a classmate in hospital? She would feel she could never again hold her head up in the town.

Unable to delay any longer, Grace used her key to get in but her mother, who must have been watching for her, was already in the hallway. In front of her, she held a long, newly acquired bamboo cane.

Grace had never been able to deal with what had happened next. Each time the image had flashed to her mind, it had skipped immediately over the beating to the aftermath. Her legs welted and sore, she had buried her head in her pillows to deaden the sound of her crying: the humiliation more agonising than physical injury.

Then the doorbell had rung.

For the rest of her life, her memories of her beloved father had been haunted by the remorse and guilt she had never been able to shift: if she hadn't lost her temper that day, the father who loved her would not have been summoned home from work to deal with this disaster, would not have been trying to make speed on the inside of a lorry turning left at a junction in the town. That doorbell would not have rung, and she wouldn't have heard the voice of the priest, the low rumble of the sergeant's.

And now Maxine was to leave as well.

The development of cancer, it is said by some, is speeded up by stress. If only she hadn't blanked Maxine. And for so long . . .

She dried her eyes and began, wearily, to empty the shopping bags and to assemble the items for packing into her suitcase. But she couldn't stop thinking of Max, of the last time they'd met in Arnotts, that first Thursday in December.

She had snapped that day when Maxine had taken off on the wings of her well-worn reiteration that Grace's handling of her daughter needed revision and became increasingly vociferous in advocating that she should change her own behaviour.

Sometimes, when everything seemed bleak, she would admit to herself that those words had hurt so much because their quantum of truth was high, highlighting how trapped she and Leonie were, shackled together.

That day, they were still on their starters when Maxine took the reins of the conversation, while Grace had responded as she usually did, quietly holding to her own position, although internally already seething: 'I do understand what you're saying, Max, honestly I do. What would you *actually* have me do, though? Abandon her? Go to Australia and forget about her? Harry and his wife certainly wouldn't take her on, I'd bet on that, and as for her sisters ...'

'What about her looking after herself? That's the whole point of this conversation, Grace. You're too soft. You have to harden up. That young woman has to be made to realise that the world doesn't revolve around her. She has to grow up but she won't, or can't, Grace, until you cut the apron strings.' Angrily she slapped butter on her bread.

'And, believe me,' she picked up another slice, 'she's damaging you, Grace. She's going to ruin your life – she already has, to a degree. I can see your spirit dying because she's bringing you down with her and in a way that's what she wants because, as we all know, misery loves company.' At last, she looked directly at Grace.

'Sorry, I know this is hard and I hate to be so blunt because I know she can't help the way she is, but someone has to say this. It's you I'm thinking of.'

Abruptly, Grace had jumped to her feet: 'I've to go to the Ladies.'

There, she had surveyed herself in the mirror above the

roaring hand drier. Was Maxine right? Had the real Grace disappeared beneath the two parallel frown lines over the bridge of her nose, the grooves curving from the sides of her mouth to her chin, the feathering around her half-dead eyes and above her top lip?

And what about the all-too-visible pink parting line in her hair, once so abundant, now limp and thin?

She combed it sideways over the parting, fluffed it up and steeled herself to go back to the table. Once she was sitting down, instead of telling Maxine to go and jump in a lake, as she wanted to, she said she wasn't feeling well, and asked if, for this year, they could skip the rest of their routine because she needed to get home. There had been just that one phone call since then, when Grace had hung up on Maxine, and the freeze-out had followed. But now, in just eleven months, the tide sure had turned.

She flung the new clothes for the Arctic into the suitcase but could barely see what she was doing through tears of frustration, sorrow and fear.

How was she going to be true to herself during tomorrow's phone call to Max? True to both of them?

And why the hell had she agreed to go to the bloody Arctic in the first place?

She pulled the suitcase off the bed but she hadn't closed it and everything – nightdresses, toiletries, underwear, dresses, jumpers, jeans, phone chargers, adapters – spilled out onto her new boots, new clothes and meagre stash of jewellery. She gazed at the jumble, then gave in to the tears and threw herself back on her bed, this time climbing under the duvet and pulling it up to her chin.

The mess on the floor characterised the state of her life.

10

In the boarding hall at the port of Kiel, Ben Brady, passport and boarding pass in hand, was spending his time as he normally did when standing in a crowd: he was watching for behavioural tics and quirks that he could employ to add colour and authenticity to characters in future novels. Plots were to be found everywhere.

Why is that man fidgeting and looking around so much – something to hide?

That's a weird, mismatched outfit that woman's wearing – what does it signify? Rebellion? From whom or where?

The observational habit persisted, despite his publisher having dropped him after two books of a three-book deal, dashing his ambition, like many another's, to be 'the next

John Grisham'. He was sad about that, but the urge to keep writing was strong. He was taking the cruise courtesy of his uncle, also his godfather and his only remaining relative, who had offered it as consolation and distraction.

Marcus, a comfortably-off businessman, had always been aware of Ben's interest in the environment: his nephew's distress at, for instance, the melting of the polar ice caps had been the trigger for his choice of the Arctic as destination. He had also suggested that this might serve as an opportunity to change direction with his novels. 'Maybe you could write one with climate change as the theme. When you see for yourself what's happening up there, the danger we're all in, at least you'll be able to portray it with authority. I know your interest is in crime writing but you could maybe start with a body surfacing from under the ice when it melted prematurely?'

Ben, who had promised he'd at least think about it, was now otherwise engaged, his attention caught by two women in the line parallel to his but a good way ahead. He judged the taller of the two, towering over the other, to be the older – something about her posture brought the word 'statuesque' to mind.

Like many Americans, even those educated to college level (English, with a minor in environmental studies), Ben's knowledge of the physical geography and topography of Europe had remained sketchy. It was based largely on TV news bulletins and movie locations: the Eiffel Tower, Big Ben, the Berlin Wall, the Steppes of Russia and, with his distant Irish lineage, shootings in Belfast, the Cliffs of

Moher, the Blarney Stone and Dublin's fair city where Bono and the other members of U2 hailed from.

This was his first trip to Europe, and before his arrival at Kiel port a quarter-hour prior to going into the terminal, he had expected that the town would be encased in a sort of watery Ruhr Valley, surrounded by smoke stacks and cranes.

There were a few of the latter, he saw, but the city in which the port nestled, reborn from the ashes of extensive bombing during the Second World War, was pretty but not spectacularly so: a low-rise city in a level hinterland.

That day, most of the port's larger berths were empty, except the one holding a massive luxury liner moored directly behind his ship. Its bridge projected over its sides, a shelf seeming too large for its supports, and the flanks of this mammoth carried an eight-storey stack of balconies, like festoons of white lace.

By contrast, although just as white and shiny as the liner, his ship the *Magyar Bla*, minnow in the shadow of a whale, was modest.

The line containing the two women was moving faster than his. A couple of things about their stance, the slight distance between them and the fact that they weren't conversing, indicated they were possibly related – in his experience, friends tended to be, well, more *friendly* with each other in situations like this. The older woman's hair was fair, the younger's so dark as to be almost black, had been cropped boyishly close to her head.

It might have been the shortness of the hair and her small

frame but, for Ben, she brought to mind Sinéad O'Connor, the Irish singer with the electric voice, when she'd been at the height of her fame in the US.

Although he had been only four years old when the singer had famously ripped up a picture of the pope on *Saturday Night Live*, his Catholic mom – perhaps because O'Connor was Irish, perhaps because she had simply admired that gorgeous voice – had remained faithful to her music. Her huge international hit, a cover of Prince's 'Nothing Compares 2 U', had been played a lot in their apartment while he was growing up. When he was clearing it out after his mom died, that record was one of the few things he had kept.

While the line holding the two women moved ahead again, his remained frustratingly static because of what was going on with a couple at the check-in desk. The guy, almost as wide as he was tall and wearing cowboy boots embellished with heavy silver, was arguing heatedly about something in his paperwork while she gazed off into the middle distance as though she didn't know him.

The women Ben had been observing turned round simultaneously as though they'd heard something behind them, and before the O'Connor lookalike turned back, her eyes met his.

Coup de foudre!

Such a cliché, he scolded himself, but there was no other way to put it. He had experienced it before but, sadly, the fire had never lasted, although if he'd managed to follow it up, there had been a few nice months each time. It happens

– your heart suddenly misses a beat, takes an unexpected, almost nauseating leap, pausing as though in mid-air, then resumes normal service.

So he was familiar with the phenomenon from fiction, songs, movies and his own experience, especially when he was a teenager and it was happening every month or so. It became rarer when he was a student at college, where, tall and athletic enough, he'd been inducted into the basketball squad and as a reserve on the swim team.

As an acknowledged jock, he didn't have to try too hard with the girls because he could take his pick – and did – of those available, and some who weren't.

But he continued to fall in love quite often, or thought he did, even after graduation when he had stuck around Loyola's Chicago campus on Sheridan Road, covering the rent on his studio walk-up by taking shifts in the college library – where, again, it was easy to find dates.

But he was thirty now and a little taken aback to experience the phenomenon again. He hadn't been watching for it.

Brief as that flash glance had been, he'd registered that this girl's face was heart-shaped with a delicate chin, and even at that distance, in her pale face her eyes, large, with a cat-like upward slant at the outer corners under a widow's peak, were extraordinary. How would he describe her in a novel? Even if Ben's literary themes were more Tom Clancy than Anita Shreve, if he *were* to write about her in a novel, if this cruise proved to be the catalyst that his uncle hoped it would . . .

A title occurred to him: *The Eyes Have It.*

He couldn't wait to meet her. He could, of course, simply walk over to the women and introduce himself, though that would be pushing his luck. They'd have plenty of opportunities to encounter one another on board. Their ship held just 805 passengers, according to the bumf, and they had ten days, nine after today, which the brochure had classed as Day Two, the overnight in Hamburg being Day One. (Bit misleading, if you asked Ben. They weren't going to be properly at sea, it appeared, until Day Three.)

He watched while the girl and her companion progressed to the check-in desk, then headed for the entrance to the ship. As they left, the older one turned briefly as though surveying the hall and, unless he was mistaken, caught his eye. But her glance took just a second or two before she turned away and followed the girl.

He was dying to describe this girl to Marcus. Even as a child, and then a teenager, Ben had found he could talk far more openly to his uncle about all sorts of things, particularly his feelings, than to his mom, who had raised him on her own and whose instincts, worn on both sleeves, had always been to protect him at all costs.

The smallest indication of trouble in Ben's life frequently turned into a major event and meant she would instantly whirl into fix-it action, taking on his problems and making them her own. He had learned to be cautious, not to involve her unless in an emergency. Normally he confided only something positive, an A for his high-school poetry assignment, a goal scored for his soccer team . . .

By contrast, Marcus, his mother's only sibling, was a quiet, steady mentor and, with no children of his own – and an early, messy divorce from an unwise marriage – he had always been part of Ben's life and had had plenty of time to devote to him. Marcus, Ben had always thought, was the lucky possessor of a compartmentalised brain, unlike his own, which skidded and hopped from subject to subject, no matter how hard he tried to control it. This drawback could be discerned in his writing, his publisher had told him, when giving him the bad news about his third book. The man had delivered it face to face, urging Ben to take courses or, at the very least, attend writers' workshops. 'Then come back to me,' he'd said. 'We can work on the damn thing together. It's not *all* bad.'

While not wealthy in the general US understanding of the word, Marcus was entrepreneurial and had deep pockets. His response to Ben's repeated childhood remark that 'Mom says you're rich, Marcus' had always been 'I'm at the upper end of comfortable, kid! And that's enough for me. Enough for anyone.'

Even when still a barman, however, Ben's godfather had never left his sister wanting for a little extra money around Christmas or Thanksgiving or during periods when her rapidly growing son needed new and ever-larger sneakers, sports gear or weather-proof jackets to tide him over Chicago's vicious winters.

He was equally generous with Ben directly. Gifts for birthdays, Christmas and other gala occasions were bountiful but offered in two parts: a third in cash to Ben, the other two-thirds by cheque directly into a college fund, thus proving that Marcus was not just a great godfather-uncle but showing by example where his godson-nephew's priorities should lie. Ben's mother had chosen wisely.

With the travel documents between them on Marcus's desk in the den-cum-office of the duplex he maintained on Oak Street, just off Lake Shore Drive in Chicago, uncle and nephew sat opposite one another.

The desk was messy, piled with business files, photos of Ben's mom, Ben in his graduation gown, and in an ornate frame, an age-spotted portrait of a stern-faced couple, she sitting, the strings of her bonnet tied under her chin, the toes of her buttoned boots peeking from under the hem of her long dark dress, he heavily moustached and clad in an equally dark suit, standing behind her. Ben's great-grandparents.

Also amid the clutter on the desk was a humidor, apparently the only surviving object of note handed down the Brady generations. It was believed to have been carried across the Atlantic from County Mayo in Ireland along with this couple's other chattels sometime in the 1900s.

Ben had already thanked his uncle for the gift of the cruise and they had graduated to chatting about more general matters. He noticed that his uncle was fiddling with the object, running an index finger across the plate, opening and closing the lid; he had noticed before that this was a habit his uncle indulged when he was uncharacteristically nervous, or had something important to say.

He waited quietly.

Eventually Marcus closed the humidor's lid. 'I've something to tell you, kid.'

'Sounds serious.'

'It is, I'm afraid.' His uncle got up from his chair and, from a percolator on a side table, poured coffee for himself. 'Want one?' He held up a second cup.

'No thanks.'

Marcus sat down again and, while the coffee grew cold, told his nephew that he'd had an offer for the Brady Group – three 'Irish' pubs in downtown Chicago and two hotels in Indiana, one in his hometown of Gary, the other in Indianapolis, both at the centre of commerce. In addition, as part of the overall package, he owned development sites in both cities, with ready-to-go plans in place to expand one of the pubs and build a third hotel. 'It was a good offer and there's money enough for me – and you, of course – to live comfortably for the rest of our lives. I'm going to take it.' Then, grasping the humidor, he confessed. 'Actually, that's bending the truth a little. I've already signed. I didn't want to tell you until the deal was done. I was worried you'd be upset and that maybe I'd change my mind. But this is something I really want. Sorry if I've upset you.'

'Wow!' To say that Ben was taken aback would be an understatement. He had braced himself for yet another lecture from his godfather about there being no future in writing novels unless you actually *were* John Grisham or Tom Clancy. 'But I always got the impression your heart and soul were in your business, Marcus?'

'They were, probably, but no longer. I detest the way this

country is going now. I know the economy's good but that's on the surface, in my opinion. It's not filtering downwards, and I know it's easy for me to say now, but the discovery that there's more to life than making money is not a new one for me. This hatred and faction fighting, the open racism you see these days, and the death of civility, everything's getting to me beyond endurance. I can't turn on the TV any more – except for *The Simpsons*!' The knuckles of the hands grasping the humidor were now white.

'I didn't know you were so unhappy – you never said a word!' Ben tried to sound empathic, but it would take him a while to come to terms with this. It was change on a momentous scale and not just for his uncle. Why hadn't he noticed this before of Marcus? Had he been that self-centred?

'What was the point of talking to anyone about it before the deal was done?' His uncle shrugged. 'I would have upset you for nothing. Anyway, neither you nor anyone else has had any way to change what's happening in American society. Nobody does now, it appears. And that's another pressure, the feeling of individual helplessness. This offer, which came out of the blue, felt like someone was throwing a lifeline to a drowning man. Sorry to be so pompous.'

'You're far from pompous, Marcus. You're definitely planning on leaving?'

'No plans made yet but I can. I need to find what I'm looking for and I don't know yet what that might be, but I have the money to do almost anything I want. And, guess what, I have an Irish passport – I've had it for years because I discovered I was eligible, through these two.' He touched the photograph. 'On a whim, I thought, Why not? Never pass up any opportunity! I was always too busy to take trips but now the whole of Europe is open to me, to get my feet under the table of another venture or simply to live a calm life someplace nice.'

He went on to reassure Ben, telling him that while he was already prospecting online for suitable sites or venues to fulfil his dream, he wouldn't immediately be doing anything rash, like selling his duplex: given the apartment's location, plenty in the city would bite his hand off to rent it. 'If I sold it, I might even rent it myself from the new owner to have a place here to get back to from time to time.'

But more was to come, even more startling: Marcus went on, shyly, to reveal a pipe dream he'd cherished for years but had never spoken about to anyone until now. 'I couldn't be an astronaut, never going to happen, ever,' he grinned, 'but I've always wanted to build a little place for myself somewhere by the water – river, lake or ocean, it doesn't matter – and hire someone to teach me to fish.'

He'd always figured, he said, this would be in Montana, Washington State, or even Alaska. 'But now,' he added with a passion Ben had rarely seen, 'no way in the USA. Not any more. America is no longer good for my soul or my mental health. There are many places on this planet that I think would be better, countries like Scotland, Ireland, Switzerland, or almost anywhere in Scandinavia . . .'

Sighing, he let the humidor be. 'So, what do you think?

You might come visit? Or even to live? You know my views on that dead-end job of yours in the library. You never know, you might like what I find, or what I build. Peace for your writing, lots of nice landscapes? Healthy food?'

'Let me think about it.' Ben was still flummoxed. He'd had his own dream – the foundations of which were now toast, following his publishers' lack of faith in him. Should he accept Marcus's dream for himself too, a puppy following his master to Europe, being cared for as though he was still a child? Or was this the wake-up call he'd always known would come some day? The prospect had been fearsome and exciting in equal measures. He had just been too lazy and too comfortable to hasten it.

He was by now out on deck. It was dark, all the pier lights illuminated and in the town, traffic presumably homegoing, was increasing.

His ruminations were shattered when the huge liner behind, its rails and balconies lined with passengers, emitted a monstrous, three-toned blast of its horn. Then a second and a third: it was about to leave.

Ben decided to cease this navel-gazing. He would have time during the cruise to do some serious thinking about his life.

Right now, though, it was time for him to go inside where his girl waited to be found. As early as this evening? In just another couple of hours ...

II

Having arrived early with Leonie at the ship's main dining room on their first evening on the *Magyar Bla*, Grace approached the affable maître d', and managed to secure a corner table for two rather than being placed at any of the larger tables for four, six or eight. This was lucky because there weren't many 'couples' tables', and as the room filled, tables seemed to be allocated as the diners came in, without much checking of nationality or language compatibility.

She still hadn't properly relaxed. While so far everything had gone smoothly, far better than she had expected, she was half afraid to ride this wave. She had feared how her daughter might react if they were placed at a larger table: at first glance, while there were a few young couples, this wasn't a family cruise. She didn't see a single child or teenager, and the average age seemed weighted towards the forties and fifties.

The room, although rather old-fashioned, was lovely, lit by strategically placed lanterns and a massive central chandelier of multicoloured glass, giving everything a festive atmosphere. 'We're lucky! This is a great table, isn't it?' she said to Leonie, as they settled themselves. 'Nice to be beside a window too, although there isn't much to see outside now it's dark.' She looked around. 'I'd hate to be stuck out in the middle – it must be like sitting in the Tower of Babel, all these nationalities!'

'Whatever.' Leonie's response was sulky, as her mother had feared. Her sunny mood hadn't lasted long. 'And by the way, you needn't think I'm on for a chat. I'm peed off that I'm not in the Shelbourne with Cherry. Tonight's her night and they must all be arriving at this stage.' She would probably have said more but the waiter had arrived at their table with his little notebook and proceeded to give his spiel about the chef's specials, wines, extra charges and so on. He was friendly but not particularly handsome and Leonie didn't bother with him.

After he had left with their order, Grace, taking another look around the tables, spotted the very tall guy who, she thought, had been eyeballing her daughter in the boarding hall. That's all they'd need now, she thought. She'd have to keep an eye not just on Leonie but on him too. *Please, God,* she prayed silently, *let him find some other woman he likes or, better than that, let some other woman find him!*

69

At present he was sitting at a table for four with three elderly people, two females (one in a wheelchair) and another male. To judge by the rapt body language of the three as they leaned forward to listen to what he was saying, he'd made an instant impression. Full of himself, no doubt. It was difficult to guess his nationality – maybe Eastern European. Weren't a lot of them very tall? This young man was certainly the tallest in the room, as far as she could see . . .

A second waiter came with the wine she'd ordered from the most expensive wine list she'd ever seen (she was worth it! Feeling her oats, as her late father would have said). She'd settled on a Bordeaux, mid-priced, by Norwegian standards, thinking that she could have bought a coat in Dunnes for what it cost. This was her first dinner on board, and it had finally struck her that she was on holiday. Holidays meant getting off the island so you shed your normal skin to become whomever you chose. At home, their little estate was a mini-community in which the residents of each house knew the business of those in the other six.

The only drag on her during this cruise was sure to be Leonie, and while it wasn't wonderful that she had to be on watch, she would make sure there was time for her to do her own thing. One of the activities on offer involved bridge sessions at every level, no matter how inexperienced. She had started to learn before Harry had left her but then, having drawn into her shell, she had given it up. It would be good to get it going again.

Right now, she decided, glancing over her wineglass at her daughter, determined not to let Leonie's capricious mood-changes dominate her, she wouldn't attempt conversation. Leonie would talk when she was ready to do so. Their starters arrived and Grace concentrated on the food.

*

The meal finished, the remaining wine labelled with their names for tomorrow's dinner, Grace saw that the crowd in the dining room had begun to thin out and suggested that the two of them should go for a walk around the decks. 'Let's get our jackets and gloves.'

'I'm tired.' Her daughter yawned.

'I am too,' Grace said, 'but it's very bad for your health – and for your figure, Leonie! – to go straight to bed after a heavy meal. Did you enjoy it by the way?'

'It was all right.'

'So will you come? I promise that if it's too cold or windy – I can feel the ship moving a bit now – we'll be straight back in. We haven't had much fresh air today with all the travel. Guess what? We're on our way to the Arctic, Leonie! To see nature at her most pure and, with the rainforests, most damaged, thanks to us humans. Surely that's of interest to you? If it's not, it should be. It certainly is for me.'

'It's your generation that's doing the damage, not mine. Oh, for God's sake,' Leonie grumped, 'is this how it's going to be? You ordering me around every half-second?'

'We could have a nightcap in one of the bars?'

'So you can give out to me about the no-alcohol rules because of my meds?'

'Look,' Grace was losing patience, 'I don't want to be controversial or to re-start old arguments, but with that medication – it's even written on the label – you know the score, Leonie.'

'Would you ever let me forget it?'

'Right.' Grace stood up. 'You do what you like. I'm going for a walk to get some air into my lungs and do a bit of exploring. It's my first time on a cruise ship and I'm going to make the most of it. See you later.'

She walked away from the table but had got only as far as the doors when she heard Leonie behind her: 'All right, all right, you win. But I'm not promising to be happy about this. About this whole thing! I should be in the Shelbourne.' She followed her mother through the doors and into the lifts so they could go to their cabins and fetch their outdoor clothing.

Abruptly, Grace felt sorry for her daughter. She couldn't say it because it would mean showing Harry up, but Leonie *should* be in the Shelbourne.

As for herself, while she had been truthful in saying she was going to make the most of the trip, she was a bit sorry for herself too. Perhaps it was the effect of the half-bottle of wine she'd consumed, but she felt an upsurge of resentment about her station in life. Why should she be carrying every inch of what she hated to think of as 'the burden' of caring for Leonie, especially while she could glimpse what freedom might be like, should she have been here on her own.

Yes, she was officially on holiday, but she remained on permanent sentry duty, while Leonie's other parent blithely got on with his life. No doubt, in tuxedo and dicky-bow, he was at present the life and soul of Cherry's party, with other guests going up to her to say, laughing, 'Your husband's a gas!'

She had to acknowledge, though, that in this case, while Harry did the heavy lifting, Charlotte Burns was the driver, so maybe she should feel a little sorry for him too. He clearly didn't run things at home and maybe this was why he played so much golf. And should he encounter a new Cherry who 'needed' him, would he abandon her and Jasmine too?

But feeling sorry for Harry didn't last long. And as for Cherry, unless he had performed a complete con job on her, she must have known that her new husband hadn't arrived unencumbered.

She didn't like this line of thought. It was beneath her and was certainly not healthy. Actually, right now, there was very little that was enjoyable about walking around the deck of the ship. Wind, the kind that bit into your face and watered your eyes, was blowing directly from the north, it seemed, and both women gave up after just a few minutes, retreating to a brightly lit bar. It was thronged, its customers clearly enjoying the performance of a piano player, who was entertaining them with a selection of popular songs, requesting everyone to join in the choruses, prompting them with lyrics.

Among the audience Grace saw the tall young man she had quietly worried about.

And to confirm her fears, having obviously spotted them coming in, he immediately crossed the floor to them when the pianist announced a short break. Close up, he reminded her starkly of Jaden, Las Vegas, that short-lived marriage, Sharon's understandable defection – the whole nine yards. More dangerously, beside her, she could feel Leonie sit up straight, either thinking the same or reacting physically to his presence.

There wasn't much Grace could do except be polite when he spoke first to her: 'Hi, there. I'm Ben! We were together in the boarding lines earlier. Great to meet you guys.'

'You're American?'

Horror piled on horror for Grace as he grinned. 'Got it in one! And you are?'

This time he had addressed Leonie, who responded immediately. 'We're Irish. I'm Leonie, and this is Grace.' She indicated her mother.

'You guys Irish? That's really cool. Mind if I sit down?' Without waiting for an answer, he folded himself into one of the seats vacated by a couple beside them. 'I'm second-generation Irish, as a lot of Americans are, I guess. And, hey, Leonie, you remind me of Sinéad O'Connor. That's what I thought when I saw you during boarding, and for a couple of seconds I actually thought you might be her! Anyone tell you that before?'

Grace, suspecting this was one of his chat-up lines, nevertheless saw that her daughter was captivated, and intervened curtly with the first thing that occurred to her: 'Sinéad O'Connor would be much older, I think, Ben.'

'Oh, I know that, Grace.' He wasn't fazed. It wasn't the first time she'd noticed that Americans overuse names. 'She was my mom's favourite singer. Can I get you guys a drink?'

'Gin and tonic,' Leonie said immediately.

Simultaneously, Grace shook her head and darted a warning glance at her daughter. 'No thanks, Ben. We're probably leaving shortly anyhow.'

'I'm not.' Leonie smirked at her. 'You go if you like, Grace.'

'I might just do that.' Grace had spoken more sharply than she'd intended, the edge too evident. He had noticed the by-play, she saw, and was looking a little puzzled.

'You know what, Ben?' She smiled warmly at him. 'I've changed my mind. I'll have a glass of red wine, please.'

As he went off to negotiate the crush around the bar, she glanced at Leonie, who was avidly following his progress. 'He's very nice, isn't he, Mum?' Those eyes of hers had lit up.

'Seems to be all right,' she said coolly, 'but Americans, as you should know better than most, Leonie, can be very plausible.'

'You're on about Jaden again, aren't you?' Her daughter bridled. 'Are you ever going to let me forget that?'

'It was less than a year ago. Are you surprised that it's lodged in my memory? Yes, this chap seems nice, but I'm not sure I'd trust him.' She knew she was playing with fire: her disapproval might prod Leonie to go for the American

75

because her mother disapproved. 'So let's wait and see,' she added. 'So far he's certainly polite. And he has the gift of the gab, like Jaden did, you have to admit that.'

'So that's a crime now, is it?'

'You don't have to be so defensive. I'm not attacking him or you. We're just talking. About someone we don't know, who, for some reason, has singled us out to buy us a drink. Neither of us knows a thing about him – he could be all kinds of criminal for all we know. He and one of those barmen up there could even be in league to drug us!' This was stretching it but she was desperate to kill off an incipient dalliance. 'You read about that all the time, these days.'

'Are you for real?' Leonie was craning to keep him in sight. 'I doubt he's part of a drugs cartel, Mum. He's not the type.'

'What *is* the type and how would you know?' Grace's unease was building. 'They don't have to *look* like criminals. The most successful of them look like your average next-door neighbour with nice kids. And before you yell at me,' she held up her hand to prevent the response, 'we're already at top volume because of the din in here. All I'm asking is that we wait a bit. If he's on the level and just buying us a drink, that's fine. But we have to be careful.'

Leonie was no longer listening. 'He's got a great body,' she said, her words almost lost in the uproar. 'Wouldn't you say so, Mum? I'd say he's an athlete.'

'Maybe. Although I wasn't looking at his body, Leonie.' That wasn't strictly true. She had noticed the lean flanks, long legs and how the tight jeans flattered him. In fairness, she hadn't been the only one because, while he waited for the barman to take his order, she had seen that several women and, indeed, a few men were studying him, not just because of his height. Beside her, Leonie's eyes were out on stalks.

'Leonie, honey,' she took her daughter's arm, 'be sensible now. Given what happened last Christmas, the last thing you should be doing now is admiring the body of a man you know nothing about.'

Instead of answering, Leonie gave her a look that would have killed a bramble.

It didn't kill Grace's alarm bells.

12

An hour or so later, those alarm bells were still audible at the back of Grace's brain although she had to admit that they weren't as loud. The young man was no Jaden, as far as she could judge in that crammed bar, with its over-enthusiastic pianist and ever-eager, raucous audience for whom no high note was too challenging. Private conversations definitely were, though, so the two women and Ben had to confine theirs to conventional swapping of small-talk.

They discovered he was originally from Gary, Indiana, but lived now in Chicago; this cruise had been a gift from his (very) generous uncle, who was also his godfather, a businessman with a small chain of hospitality venues. His own flat was near Loyola University, where he worked in the library. And he was a published author of two novels.

Leonie, beating Grace to a response, told him they lived in a suburb of Dublin with a wonderful sea view; since college, her career had been in journalism and she had been commissioned to write an article about her experience in the Arctic.

Grace, keeping a straight face, got as far as telling Ben she used to work for Aer Lingus, had taken early retirement and that Baldoyle was the name of her suburb. She was about to describe it when a particularly raucous chorus of 'Delilah', evidently a crowd favourite, rendered the transmission of any other details moot. Instead, she stood up and yelled she was buying them another round.

It took a fair amount of time to get close enough to the bar to order, and when she did, she asked the barman to go easy on the gin in her daughter's glass.

As she wove through the crowds, trying to keep the three drinks steady, she was dismayed to see that in her short absence Leonie had moved into flirting mode, not quite as audaciously as she had on that lethal night in the restaurant, but obviously enough for it to show. She was sitting very close to Ben, linking her arm with his. Even from that distance, her mother could discern she was using those eyes of hers to fullest effect. Déjà vu. Her heart sank.

To be fair to Ben, though, while he was smiling down at her, reciprocating the locked-eyes thing, he didn't seem to be fully engaged. Perhaps, unlike Jaden, he was holding back because the venue was so public. Or maybe he was just more of a gentleman and had recognised that Leonie was vulnerable.

Or maybe, she hoped, he just wasn't into her daughter.

He detached himself when she arrived with the drinks, leaping to his feet to take them from her. Thankfully, Leonie behaved properly (perhaps, thought her mother, because she knew that Ben, like herself, was a captive on the little ship for days to come and she'd have plenty more opportunities with him).

She was ignoring her mother, her back turned completely. But Ben noticed and made several efforts to include her in the conversation, talking across Leonie. He had manners.

The uproar increased in volume as the bar's patrons continued to drink, and while Ben said he'd stay for just one more, Grace called it a night at around nine o'clock. 'You said you were tired, Leonie,' she reminded her. 'You must be now – it's been a long day.'

'I am actually.' To Grace's astonishment, she agreed.

Ben stood up, helping Leonie to her feet. Then he bent to extricate her handbag from under her chair. Before he could straighten up to his full height, she had pulled him towards her, planted a kiss on his cheek and, giving him a little wave, followed her mother into the relative peace of the ship's main concourse.

In the lift down to their deck, she was hyper, bubbling over, even, to Grace's near-stupefaction, thanking her for bringing her on the cruise. 'I was *sooo* afraid it would be boring, boring, *boring*, but now that I've met Ben – I think he likes me, Mum! What do you think? You should stop reminding me about Jaden. Ben is a terrific person and he's gorgeous too – even you must see that.'

She wrinkled her beautiful eyes and, with one hand, swiped at the air. 'Take *that*, Jackie, with your little midget Mick! Mum, Ben's The One, I'm sure of it, and when you were up at the bar getting those drinks, you'll never believe what he told me!'

'Take it easy, darling.' Grace simply couldn't let her go on like this, memories of that middle-of-the-night phone call she'd had from Las Vegas still being all too fresh. Her daughter had been happy then, too happy, soaring on the upside of her unique, oscillating world. Grace knew that the more dazzling that summit, the darker the abyss after the fall, as Leonie had so tragically discovered but had now conveniently cast aside. 'Here's our floor,' Grace said, as the doors slid open. 'And it's not fair to call poor Mick a midget.'

'He's smaller than Jackie, though.'

'And what size are you, may I ask? With both of your sisters nearly as tall as me, how would you like it if the neighbours referred to you as "the midget of Winslow Close"? Wouldn't you think that might be a bit cruel?' This was provocative, deliberately so. She was risking an outburst – anything, though, to distract her daughter from unrealistic and untenable heights, thus saving her from the inevitable crash.

As predicted, a huge row did ensue. As they made their way along the corridor towards their adjacent cabins,

Leonie raged at her, calling her names, accusing her of making her life hell, of driving away everyone she'd ever loved, her dad, for instance, and now Cherry. 'It's you who did this, isn't it? You fancied this fucking cruise and persuaded Dad to give you the money because you were jealous of me being invited to the Shelbourne and you weren't!

'But you did let Adeline and Jackie go, didn't you? You never wanted me. I'm surprised you didn't have an abortion.' Then, forestalling Grace's reaction, 'It's true, it's true! I was the accident, wasn't I? And that's why you always liked the other two before me. What's wrong with you, Mother? You have to drive everyone away from me. Is it that you're so fucking lonely and abandoned that you want me to feel the same? Well, it's *over*, Mother. Suck it up! I'm no longer your go-to punchbag. You'll have to find someone else to be your daughter in your exclusive, mother–daughter fantasy castle. So tell me – tell me the truth, Grace, why do you always want it to be just the two of us? That's sick. I resign!'

Leaving Leonie to huff her way into her cabin, Grace was happy to enter hers, delighted to see her bed had been turned down. She undressed quickly and slid into its smooth depths, while re-running the evening and the row.

That mother–daughter scenario had been new, and she asked herself if it could have arisen because both she and Leonie had suffered failed marriages, had been abandoned by their spouses, and were somehow permanently bound together in failed-marriage hell. But she'd managed to suffer it in silence, along with all the other insults, again without overt reaction. Despite the stoicism she was hurt but: *No expressed emotion!*

The distraction created by the row wouldn't hold for long, she knew, but she might have gained a bit of time to explain the situation to Ben. She'd have to avoid giving him the sense that she was criticising Leonie, even dumping on her, but was merely trying to be helpful. She could impart a short, judiciously edited slice of her daughter's history and vulnerability, citing the Las Vegas episode and explaining that Jaden had been a predator, dallying with Leonie's impetuous desires and ambitions while feeding on her very obvious beauty.

And while as her mother she accepted her daughter's right to fall in love with whomever she chose, Grace's watchfulness existed mainly because something within Leonie did not, could not, recognise what was good for her.

Ben would believe, correctly, that this was a mother interfering, but she'd earned that right. If she handled this properly, she hoped he would see that she was acting with the best of intentions towards not just Leonie but him.

This young man seemed to have been well brought up but one short encounter in a noisy bar, while being forced by a rowdy crowd to become lip-readers, was far from conducive to making judgements on someone's character. Already, however, Grace was willing to wager he wasn't a second Jaden.

Physically, he was gorgeous (Leonie's word), and Grace could certainly understand why her daughter had been so instantly attracted. In fact, that night there probably hadn't been a woman in the bar (maybe a man or two as well) who hadn't covertly thought they wouldn't mind a shot at him.

A piece of paper was slipped under her door. She got up to check it out.

I'm in love with Ben, so stay away from me, Mother, and stop interfering. I have my rights and I've decided I want nothing to do with you. You don't support me, you don't love me. Well, news for you, Grace. The feeling is reciprocal. L

So! Gorgeous, yes, but Jaden had been gorgeous too. Caution still to the fore.

13

It was two in the morning and Grace had been in bed for four hours and eleven minutes but there was no sign of sleep. She'd had her warm shower, she'd read six chapters of her book.

TV, which usually helped her drop off, hadn't been an ally this time. There seemed to be no end to the number of shopping channels, and while she was very interested in environmental issues, even when she'd found a nature programme, the constant interruptions with commercial breaks had become very irritating.

It didn't help that the altercation with Leonie kept repeating itself word-for-word in her brain although by now she would have thought she'd be inured to the rows.

Anyhow, she had gone beyond the point of sleeping, and as the ship chugged along, asked herself again what the hell she was doing here. She was angry with herself for being such a pushover. Eight more days of this? Could she stand it?

The cabin was warm, so that was something. The bed was comfortable too – and Leonie had left her target man and had come back to her own cabin, another bonus.

Her cabin offered a minibar, housed in a cupboard under the TV, so she decided to have one more try at sleep. She got out of bed, chose a miniature gin and a carton of orange juice, poured both into a tall glass and, going back to bed, drank half of the concoction as though it were lemonade.

Should she call Max? But it was after one a.m. at home – and, anyhow, they were at sea. No coverage.

How had it come to this with her friend? Those first boarding-school days, where they'd stuck together like a pair of orphan kittens, seemed very far away – those days when they'd confided in one another about their less-than-satisfactory home lives, but had been also, strangely, suffering from homesickness.

They'd complained routinely to each other about the nuns, while acknowledging they were decent and very good teachers to their small classes, but even that was frightening to Grace because it meant individual attention and fewer opportunities to hide from the herd . . . But despite all that, she had felt safe in that school, not just because the nuns were civilised, but because she knew Maxine had her back.

They were so close that the nuns worried about it, making sure that their beds were in different dormitories. This had been a mystery to both girls as it seemed like a punishment, and it wasn't until several years after her marriage that, for Grace, the penny had dropped.

She had immediately rung Maxine, who'd been in Germany at the time, and the two of them had regretted not pushing for an explanation at the time. They'd outdone each other in crafting the silliest, funniest sentences.

After both had married they'd made efforts to see each other, Grace using her Aer Lingus travel pass to go to Germany. Then Max had moved to Galway with Dieter, and although both women were busy, Grace by that time juggling kids and work, they remained close and saw each other when they could.

It was so sad, Grace thought, swigging the rest of her G & OJ, that they had split over Leonie's handling. Her friend's crusade had been hard to bear, but such a friendship should not have been allowed to lapse.

She looked at her watch. She was no nearer sleep. Maybe a bit of fresh air? Another bracing walk on the deck to clear her head?

She got out of bed again, dressed quickly, and left her stateroom. Before she went outside, however, she used the spare key to Leonie's cabin to crack open the door — if her daughter was awake she'd tell her she was going out for a bit.

The bed was empty.

Now she had a purpose. Had Leonie gone secretly to

meet Ben? Had they taken advantage of the noise in the bar to make arrangements, knowing that Leonie's mother wouldn't hear what was said? She remembered that for a lot of the time they were there Leonie had had her back turned to her.

Grimly, she went up in the lift, her 'bracing' walk now a search mission. If her suspicions proved to be correct, wherever they were she couldn't barge in, all guns blazing. She had to be restrained and polite – both were adults, she reminded herself – but she couldn't help falling into catastrophe mode. He had a cabin too (he hadn't mentioned a companion) so they might be in bed.

Supposing Leonie got pregnant! Grace, not privy to her daughter's contraception status, had worried about that with Jaden. She wasn't stable enough to handle a child and, de facto, Grace would become the resident granny-childminder, wouldn't she? Was that thought too selfish?

She arrived on the top deck, her face pulverised by the blast of cold wind generated by the ship's brisk progress on the sea, now choppy, so she pulled her woolly hat down over her forehead and, with gloved hands, pulled it as far as it would go over her cheeks. Where would she start the search?

If she went to the desk in the main concourse, would they give her Ben's cabin number? Hardly – everything was about privacy these days.

She decided to think outside the box. This was Leonie's first night on a ship. She was a fan of the *Titanic* film, having seen it twice, and being of a dramatic nature, wouldn't be beyond urging that Ben and herself replicate the scene where Kate Winslet and Leonardo DiCaprio stand in the bow of the liner, arms outstretched as though flying.

There were very few people around, naturally, but as she approached the bow she noticed a figure on the rail just in front of it. Her eyes were tearing up as a result of the cold, blurring her vision. Was it?

It was. Leonie. Alone. Wearing her pink jacket. Open.

Grace walked calmly up to her. 'Here long, Leonie? You couldn't sleep? Me neither.'

One of the ship's outdoor lights illuminated her daughter's face as she turned. 'Oh, hello, Mum.' Her expression was dreamy, her speech unnaturally slow.

Had Ben given her something? Cannabis, maybe? Had they been in bed and was this dreaminess post-coital – Grace had to make a huge effort to calm her racing thoughts. 'Shall we to go back to our cabins, Leonie? It's freezing out here.'

'Oh, I'm fine. It's cold but I don't mind – I won't be long. You go on and I'll follow you.'

'I'm worried about you.'

'Of course you are. You're always worried, Mum. It's kind of your job, isn't it, worrying about me?' There was no trace of the venom she'd displayed just a few hours previously, no hint of the sentiments in that note pushed under her own door. Grace, forcing herself to be calm and gentle, asked her if she'd seen Ben after the bar. 'He was quite nice, I thought.' She reached over to zip up the pink jacket and tie on its hood. Ordinarily, Leonie wouldn't have stood for this, but now she did, like a small child on her way to school.

'Ben? Nice, yeah,' she said, still in that disconcerting dreamy voice. 'He's gorgeous.'

'Come on in, Leonie – you'll get your death out here.'

'No, I won't. I like it here – you go on, Mum.' She turned her head to gaze out to sea and Grace felt she had no option but to leave.

It was only when she was back in the interior warmth and waiting for the lift that the old fear struck. Was Leonie contemplating suicide? Was this what people talked about, that calm that happened once the decision had been made? The lift came, its doors opening. She jammed them, trying to decide whether she should go out again on deck – remembering that both Harriet and Jenny had mentioned noticing a calming down before their children's final actions, but that it had been only in retrospect that they had realised its significance.

She stepped in and pressed a button. As the lift descended, she noticed there were lights on in a bar, a different one to that they'd been to earlier. She'd passed the floor but stopped the lift and went up again. The cold and the wind had served to wake her up and it wasn't more alcohol she sought. It was warmth and light, maybe uncomplicated companionship – even a short chat with a barman would help calm her fears.

14

On entering the bar, Grace realised that its ambience was the polar opposite to the one she'd been in earlier. The windows were shrouded with heavy curtains, the lamplight was dim, white candles flickered on tables and the seating was plush, upholstered armchairs and couches draped with a selection of soft woollen throws or rugs in ecru, pale pink and hazy blue.

There were fewer than a dozen people in the place, presumably insomniacs like herself. And then she saw that Ben was among them, sitting alone in an armchair halfway up the room, a beer in front of him, his back to her.

Should she just leave quietly?

Her presumption now was that he and her daughter had

been in bed and that Leonie had gone on deck to reflect. She had to confront this, but as tactfully as she could, and not be remotely aggressive because such an approach could be counter-productive. Presumably the sex between them had been consensual – Leonie's demeanour on the deck would certainly have suggested that.

As she tried to gather her thoughts, Ben drained his glass and stood up to leave, turning towards the door and seeing her.

'Grace?' He came towards her. 'Hello again! Welcome to the Koselig bar. Lovely, isn't it?' He seemed to think it was normal to come into a bar at half past two in the morning.

'It is,' she answered, asking herself if he would be so welcoming if he'd just slept with her daughter. Wouldn't there be a bit of a *frisson* if that had been the case? Or was he a consummate con artist, like Jaden? 'I just can't sleep,' she said, 'that's all.'

'I guess that's the common denominator for everyone in this bar – here, sit down. Let me get you a drink. It's red wine, isn't it?'

'But you were on your way out.'

'I haven't been able to sleep either, that jetlag is killing me – I was going to have another try. I'm very happy that I don't have to. So – wine? I'll join you with another beer.'

'Maybe a cup of tea, if they can do that for me.'

'I'm sure they can. It wouldn't be the first time they've been asked, I'd say. I have Scottish tablemates and two of them got tea after the meal. Please make yourself comfortable, Grace. I'll go up and ask.'

Grace, watching him cover the distance with long strides, thought that, as Leonie had remarked, he had to be an athlete. Was she still up there on the deck, freezing herself to death and not noticing it?

For once, Grace parked her rescue instinct because that, again, was mother-hen thinking – but it had been one-way traffic for so long that giving up her watchtower was difficult.

She still hadn't made up her mind about Ben. A chat could tell a lot. Maybe he could be a boyfriend for Leonie. Ease her isolation and loneliness?

But there she was again, trying to fix things when landed with yet another crisis surrounding her daughter. The content of that note on her bedside table, allied to the rare appearance of calm on deck, had left her in no doubt that, whatever had gone on between her daughter and Ben while she was out of the way, Leonie believed she was in love.

But first instincts to jump into action aren't always the cleverest and, watching him return to her, carefully bearing a small tray with sugar basin, milk jug and cutlery wrapped in a napkin, Grace decided she'd tread warily around him, not to speak of her daughter, in case she triggered something nuclear. 'No big deal,' he said, placing the tray on a side table beside her armchair. 'He'll bring the tea down to you.'

'Thank you. You're right, this is a nice place.' She eyed her surroundings.

'Yeah.' He folded himself into the armchair opposite. 'Did you read the notice at the door giving the meaning of "Koselig"?'

'No.' She shook her head. 'Tell me. Obviously it's a Norwegian word.'

'It's this country's equivalent to the Danish *hygge*. Heard of that?'

'Only in magazines. Something to do with comfort and cosiness?' She looked around at the plumped-up cushions, the heavy window curtains. 'Is that it?'

'Absolutely. I know about it because my uncle has done up one of his hotels, the one in Gary, with that concept in mind. It was a good bet from the get-go, a real hit in Hoosier town. The locals had never seen anything like it. He launched it in winter – and winter's really terrible in Gary. Folks majorly hibernate.'

Was she really discussing décor with a young man in a bar at this hour of the morning when her daughter was hanging over a ship's rail gazing into the sea? 'Tell me about this uncle of yours,' she said. 'From what you were saying to me and Leonie earlier in that singing pub, he sounded lovely.' Having deliberately brought her daughter into the conversation she watched for a response, but didn't detect anything in particular. Instead, he smiled fondly. 'He sure is – oh! Here's the tea!'

On the second tray, with teapot, teabags in a small dish beside it and little biscuits, there were two cups. 'You're having tea too?' She thanked the waiter on behalf of them both.

'Tea for two.' Ben laughed. 'I'd hate to know what some of my buddies at home would think of the tea-drinking! I just thought I'd keep you company.'

The light in the Koselig was low because it came mostly from candles and lanterns, but afterwards, when she was reviewing the evening, Grace could have sworn he'd blushed, and she was further reassured. Con artists don't blush.

*

It was after five when she got back to her stateroom, and before she let herself into it, Grace checked Leonie's.

Her daughter was lying on her back, snoring quietly, both arms flung cruciform as though welcoming the world (or appealing to it?). Her bedside lamp was still on and, under its beam, Grace noticed her open notebook, offering evidence of the torn-out page that had come under her door, but also something further. Another note?

The temptation was too great to resist and while listening and watching for any change in her daughter's breathing, she tiptoed silently towards the bed.

> *Mrs Leonie Brady invites you to afternoon tea.*
> *Mr and Mrs Harold McGee invite you to the wedding of their daughter, Leonie.*
> *Ben and Leonie invite you to their wedding.*

Then, columnar:

> *Beleonie . . .*
> *Brelonie*
> *Bramagee*

The third amalgamation sported a huge red tick and 'Yesssss' the line of *s*'s trailing all the way off the edge of the paper.

Compared with the page she'd delivered to Grace, this one was so childlike, and so full of hope, that tears rose to sting her mother's eyes.

Silently, continuing to listen and watch to make sure that her daughter was still deeply asleep, Grace took a step towards her bed and, afraid that a kiss might waken her, placed a hand, very lightly, on her shoulder. 'I love you,' she whispered. 'I love you so much, Leonie.'

*

Back in her own bed, exhausted but sleepless, Grace considered the events of that evening. So much for coming on holiday to escape the vicissitudes of life at 7 Winslow Close. The situation there had, it seemed, transferred seamlessly to the *Magyar Bla*.

It was entirely possible, she thought, that she'd jumped the gun. Got the Leonie/Ben axis wrong. Certainly not where Leonie was concerned, on the evidence of those notebook fantasies, but in his case?

With this young man representing such a worry to her, the questions she had to ask herself now were, firstly, why, on entering that bar in search of passing company, had she stayed to talk to him, of all people? And secondly, during that chat, why had she failed to capitalise on their meeting to fulfil her basic mission of warning him off Leonie (even, very briefly, entertaining the thought that he might, after all, not be such a bad prospect for her daughter!).

She wouldn't be a sentient female if she didn't viscerally understand Leonie's attraction to Ben Brady. And since he seemed to be such a decent sort as well, she now felt a bit odd about continuing to warn her daughter off him – and as for warning him off Leonie, was that fair?

This was complicated. She had a tightrope to walk.

15

In the ship's library at around half past ten the next morning, after a fitful sleep, with only coffee for breakfast and having checked that Leonie was still out for the count, Grace was searching for books about the Arctic, manageable ones, rather than the huge and heavy photographic volumes on the display tables.

It was still dark outside, of course, and the wind had whipped up so that the ship, ploughing through a restless sea, was rocking a little. In here, however, it was warm, there were plenty of comfortable chairs and the shelved books were well catalogued, so she was enjoying the peace. She felt cocooned.

For a while she'd been the library's only visitor –

standing at a display plinth and paging through a beautiful photographic book about landscapes in the Arctic – until Ben walked in. 'Well, hello again!' she said brightly. She had already let go many of her worries about him. If he and Leonie had been in bed together, so what?

'They're probably talking already,' he responded. 'Depends on the discretion of our barman. I can hear him now: "You won't believe it, Sven, two cups of goddamned tea, at that hour!" I wonder how it would sound in Norwegian.'

'I think "Sven" is Swedish.'

'Whatever, I don't know any Norwegian names, never needed them, probably never will. Anything decent to read here?'

'I'm being specific. Telling myself I need to know something about the Arctic before we actually get there. I think the novels are over there.' She indicated the section marked, helpfully, *Novels in English.*

As he moved away, the thought did occur to her that he might have been searching for her, perhaps building up to seeking more information about Leonie.

There were only the three of them present: Grace, Ben and the library assistant behind a desk. 'I'll leave this, I think,' she said. 'It's gorgeous but I'd need a wheelbarrow or a trolley to get it to my stateroom – I don't know what your cabin is like but I can't swing a cat in mine.'

'I'll carry it for you, Grace, my pleasure.'

'Ah, no thanks. I was just killing time.'

'My cabin's fine,' he confided. 'But it's pretty small and

there's only me in it even though it's supposed to be a double. Must be tough to share.'

'Leonie and I have separate cabins, side by side. Makes for family harmony! I don't mean to get personal,' she added, 'but I've been dying to ask you. How tall are you, actually?'

'Six eight, maybe a little more. Don't know how much that is in centimetres, maybe two hundred and ten or something – and, yes, before you ask, I did play basketball for my college, and although I didn't quite make the swim team, I did make it now and then for relay. Sometimes a long body and long limbs can be helpful there. Swimming's the only fitness exercise I take these days, although I know I should run or something because my job is so sedentary. I never thought to ask if there was a pool on board this ship. I just assumed there would be an indoor one – betraying my ignorance of what kind of a cruise it was going to be. Turns out it's more like a long educational infomercial, isn't it? All those lectures and workshops! Not much action in the nightclubs on board the *Magyar Bla*! God, I'm talking too much!'

She laughed. 'I don't see you as a clubber, Ben – I could be wrong? My jury's out about whether or not I'd prefer to be in the Caribbean. But apparently we can expect to see polar bears in some of the more northern towns, coming right in to raid the rubbish bins and even trying to get into people's houses.

When I was young, I always felt desperately sorry for the poor solitary thing in Dublin Zoo, all on its own in a little pool, its fur grubby and nothing to do. I gather they're more enlightened now and don't have one, but isn't it hard to know if they're any better off in the wild? With the ice melting, they're starving. I was reading too that even the reindeer are in difficulty because there's more rain than before. It penetrates the snow, freezes and makes it very hard for the poor things to graze. Now I'm the one talking too much?' She laughed again.

'So why *did* you decide to come to the Arctic? I wanted to ask last night.'

'It kind of sneaked up on me, and I didn't really get the opportunity to think it through. I knew it would be dark – but hadn't imagined *how* dark and for how much of the day. It was a last-minute gift to Leonie from her father.'

'Just like me getting it from Marcus. It's a bit of an adjustment on all fronts, all right, no pun intended!'

'Another thing I could ask you, never having met a basketball player before, I've always believed basketball players were of African heritage?'

'They were, and during my time, I was the only white guy, but there are plenty now. Almost all of my teammates were taller than me. The other guys were fine about me being there but when it suited them they gave me a hard time about my red hair, particularly if I missed a shot!' He grinned.

'Well, I like red hair. Makes you hard to miss or easy to remember, take your pick. My best friend is, or was, a blazing redhead when we were all young but, alas, not so much now. Anno Domini catches up with us all.'

'If I may return the compliment, it's hard to miss you. You're not so small yourself, are you?'

Despite the lightness of the chat, with just the two of them (and the desk clerk who wasn't paying them any attention), she wondered if this could be an appropriate time to seize the moment concerning Leonie – her vulnerability, instability and so on. To give him at least a hint of reality, but for some reason it didn't feel right.

She closed the book and stooped to set it back on a low wooden shelf inbuilt under the table. It was so heavy and the slot so snug that its dustcover snagged on a rough corner of the wood and she hunkered down to extricate it without causing damage.

He bent to help her and, steadying her resolve, she took the bull by the horns: 'Would you be interested in getting together for a coffee or a drink later, Ben? My bridge session starts shortly, but could we say the Koselig again? Maybe about two?' She didn't look at him.

'That's fine. I've my photography class on deck but it should be well over by then – there! That's it!' He had managed to free the book and they straightened up.

'Thanks for the help. Yes, Ben, that would be nice. I'll look forward to it.' She turned for the door. 'Nice chatting to you. See you later!' She left.

16

At five minutes to two Grace, mentally primed on what she had to say to Ben about Leonie, was once again in the Koselig, waiting for him.

She'd had to be a little devious in making sure that her daughter was otherwise occupied at this time. She knew Leonie loved spa treatments and had made a booking for her to have a facial and a massage at 1.45 p.m.

In the spa, after her hour-long bridge lesson, an introductory lecture geared towards beginners like herself, she saw that the equipment had been ingeniously slotted into quite a small space, although it covered almost half the width of the vessel.

Then, confident that Leonie was in her stateroom,

because she could hear her moving about, and knowing she herself was persona non grata (so what else was new?), she didn't deliver the spa booking in person. Instead, she pushed the confirmation slip under Leonie's door, then listened for it to open, which it did at around half past one.

In the Koselig, she had positioned herself alongside the huge windows, where Ben would see her immediately on entering.

She had a view of the ship's ramp, the pier to which it was now moored, and the little village beyond, its small shops and village houses straggling along the shoreline, some even clinging to the flanks of a towering mountain.

Seeing all this, she was a little ashamed that she had not yet gone ashore to savour the beauty of the fjord and its surroundings.

But she brushed that aside. She was sick of being guilty – if two flies walked up a wall and one fell off, she'd somehow blame herself.

Although ready for the conversation with Ben, she was now worrying that Leonie ('Did you not read my note, Mother?') would not take advantage of the spa booking and find the two of them talking in here. Right now, she was in no form to have another go-round with her daughter.

It was too late, of course, but she had begun to regret that she had chosen this venue because it was so open and even obvious. There had to be quiet nooks in other parts of the ship. It also struck her that she had sunk to the depths of deceit for what, in her terms, were Leonie's best interests. This had to stop.

In here, the candles and lanterns had been lit but the curtains had not yet been drawn, and through all of the windows, here and facing the waters of the fjord, she discovered it was now snowing, thick flurries drifting through the darkening sky into the ocean and accumulating on the surfaces of the ramp and the pier.

The ship's cleaning staff were already busy on both, working around the passengers who had gone ashore and who were now scurrying back to the warmth and shelter of their vessel, not due to cast off for another fifty minutes.

By a quarter past two, she was on the brink of becoming irritated but then Ben rushed in, full of apologies: 'Sorry I'm late – the session ran over. But the big news is that I now know all about DSLR and HDR and what ISO is. Care to speculate, Grace?'

'No, thanks!' She relaxed a little, enough to smile at him.

'I also learned two other things.' He smiled back. 'One is that it's a waste of time to use a flash when taking a portrait of someone while it's snowing, and the other is that my camera's pretty crap!' Wreathed in the smells of outdoors, he plopped beside her onto the couch. 'I'd planned to be here at two, honest. Is it tea again, or would you like a drink this time?'

'Let me get it.'

'Absolutely not.' He jumped up again and she asked for a gin and tonic.

'No ice, Ben, please. There's nothing worse than watery gin!'

As she waited for him to return, she was conscious that

it was far from this she'd been reared, and although the Arctic still would not have been her first choice (maybe in summer when it was bright all day and night), she was glad she was here. It felt deliciously decadent to be sitting in such luxury on an ordinary afternoon, on a ship somewhere in the Arctic Ocean, snow falling picturesquely outside and a handsome young man on hand to fetch her a cocktail. All that was needed to complete the feeling of having stumbled into a scene from a forties movie was a long cigarette holder, a fashionable hair-do and a suite of diamond jewellery enhancing her grey silk dress.

'Thank you.' Ben was back, again with a little tray, and as she accepted her G & T she saw that he, too, was having one.

'I'm usually a beer man,' he said, 'but they do these things so nicely here.' Instead of the usual slice of lemon, each glass held a spiral of cucumber peel. 'And they also come with these.' Along with his own glass he unloaded two small bowls, one filled with nuts – 'flavoured with sea salt, I'm told' – and another holding tiny pearl onions. 'Dig in!'

Grace took a large sip of her drink, to discover it was delicious, heavily weighted towards the gin.

As the bar filled with returnees from the shore excursion – refugees from the snow – they talked easily for a little while. Then he asked if Leonie would be joining them.

This was her chance – she took it.

'Look, Ben, there's something you need to know about Leonie.' She glanced at her watch, saw it was now 2.25, Leonie would be due for spa-release within the next quarter of an hour or so. To be safe, Grace had to get a move on.

'I do know she's absolutely beautiful, Grace, a knockout,' he said quietly.

'That's just it. It's hard to explain it but she doesn't really know how beautiful she is.' She hesitated. 'Maybe this is a little hard to understand but it makes her vulnerable to exploitation. She's not all that sophisticated, although she behaves as though she is. For instance, I saw her flirt with you just last night in that singing bar. She does that, and in the past it's got her into serious trouble. I won't go into it, but her father, my ex, and I, continually worry about her.'

Again she hesitated. 'I don't mean to imply anything earth-shattering,' she continued, 'although that depends on how you look at it, but she's not very stable and is sometimes liable to, well, fly off the handle . . .' To her horror, she felt the ooze of a tear rolling down one of her cheeks and apologised profusely. 'I'm so, so sorry, Ben. This is unforgivable,' she dashed away the tear, 'moaning about my daughter like this, but you're a good listener and this isn't fair on you. It's been hard, you know. Especially since my husband left us. Sometimes I—

'Oh, for God's sake! This is terrible. Of all the emotions in the world, self-pity is the worst, in my opinion.' She blew her nose on the little cocktail napkin that had come with her drink.

'I don't for a second think you're self-pitying, Grace,' he said, his expression unreadable. 'Honestly. That's the last thing I'd think about you. Poor Leonie! Poor the two of you .

. .' He reached out and took her hand, squeezing it as though he was her brother, if she'd had one, or even her father. Then, abruptly, he let her hand go and, his expression changing, was gazing beyond her towards the doors.

She turned to see what had attracted his attention. Her daughter was walking towards them, her face thunderous. 'Leonie! Grace cried. 'Great.' She rose to her feet. 'Won't you join us? What'll you have, sweetheart? We're having gin. It's lovely the way they present it. Sit down there now with Ben and I'll go up and order the same for you – you'll have another, Ben?' He nodded, looking as though he didn't quite know what was going on. 'So,' she cried, 'I'll get the drinks.'

Her eyes like black stones, Leonie didn't respond to any of this so Grace, trying hard not to run, made her way to the bar. She'd gabbled. In other words, although she had no reason to feel guilty, she was behaving as though she had plenty.

At the counter, the barman was busy with orders, giving her an opportunity to calm down. Why the hell should she feel guilty? she asked herself. She and Ben had merely been talking, that was all. *Talking!*

Yes, she had let the stoic's mask slip for a minute or two, but how could she convince her daughter that she'd been looking out for her so she wouldn't make the Jaden mistake twice? And that this young man was just being kind to her.

But she had to admit that, from Leonie's perspective, it might have seemed that the man she thought she was in love with had been holding hands with her mother.

And who to blame?

The mother, of course.

But why had the universe allowed him to take her hand at the exact moment Leonie had walked in to see it? Grace, angry now, felt she was never destined to catch a break.

The barman came to her at last and she ordered the three gins. While he was pouring them, she looked back at Leonie and Ben to give them an encouraging wave.

Neither of the two was there.

17

Grace had searched what she believed to be every accessible part of the *Magyar Bla*, all corridors, the restaurants, both bars, the activity rooms, the cinema, the spa (where, having listened to her description of Leonie, the receptionist remembered her but hadn't seen her since she had left after her treatments. 'I'd have noticed. She was beautiful!') with interim dashes back to Leonie's cabin to see if she'd returned there.

It had been more than twenty-five minutes since she'd turned from the Koselig's bar to see a couple about to sit on the couch where she and Ben had been talking and no sign of either him or her daughter.

She had immediately embarked on her search, had

retraced the routes she had already checked and was now walking the top deck. The ship was under way in darkness, bumping through a heavy sea, scoured by a cold, keen headwind from the north and she was having to hold on to the rail for fear of losing her balance. Luckily, the decks had already been cleared of accumulated snow, which had ceased falling.

And where was Ben? Was he with Leonie? Could they be in his cabin? Instantly, she discounted that idea: Leonie's disgust on seeing them holding hands had covered both of them – and who would blame her? In bed one night with him, then the very next day he's ticky-tacking with her mother?

Despite the wintry conditions, there were a few stalwarts, including joggers, still on the deck and she waylaid everyone she encountered, describing her daughter. Everyone had been sympathetic, most had offered to watch out for Leonie, and an elderly man had offered to accompany her on the search, but he was using a stick and Grace, thanking him, knew she'd be faster alone. Anyway, it had become clear during her first tour of the ship that nobody at that time outdoors had seen a lone young woman of Leonie's description.

Grace's distress quickly deepened to panic. She now had to fight vivid images of Leonie struggling beneath the waves, allowing herself to sink into the silent depths, bullied by currents and upwashes.

What would her daughter have been thinking as she gave up the battle? Had she remained true to her nature as a mind-changer and, at the last minute, managed to get to the surface again – only to discover that her ship was just a dot on the horizon?

On the top deck for the second time, Grace's next move had to be to approach officialdom; someone in the ship's central concourse would know of any out-of-the-way nook or cranny to which her daughter might have retreated to hide from the world. It was time to report Leonie as missing. And if that didn't work, she was going to insist they turn the ship around to go back the way they'd come.

As she made her way to the lift that would bring her down to the concourse, she tried to remember whether or not the ship had left its village berth before or after Leonie had come into the Koselig. But frantic as she was, her memory simply wouldn't work, and all she could think of was the possibility that Leonie had bolted out of the bar and, with the ramp down, straight off the ship. That she was now sitting disconsolately in an onshore coffee shop or restaurant, trying to figure out how to get in touch. Grace had checked her own phone and, with the *Magyar Bla* at sea, there was, as usual, no network coverage.

*

Despair upon worry: suppose Leonie was repeatedly ringing her mother's phone but it was going direct to voicemail? She might have concluded that she'd been blocked.

Those awful drowning images recurred, overpowering all else.

She was at the lift now and pressed the call button, but

it was already ascending so she had to wait for it to come back, every passing millisecond feeling like half an hour. When it did arrive, she saw through its glass door that there was a passenger inside. It was Ben. When the door opened, Grace burst into tears and let fly. Where had he been? Where was Leonie? Had he said something to her that had made her run off? Did he care one whit that she had? He'd had no right to have sex with someone as vulnerable as she was! What kind of man was he, taking advantage of someone like her? Why the hell—

'Grace, Grace, slow down! You're not making sense.'

He attempted to put his hands on her shoulders, but she flung them off and pushed him away, hard. 'Don't touch me! It's all your fault – and now, Leonie—'

'What? I don't know what you're talking about Grace.'

This further infuriated her. 'Don't pretend you don't know! You're just like all the rest of them – devious, selfish, predatory. You're a predator, Ben Brady! You should be ashamed of yourself, but you're not, are you? Pretending to be as nice as pie . . .'

'Whoa, whoa there!' He backed away a little, staring at her. 'I have no idea what brought this on or what you're talking about or why you're so angry with me. Predator? That's a strong word, Grace, I am *not* a predator.'

She ignored him, got into the lift and pressed the button, the up one, as it happened, so the lift's cabin jerked and stayed where it was. She pressed the down button, and as she began to descend, her last images of Ben Brady were of his shocked expression.

*

He followed her to the concourse. She was standing at the reception desk, having rapidly outlined the situation to one of the supervisory clerks, who was on the phone, when out of the corner of her eye she saw him. Although he remained some feet away, he had overheard what the clerk was saying into the phone and moved nearer: 'Leonie's missing?'

She glanced scornfully at him. 'As if you didn't know! The last time I saw you, you were together.'

The man behind the desk had heard this. 'Excuse me for a second,' he said into the phone, then, 'Give me a minute, I'll call you back.' He moved a couple of feet down the counter to stand in front of Ben. 'Good afternoon, sir. You were the last person to see the young lady?'

'I guess so.'

'And where was this?'

'We left the Koselig bar together and I tried to talk to her outside but she ran off, making it very clear she didn't want anything to do with me. She was upset. I did know that.'

'Had you had a fight?' Like most of the administrative staff at the desk, the clerk's English was faultless.

Ben hesitated. 'I guess it was more a misunderstanding. There wasn't an out-and-out fight, no.'

'So you were outside the Koselig.' The clerk was now writing on a notepad. 'In which direction did she go?'

'We're wasting time,' Grace intervened. 'I've searched this whole ship and she's not on board. Unless he's lying and she's in his cabin.'

'She's not,' Ben shot back. 'I've just come from there. I went to use my bathroom and to get something warmer to wear.'

'You don't mind if we have a look?' the clerk asked carefully.

'We're wasting time,' Grace repeated, beginning seriously to panic.

The clerk moved back to where she stood. 'My colleagues are already searching, madam. You're understandably upset, but you can trust us. If she's still on the ship, we'll locate her.'

'But I keep telling you, I've looked everywhere.'

'I'm sure you have but there are many places on a ship where you wouldn't have looked. We have had stowaways successfully managing to avoid being seen for an entire voyage, coming into view only at a time of their choosing.'

'How long will this take?' The tears were again taking hold.

'Perhaps fifteen or twenty minutes. In the meantime, the captain has acceded to your request and we are changing course back towards our last stop.'

'If she's in the water, she'll be dead by then!'

He didn't respond to this, except to advise her to stay calm, if possible, and to trust the system. 'A passenger being reported missing is rare, of course, but this isn't the first time we've dealt with it and, in many cases, the outcome is positive.'

'Not always, though?' The tears were now streaming. She clutched her throat – she felt she might choke.

The man didn't answer, but Ben chipped in, first addressing her. 'You've made it clear you don't want me to have anything to do with this.' He was keeping his distance. Then he turned to the clerk: 'If it's acceptable, I'll make a search on my own. I'll be sure not to impede any of your staff.'

Rather than answer straight away, the other man stared at him, as though, Grace thought, he was weighing up the suspicion that Ben had had something to do with Leonie's disappearance. Then he nodded. Slowly.

Before walking off, Ben cast a final glance at her. 'Stay strong,' he said, his expression blank, his tone formal. 'She'll be found.'

18

Ben was deeply upset.

Leonie had run away from him outside the Koselig, giving him the impression that she wanted to get as far away from him as she could, then Grace had hurled those appalling accusations at him. This afternoon had been a nightmare.

But he had made a promise that Leonie would be found and, in whatever context, he would strain every nerve to keep it. With time ticking away and the weather worsening by the minute, his confidence in the outcome had begun to diminish. He was having to push away all kinds of images: she had climbed up to the top deck, become trapped somewhere and was going to die of hypothermia; she had gone to ground in the ship's kitchens and had been electrocuted by a shorting appliance.

Overshadowing that, he couldn't stop thinking about the vile name Grace had called him. What had happened back there in the Koselig to trigger it? While he searched for Leonie, his brain picked and worried at it, trying to figure it out.

This was not the time for analysis, though: the weather conditions had deteriorated in the past fifteen minutes or so and, from the safety of inside, he could tell they were now worsening towards becoming atrocious. He decided, nevertheless, to venture out but had difficulty with an outwards-opening glass door onto the deck. As he stepped through it, he lost his baseball cap to the wind and the sea.

The vessel was now seriously buffeted by violent gusts, driving seawater onto the lower decks and surging across the bow onto the upper ones. Fit and strong as he was, on one of the lower decks he was finding it tough to maintain his footing or even to breathe properly while negotiating all the little spaces and storage areas.

This deck held the ramp, now stowed, and three lifeboats, strung from their davits. In effect the latter were sturdy, detachable cranes to swing the craft out over the water. To help him keep his balance on the slippery wood beneath his feet, he grabbed the framework of a davit and turned his back to the sea while catching his breath.

He found himself looking through a large window into the interior of the secondary restaurant, the Marine, where guests, eschewing formality, could avail of buffet meals.

Under its bright lights, he could see that the doors to the refrigerated storerooms, normally closed, were open, with uniformed crew members emptying shelves or searching behind food containers and fish boxes. In the body of the room, chefs and waiters were pulling out tables and chairs, peering under and behind counters. This search was impressive and, whatever happened eventually, nobody, not even Grace, could claim it hadn't been thorough.

But as he stood there, holding on to the davit for dear life, he was temporarily blinded when a large piece of blue and white fabric flew at him, wrapping itself around his bare head. With his free hand he managed to get it off but it flew again, whirling and flapping in circles, then spiralling off the ship to follow his baseball cap into the increasingly wild water.

His heart had started to bang against his ribs and it wasn't because of his exertions. He'd had enough time with that piece of fabric to recognise it as Leonie's scarf, distinctive because of its repeated motif: a white lioness with a small cub, against a blue background. Ben liked lions and it was probably for that reason he'd noticed the scarf draped around Leonie's neck when she'd come storming into the Koselig.

Around his head the scarf had felt damp, even slightly warm, warmer than the freezing temperature anyhow, but certainly not sopping, so she might have been wearing it until recently. He looked in the direction from which it had come but it was difficult to see through the seawater spray, so he saw only the deck and the other two lifeboats. Yet he felt she must have sheltered somewhere nearby and maybe was still there.

He needed to tell someone, fast. Maybe not Grace, though, he'd leave that to others, because he had no idea how she'd receive him now.

The fingers on the hand holding the freezing davit had cramped painfully, and as he used his other hand to prise them off the metal, something occurred to him. The vertical support pillar of this davit rose to an L-shaped junction with the extending arm of the crane. It sported a latticework of horizontal bracings between its sides. Making it a ladder.

A ladder!

Difficult for someone of Leonie's size because the 'treads' were widely spaced – but not for him.

He flexed the freed hand and began to climb, shouting her name into the wind, then banging on the side of the craft.

There was no response.

But she needn't necessarily be in this one. Every lifeboat – he'd counted six, three on this side, three on the other – was similarly hung and supported. Full of hope, struggling once more against the wind and fearful of falling, he climbed up, again competing with the storm to shout and bang. No response.

He was about to climb the third vessel when a crew member in oilskins came running towards him, yelling at him. Every second word whipped away by the gale and the roaring of the sea, he was shouting at Ben to get away from the lifeboats right now.

They sheltered under the third lifeboat out of the worst of the gale while Ben told him he'd checked the first two vessels, but not the three on the other side. 'Thank you,' the crewman said. 'Now come with me, please, sir. I will guide you to where you will be safe until this storm blows over.' He took Ben by the arm and half dragged him towards the glass door so they could both enter.

Ben knew immediately where he was. This was the backwater corridor leading to the library. After the furore outside, in here the silence sang, and he thanked the sailor, who reassured him that, if Leonie was on the ship, they would find her. 'But we will have to interview her about why she did this.'

'Is she in trouble?' *What a stupid question, Doofus! Of course she's in trouble! She had slowed a ship, caused it to reverse its course, and involved its entire crew in a search for her, risking their own safety in a storm, not to mention interrupting their routines.* The man didn't reply.

Soaked, exhausted, once the man had departed, Ben shook himself as a dog does after a bath or a swim. There was no one else in the corridor so he took off his jacket and ruined sneakers and fell into the nearest chair because he couldn't yet summon enough energy to walk back to his cabin.

As he sat there, his emotions freewheeled: he was torn between fear that Leonie wouldn't be found and hope that she would. He was glad that he had managed to be part of the search and that, at the very least, he had fulfilled his promise to Grace, despite her outburst, even if he hadn't managed to complete the task.

But in addition to all of that, sitting in a chair alone in that corridor, his pants gently steaming in the indoor heat, he had to deal with the conundrum Leonie represented, especially given what Grace had said about her. He accepted that, at present, the attraction was far from mutual from her point of view and, while acknowledging his continuing appreciation of her physical beauty and her 'otherness' – the aura of mystery she carried with her – the more practical side of his nature was now prompting him to flee.

When she was found, how would this episode have affected her? Would she regard it as some kind of personal affirmation that an entire ship was being searched by most of its crew and staff during a storm? Or would she believe this had been no less than her due?

He hastily suppressed these unworthy scenarios. Bottom line, thinking could come later: first, Leonie had to be found.

He had been sitting in the chair for about fifteen minutes (at least his watch was storm-proof, he thought gratefully) and had just about summoned enough energy to go to his cabin for fresh clothes, when he heard his name being called and looked up. Grace, accompanied by a ship's officer, was coming towards him.

Conscious of his bedraggled appearance and that his feet were bare, he forced himself up out of the chair.

At this distance, he couldn't read her expression. Was she still mad at him? Did she still believe he was a predator? He straightened his shoulders and waited for her to reach him.

When she did, she didn't look at him but at the carpet, saying quietly: 'Leonie's found.'

'Oh, thank God.' He'd meant it sincerely and let out the breath he seemed to have been holding for a very long time. 'Where was she found?

'In one of the lifeboats. I gather you'd been searching there.'

'How is she?'

'Tired, but unrepentant.' She glanced at the ship's officer and back at Ben, attempting, unsuccessfully, to smile. Then, in a bone-weary monotone: 'Time will tell what she really feels and why she did this. They've taken her to the ship's medical bay for a check-up – and a doctor there has found a psychiatrist on board. She's a guest, but has agreed to see Leonie just for a chat. There will be official repercussions. They're going to leave that for today and see us tomorrow.'

Then: 'I've been told what you did, in the teeth of the storm. Thank you. I'm sorry.'

She turned to go but Ben grabbed her arm. 'Is there to be no explanation, Grace?'

'For what? I told you that's for tomorrow.'

'No. Not that.' Conscious of the other man's presence, he lowered his tone. 'About our conversation on the upper deck less than half an hour ago.'

She didn't answer immediately but then, back to him, half whispering: 'I told you I'm sorry, and I am.'

'We need to talk, Grace.' They stared at one another.

'All right. Not now, I've to go down to the sick bay, see how she is.'

'Then when?' he persisted.

'This evening. They said they'd probably keep her overnight.' She closed her eyes, tears leaking from under her eyelids. 'That bar again. Eight o'clock.'

19

With Leonie safe and presumably asleep in the ship's medical centre, Grace had approached the Koselig at eight o'clock that evening full of dread. Ben had every right verbally to cut her into ribbons for her attack on him that afternoon and she was expecting it. She deserved it.

During the short journey from the sick bay to the bar she had tried to analyse why she had raged at him by the lift, but could reach no conclusion other than that she had arbitrarily lost her temper and he was the available target. Under control for so many years, it had gone on a rampage, and she had used the most insulting and wounding words in her vocabulary.

When she got to the bar, bang on eight o'clock, she saw him immediately, sitting, back to the door but instantly recognisable. She paused before approaching him, trying to guess at his mood by reading his upright posture, and decided he had planned his attitude to the encounter to be formal.

When last she'd seen him he'd been wet, dishevelled, barefoot and half undressed. Now his chinos were crisp and his lumberjack-type shirt could have been tailored to his body. He'd obviously had a recent shower because, viewed from the back, some of his hair, darker than the rest, was not yet dry.

This time, he'd chosen to occupy an armchair rather than a sofa and had placed an open book on the chair opposite, signifying, she supposed, that he had reserved it for her.

'Hello, Ben,' she said quietly, going around the chair to stand in front of him. He got to his feet and, not for the first time since meeting him, she experienced the novelty of looking upwards at the face of a man.

The expression on that face was, she judged, neutral, or designed to be such, but she noticed a flicker to the side of one eye. He was nervous. 'Should I sit?' she asked.

He took the book from the seat of the second chair and sat back into his own. But, rather than join him right away, she offered to buy him a drink. 'Or a coffee, Ben. Whatever you'd like – the most expensive drink they have up there!' She'd meant it as a cheery apology but it had emerged as merely vulgar.

'Thank you,' he said, avoiding looking directly at her. 'I'll have a beer.'

She went to the bar and saw that the Koselig offered Black Russian cocktails, one part Kahlua to two parts vodka, the choice of her youthful first year when on holidays courtesy of the Aer Lingus travel pass. Hang the beer, she decided. She ordered two.

In those days the world had been wide, bright and joyful, the future filled with nothing but hope. She had met Harry in Ibiza when she and four of her colleagues were in a resort, pretending to be sophisticated, throwing back the Black Russians as though they were Coca-Cola, fooling themselves that the coffee in the Kahlua would keep them sober.

Carefully, she carried both drinks back to the two chairs in the Koselig, along with a small stack of *lefse,* Norwegian potato bread, slightly sweet, heavy on cream and butter. She'd eaten them in the dining room and had found them delicious.

Ben was still bolt upright, like a toy soldier placed there under orders by a little boy. 'I got these potato breads too,' she said, adding, 'I'm not that hungry but I fancied something.' As she bent a little to lower the heavy tray to the table between their chairs, he sprang up to take it from her but too quickly, slopping the drinks on to it. 'Never mind,' she said. 'Those Black Russians are lethal anyway, the smaller the better. Sorry about your beer, though.'

Without responding, he lifted both drinks off the tray and settled them symmetrically on the little table with the *lefse* in between, then took the tray back to the bar.

This wasn't going well, Grace thought. But, she reminded herself, he was the one who'd insisted he wanted to talk. He was clearly furious with her, and he had a right to be.

She waited until he was seated again. 'This is awkward, Ben. I know you're angry with me and, as I said up there in the corridor earlier, I'm sorry. Of course I didn't mean those horrible things I said.'

'Then why did you say them?' he flashed at her.

Although the response had been infantile, at least he'd made it. 'I can't answer that,' she said, 'because the truth is, I don't know why. No excuses for taking my anxiety out on you, but I was desperately afraid that Leonie had jumped overboard and, in my brain, that was mixed in with you because the last I saw of her she was sitting with you.'

She took a deep breath. 'She thinks she's in love with you, Ben. I talked about her earlier. She's impulsive, acts without any forethought, and she completely misinterpreted your holding my hand. I guess she reacted to that. That's my theory anyhow.'

'In love with me?' He looked genuinely startled, then puzzled. 'I hardly know her.'

'Nor she you. But that's what she believes. She hopes to marry you.'

'*What?*'

'Ben,' she said softly, 'Leonie is flirtatious, unreliable, and as I said, I don't want to go into it in detail but she's had a hard time lately, not as hard as she thinks, but that's why we're on this ship. To give us a bit of a break away from home where things had become a little, well, tense . . .'

'I'd certainly picked that last bit up – and, if you're interested,' he sounded a little bitter now, 'that was why I put my hand on yours when you got upset. If that simple little gesture was why she reacted like she did, well, I can hardly be blamed, can I?'

Grace hadn't a leg to stand on and she knew it, even though, as he went on to admit, he had been instantly attracted to Leonie. 'At the beginning, when I saw her first, but that was at a distance. What man wouldn't be? She's lovely. A total beauty – those eyes!'

'Apparently the attraction was mutual,' Grace said wryly.

'And from your point of view,' he unbent a little, 'you had to put a stop to it, right? You said that she gets into trouble.'

'You might say that,' she said.

'Yes, I'd figured out, even though I've known her for only a couple of days,' he went on, 'that there was a vulnerability about Leonie but, you can believe me or not – and I don't know what she's said about it – it was she who came on to me in the singing bar, not the other way round.'

'Hold on, Ben.' She wasn't going to let this go. 'You said you recognised she's vulnerable. Is it not bad enough that you slept with her when you *knew* that?'

'Grace!' His eyebrows shot up, and then, just as abruptly, his expression shifted again. 'Is that what you meant when you screamed at me that I was a predator? Did you think we'd had sex?'

'Didn't you?'

'No, Grace, we didn't. You're on the wrong track, and even if she does believe she's in love with me, I can assure you that I don't feel the same way in return. I don't know her. She doesn't know me either. That doesn't mean I can't appreciate physical beauty.'

Something about the way he said this reduced Grace to silence. She took several sips of her drink, while asking herself why she had got things so, so wrong, why she had taken Leonie's scribblings so literally. She tried to elongate her former stance: wasn't plausibility one of the predator's most important tools? But she looked at him, still sitting as if he'd been ordered to, almost mechanically drinking his cocktail.

Not knowing what to say next, she went for broke and downed most of what remained of her Black Russian. It hit her like a bus. These Black Russians, she thought, were more powerful than she'd remembered. Maybe they made them stronger in Norway. Or on board a ship – to give you value for the extraordinary sums you pay for them.

She noticed that at the other side of the table between them he, unlike her, was husbanding his drink, taking a small mouthful then putting down the glass, picking it up, taking another sip, putting it down again, concentrating on the positioning of his glass, then moving it a fraction before picking it up again.

The performance was unsettling in itself but, in addition, she found she was watching his hands. He had long fingers, she saw, maybe a surgeon's hands. Or a pianist's? Studiously, she watched them in an effort to focus on anything but the feeling building within her own body. Against the context of this meeting, against all of what she would have considered her own mores, this sensation, growing and expanding, seemed to have a life of its own and was utterly outside her control . . .

She raised her eyes, risking another direct glance at him – only to find him staring back. They locked eyes for what had to be at least thirty seconds and Grace knew, without a doubt, that Ben wanted to kiss her.

20

Ben had reached out across the table to touch Grace's hand, maybe twenty seconds ago, or maybe it was thirty, yet still they stared at each other. The Koselig's soft light created shadows beneath his cheekbones and intensified the sheen of his brown eyes. While she didn't know what to do, that hand did and increasingly, so did her brain and body, melding, slowly churning together.

He wanted to kiss her? She certainly wanted to kiss him . . . and something she hadn't experienced for a long, long time stirred deep in her belly.

Then, knowing exactly what she was doing, she turned her hand upwards and stroked his palm with two of her fingers. He reacted by gripping the hand but now, she thought, neither of them seemed to know how to take anything further and to deal with this new situation. He got up and, her senses confusing her, she watched him walk to the bar, watched the way some women's heads turned to follow his progress, watched his hips moving easily to accommodate his leggy strides. That rogue urge, hot, deep in her belly, watched him too. It widened, intensified, climbing through her body until it reached the lower part of her chest. The more she fought it, the stronger it got.

What the hell was happening to her?

Rhetorical question. She knew perfectly well, but it hadn't happened to her for a very long time. She certainly couldn't recall it at this level of intensity.

Through the fog of confusion memories rose . . .

She and Harry had first slept together on their honeymoon, the first time for both of them. Although it had not been knee-trembling for either, they'd known no better and had reassured each other that it had been fantastic.

Having taken advantage of Grace's staff-discounted airline privileges to fly to Rome, her new husband, at the time still on the lower slopes of his career, had been thrilled with the rock-bottom cost of their tickets and was looking forward to taking full advantage of the opportunities the privilege offered to him as well as her.

They had used up all their savings on their modest wedding reception, and their hotel had been billed by the travel agent as 'budget'. It had no dining room but offered room service. They had arrived during a rainstorm and their room, cosy enough – and clean – had been in an attic.

For the first forty-eight hours of their marriage, rain continued to pelt the roof over their heads, cascading from a broken gutter just above their window, so they'd stayed in their room, mostly in the marital bed, getting to know each other's bodies. She had been a little reluctant to expose herself, but Harry had been gentle and she had quickly come to enjoy it. Sex was not just an obligation with your husband: it was fun when you let go of inhibitions. At the beginning she was mortified each time the room-service waiter appeared, but then he took to giving them an approving wink with his deliveries: breakfast rolls at 9 a.m., pasta and/or pizza throughout the day, along with strong, bitter coffee and evening bottles of rotgut 'champagne', which was in reality the cheapest sparkling wine on offer.

They'd loved every second of it. They even came to believe that the whining and revving of what seemed like thousands of Vespas sloshing day and night through the flooded street outside was not irritating, just another exciting indication of the city's exotica.

She subdued this line of thought because, in the Koselig, Ben was returning with the drinks. Watching him again, head bowed over the tray he carried carefully so nothing would spill, the gnawing desire that had so unexpectedly overtaken her intensified. She was reminded that she hadn't been touched, except by her hairdresser, since Harry had left her seven and a half years previously.

'Thank you,' she said now to Ben, as he placed the drinks

on the table. His was the colour of burnished gold. 'What's that?'

'A Manhattan.'

'What's in it?'

'Bourbon, sweet vermouth and bitters.'

They lapsed again into silence.

Then, without raising his head, he asked softly, 'Have I scared you, Grace?'

She shook her head. 'No,' she croaked. 'I'm not scared.' Having finished the first, she swigged a goodish portion of her second Black Russian and was already feeling its effects. The Kahlua might include a coffee component but it was obviously minor.

Suddenly, for her, all the bingo balls fell into place: the cares, concerns and reticence, the parcels of self-denial all fluttering away, like autumn leaves on the wind, and she became Grace. A woman in charge of her own life. For now this Grace would celebrate what was on offer. What was to happen next. To hell with the consequences, she was taking a night off. She stood up. He followed suit. Her demon went into orbit.

*

Somehow it became an unspoken, mutual decision that, although Leonie was safely sequestered and under observation in the sick bay, it would be his stateroom rather than hers.

They were initially careful, walking separately, in single

file, towards his quarters because there were discreet CCTV cameras on the corridors. (That was how she and the officer accompanying her had known how to find Ben in the passageway leading to the library.)

As she padded along about twenty metres behind him, the secrecy served to increase her excitement, although her observational powers didn't desert her: again she admired how his limbs moved, as though he was a trained actor or a catwalk model, all body parts beautifully aligned. She couldn't remember ever, *ever*, feeling as alive or as desirous of a man.

At one point he turned and waited for her to catch up, and she ran to him, lips, limbs and torsos colliding and, as they kissed, she felt that if the world were to end around them right now, her body could not be parted from his.

Inside his stateroom, they had torn each other's clothes off by the time they'd got from the door to his bed, on which they fell together, and it was a revelation to Grace to find how wonderfully well their bodies so naturally fitted together. While it might be disloyal to make comparisons – but who'd know? – she couldn't help but contrast this experience with that of her only other partner. It was probably 'coarse', as the nuns used to say, to describe how she and Ben had come together as a hand fits a glove and how his body had so perfectly covered hers, as though they had been specifically tailored for each other.

'I have to apologise that it wasn't you from the beginning, Grace,' he said, when they had taken a rest and were comfortably relaxed in each other's arms, 'but you have to admit that Leonie dazzles. The more I saw of you, though, and the more we talked—'

'Ben, stop!' She put her hand over his mouth, whereupon he opened it, taking it on his tongue. 'I'm serious,' she protested, removing it. 'What you thought then doesn't matter one iota, and I don't care who came first. Now, where were we?'

With this man, she'd discovered many parts of her body she hadn't previously imagined could be responsive to touch, thanks to his inventive (*Must come with being a writer,* she'd thought) and confident use of his hands and other parts of his anatomy.

And the encounter was not just physical: it raised her sense of self, and renewed the discovery that, yes, she was a sensual woman.

He even caused her to giggle when he had shown her that ears, too, can trigger desire.

At one stage, she had the sheet pulled up to her chin when they were chatting, each offering a précis of their life stories so far. She included a truthful but heavily edited account of her life with Leonie – she didn't want to let her daughter down, she'd already said enough about her to him. He asked her how long she'd been married. When she told him it had been twenty-six years, he said, pulling the sheet down to expose her breasts and kissing them, 'I could have been your flower boy!' He'd been dead right. But, somehow, that aspect of their encounter hadn't mattered at all.

Nor, throughout, had she cared one jot that she was

probably the umpteenth woman to benefit from Ben Brady's lovemaking techniques. Willingly she'd set herself up for him until, feeling gloriously wanton, the bad girl, the one who has all the fun, she'd found the *cojones* to manoeuvre herself on top of him from where she firmly took charge.

*

Next morning she was careful not to wake him, sleeping blissfully, feet dangling over the end of a bed that was barely adequate to accommodate him, never mind a second person only seven or eight inches shorter than he was.

It took a little time to disentangle her feet from the bedclothes twined around her legs (and, without disturbing him, to remove his arm from around her waist), but she managed both, then slid quietly to the floor and tiptoed to his bathroom. She waited until she was inside to extend her arm to the control on the wall outside and activate the light.

She closed the door as quietly as she could and put on one of the two robes hanging there.

Having been engaged in so much unaccustomed and enthusiastic activity up to a couple of hours ago, many of her muscles were complaining and as she tied on the robe, she discovered that one of her breasts was a little tender, nothing major, but it was an acute, but pleasurable reminder of the physicality of it all.

Her brain, however, was less than alert because, having

had so little rest, it was slopping around in an ooze of relaxation, unwilling, even unable, to turn on its worry switch, even to search for it.

In front of Ben's mirror, identical to the one in the bathroom of her own stateroom, her image smiled widely at her, joining her in celebrating what had happened throughout the hours of that glorious night.

Although she was more tired than she'd been for many years – 'hollowed out' was the phrase she would have used, if asked – she was exhilarated, minded to climb a mountain and, from its peak, to declaim through a loudspeaker that, yes, she was completely a woman. That, yes, someone was attracted to her! That, yes, she'd had wonderful (wonder-filled) sex for nearly a full night with a beautiful man who thought she, too, was beautiful.

In his bathroom now, she splashed water on her face, then squeezed some of his toothpaste onto the tip of her index finger, rubbed it on her teeth and gums, then rinsed it off. The Grace McGee in this mirror, and recently in Ben's bed, had been so different from the woman she'd known for most of her life, so very far off that scale, she found it amazing to realise how quickly she'd metamorphosed in his accomplished hands.

Had she been able to behave so freely because she was far from home and on a ship in the middle of what was essentially nowhere? Because of the effect of two Black Russians? Because Leonie was safe in a hospital bed and not occupying most of her mind?

Had she (temporarily) escaped and was this what freedom felt like?

Extraordinarily satisfying as it had been on many counts, like a passing comet, the experience seemed already to be spinning away from her, leaving her with a sense of sadness that it was already out of reach. She pressed the sore spot on her breast again to confirm that all this had happened. 'All right,' she murmured, to her mirror image. 'I get it. It was a fairy tale but I'll never forget it. I'll probably never get over it either.' Because even as she'd crept out of his bed, she knew there could be no repeat performance: this had been a one-night-only event. Just as *What happens in Vegas stays in Vegas*, what had occurred between them on the *Magyar Bla* would have to stay on the *Magyar Bla.*

A brief vision of Leonie's furious face rose to warn her of how her daughter would react should she get even the smallest whiff of what her mother had been up to with the man she had earmarked as a potential husband. But there and then she made a decision to lie and dissemble until her teeth hurt.

Ben was demonstrably secure about his sexual prowess, so she believed there was no danger he would blab. He had no need to boast. He hadn't mentioned any of his ex-girlfriends, and there had been no showboating about how skilled he was with women – at that thought, her demon stirred again, but she instantly smothered it.

In his mirror she looked like a woman who'd been

dragged through a hedge backwards but also like a woman who'd had a great time.

Would she have liked more of it? Yes. But that was to move into La La Land and she had decided some years ago that the best plan for her, always, was to move forward from all experiences, bad, good and even exquisite, like this one. It had been like cracking open a hazelnut and finding a nugget of solid gold. It had been perfect and that was enough.

She thought it unlikely, but if Ben wanted a rematch, she'd explain, truthfully, that declining meant only that she couldn't, not that she wouldn't, had her own life circumstances been different. The truth was that if she'd had to have a fling, she had lucked out that it had been with Ben Brady. She touched her image in the mirror and smiled at herself, for once not being critical, despite the state of her hair, saturated by wind and rain earlier that day, and then, when she'd gone to all the trouble of washing and drying it, tangled up by Ben's hands.

The next exercise was to get out of his stateroom without fuss. The exact location of her clothes was a mystery since they had been deposited on his floor with no plan for retrieval. So she opened the bathroom door a little, allowing a sliver of light into the bedroom. Her handbag was on its side by the door, her jeans and sweatshirt on the floor by the bed, but she couldn't see either her bra or her shoes – while her pants had to be somewhere within the maelstrom of bedclothes.

The first three would have to do.

She stole into the room, quietly picked them up and went back into the bathroom to put them on. It was still very early, there should be few people about, but his cabin was in a corridor above hers and at the opposite end of the ship, so there was quite a distance to travel. She left the room barefoot, carrying only her handbag. Once outside, she strolled casually along the carpet, enjoying the sensation of its softness through her toes, and got safely into her own stateroom, relieved that she'd made it unchallenged although, in her current mood, she didn't give a fig for what the CCTV might show. She couldn't have been the first woman observed coming out of a man's cabin at that hour of the morning. But if she was being truthful, she had been fearful that she might encounter Leonie.

That was nonsense. Leonie was safe in the hospital bay, with the prospect of seeing a psychiatrist in a couple of hours. Although she knew she was being unfair, based on Leonie's history – and her own lack of success when seeking information about her daughter's progress or otherwise – she couldn't say she was an ardent fan of the profession. She would admit, if pushed, that she and Leonie might have been unlucky because there were undoubtedly those stories of miraculous psychiatric or social interventions and rescues.

She unearthed her mobile from the handbag and switched it on. Although there was no coverage at present, there had been some time during the night because she'd had a text message from Harry, asking her to call him at her 'earliest convenience'. The time stamp was 22.46, just after a quarter to ten in the evening, Irish time, when, she smiled, his ex had been tumbling into bed with Ben.

It was now just after six in the morning here but, even if she did have a signal, nobody should call anyone at five in the morning, unless it was a matter of life and death.

Anyhow, in her present mood, and with ghostly traces of Ben's hands all over her body, she really, *really* didn't want to talk to Harry. She pulled off the jeans and sweatshirt and went into the shower but, luxuriating in the flow of hot water, she couldn't avoid speculating on the reason for his text.

Probably, under the guise of asking how she and Leonie were getting on in the Arctic, he had wanted to disclose something amazing about himself, like he was now installed as captain of his golf club or something like that and that everyone had said how brilliant and witty his speech had been at the club's celebration dinner.

She lay down on her own bed and remembered how, before she left Ben's stateroom, she had come out of his bathroom to take one last look at him in the bed they'd messed up together.

Although still glowing with physical joy on one level, she was also sad that she and he would not get together like that ever again.

There would be no coming back here.

21

Grace, in bed in her own cabin, her alarm set for an hour hence, was almost asleep when she remembered that today at 11 a.m. they were to dock at the town of Longyearbyen. To facilitate those going ashore, the timings of almost everything on board had been moved forward.

The early-bird breakfast was to be served at six thirty (normally seven o'clock to let the fitness freaks load up on their carbs after their 6 a.m. workouts) and her bridge session had been moved to nine thirty. That, she figured, would have to bite the dust today because of the two potentially fraught interviews facing Leonie and herself: one with the onboard guest-psychiatrist, and the other, potentially very difficult, with the ship's authorities when the two of them would face the music about yesterday's disruptions. She dreaded that one, but Maxine's accusations that she was still treating Leonie as though she were a child rose to confront her again: it had been her daughter who had caused the confusion the day before, not herself, yet here she was, no doubt far more worried about what was to come than Leonie was. She had spent far too much of her life living the consequences of Leonie's behaviour, trying to head them off on her daughter's behalf. Yesterday's incidents had not been just a few dishes and a packet or two of cereal thrown around in their own kitchen: this had affected not just her but every crew member and every passenger on the ship.

Fully awake now, her elation trampled, she was back in Leonie-land. She also discovered that she was very hungry and remembered that, even during her ex-husband's era, sex had always had that effect on her. In this case, the signals from her stomach were particularly strong because she hadn't eaten since lunchtime the previous day.

She lay there for a minute or two while she considered her options and then, having realised she had none, dragged herself out of bed, accepting that, although she was reluctant to let the elation of the past eight or nine hours dissolve, she had no option but to return to reality. She'd get through the morning somehow and, all going well, could take a nap in the afternoon.

All going well? What the hell was she thinking?

She dressed quickly in jeans and a fresh sweatshirt,

dragged a wide-toothed comb through her hair and, feeling far from ready for what was ahead, left her cabin, heading for the dining room. She'd eat quickly and head to the hospital bay to make enquiries about Leonie. Although she believed her daughter was probably still asleep, there might be something to report. First things first, though: she needed calories. Energy.

She arrived as the doors to the dining room were being opened to find that quite a number of early birds were already waiting. They all piled inside and, without selecting tables – it was free seating at breakfast time – headed straight for the buffet to stack their plates.

She dropped hers off, piled with fruit and yoghurt, on the corner table she and Leonie had used that first night, then went back to the hot-food area to load up with 'American bacon' and scrambled egg. On the way back, she was intercepted from behind: 'Hello there, Mrs McGee!'

'Ben! What are you doing here?'

Damp hair combed close to his scalp, white sweatshirt pristine, he was grinning widely and certainly didn't look as tired as she felt, although, she allowed, he had slept a little more than she had and, crucially, he was young and fit. His grin widened. 'Having breakfast? I'm hungry. Mind if I join you this morning?'

On seeing him her instinct, tired as she was, had been to drag him back to his bed, but now, here in Leonie-land, her mind automatically swept the probabilities before she answered. It was only six thirty. How likely was it that her daughter, with an important interview to come, had been discharged at this hour, even on a promise to come back to meet the psychiatrist? 'Sure you can join me,' she said cheerily, hoping to deflect others' suspicions that she and Ben might be more than mere social acquaintances. 'I'd love some company!'

'You're actually good at this.' His grin, now knowing, widened and she blushed. The attempt at pretence had been ludicrous, not to speak of unnecessary: these strangers, many in flashy neon gym gear and busy filling plates and bowls or queuing at toasters and coffee machines, were of course thinking only of themselves, like most people do most of the time. 'Sorry,' she said, in her normal voice, 'I'm a bit hyper. Not much sleep, I'm afraid.' She hadn't been able to resist it and glanced up at him.

'Oh dear – that's awful, Mrs McGee,' he bought in. Then, deliberately overbuying: 'Let me take that to your table for you.' He reached for her tray.

She handed it over, then led him to her table, his presence so close behind her again magnetising every treacherous nerve in her body. If she was to stay sane, she thought, she'd have to find a way to put a stop to this. She had already decided it was the only way forward for them, but that had been her brain talking. Her body, it seemed, had decided otherwise.

She watched him go to the buffet. As usual, he stood out from the herd, with two of the women near him reacting.

He seemed absolutely unaware of the effect he had on strangers. Perhaps he'd simply become so accustomed to it during his sporting career at college that he no longer noticed the attention he garnered. For her, this modesty, unpretentiousness, whatever it was, fuelled the attraction.

She repeated to herself that she had to stop thinking this way. She just had to, end of story. When he came back with orange juice, muesli and sliced apple, she immediately launched into her fears about Leonie as a result of being hauled up in front of the authorities. 'What do you think will happen to her? To us, I suppose? They're hardly going to ask one of us to leave without the other.'

'I don't know,' he said simply. 'And I don't know how to find out, either, without making things worse for you both. Best to play things by ear. But,' he drank some of his juice, 'it's not my business, I know that, but she is an adult. You're not remotely responsible for what happened yesterday, Grace.'

No, she mourned silently, *not you too.* 'I do know that. But she is vulnerable, Ben, and I am her mother. She has no one else.'

'Her father, maybe?' he asked tentatively. 'Her sisters?'

'They're not here, are they?' That had sounded like a rebuke, and she rowed back: 'Sorry. I know you're only thinking of me.'

'Grace, did you launch so quickly into all this serious stuff to put me off you? Are you saying you and I don't have unfinished business?'

'Ben, you know our business has to be finished.' She almost took his hand but, at the last moment, held back. 'I wish it wasn't, honestly. For me, with the exception of the nights spent having my three children, last night was probably the most intense of my life, and certainly,' she laughed, trying to lighten things, 'by far the most physically enjoyable. I won't be so stupid as to ask you how it was for you but you taught me a lot. So much that you might have ruined me for ever!'

He didn't smile, instead had another swig of his juice, then a spoonful of the cereal. Then: 'Would you like me to be there with you later? For you, Grace, not for Leonie. In the background. As a third party so that these people know they can't bully her or you. If they try anything like that with either of you, there'd be a witness.'

She told him she was grateful, but didn't accept the offer, believing Leonie would freak if he was there, having assumed correctly that something was going on between her mother and Ben. She'd known the signs before Grace had. Despite all her difficulties and narcissism, she was intuitive, and if Ben showed up in a supporting role this morning, she was likely to figure out, rightly or wrongly, that he was not there for her.

If he thought she had acted badly before, he hadn't seen anything like the havoc she could wreak, in an instant. 'You're a very kind young man, Ben—'

'Less of the young, please,' he said, but he wasn't smiling.

'Are you upset, Ben? Did you really think we had any kind of a future together? I certainly wasn't leaving my family and going to Chicago, or Gary or wherever. Were you going to come and live in a small Dublin suburb?'

'So it was only the sex, was it?'

She hadn't thought of it that way, but he was right. She

steeled herself. 'I'm afraid so. I'm sorry. I hadn't planned it, or thought it through, it just happened. You are a beautiful man, Ben, body and soul. I hope you know that, and I'm so sad that—' She stopped. He was no longer listening. A look of horror on his face, he was gazing over her shoulder. She knew that look.

She turned. Leonie was not just walking towards them, she was marching. Fast.

She stopped beside Grace and, looking from one to the other, and on a rising scale of volume, said, 'I fucking knew it, I knew it, I knew it, I FUCKING KNEW IT! You are a sickbag, Grace McGee, a vicious, thieving, lying, psycho shit!

'And as for you,' she screamed at Ben, 'you *turd*, you piece of junk!' Quick as a striking snake, and before Grace could react, she had snatched the bowl of fruit and flung it at Ben's head. His reflexes came into play and he was quicker, ducking sideways so the bowl landed on his lap, contents spilling all over him and the floor, spreading like a colour-rich and messy artwork. Screaming incoherently with frustration, Leonie grabbed the edge of the table to upend it, managing to raise it a couple of inches, but Ben was on his feet, and before she could get full purchase, he had grabbed her bodily, swinging her into the air and out into the aisle while Grace clamped down on the table, managing with both hands to prevent any more of what was on it, falling off.

'Let me down, let me down, sicko, sicko, shit!' Leonie struggled to escape but, with her arms tightly fastened between his, and her feet bicycling several inches off the floor, she was held like a pinned butterfly to his body.

'What'll I do?' he asked Grace over Leonie's head, as she twisted from side to side against his chest, while, from all sides of the room, waiters and other staff, helped by a few of the passengers sitting nearby, rushed to clear up the mess.

'Carry her out into the concourse,' Grace yelled, over her daughter's screeching, but there was no word adequately to explain how embarrassed, humiliated and helpless she now felt as, apologising to everyone around her, she followed from the dining room, her daughter semaphoring with hands, feet and head to get out of her fetters. 'Put me down! Put me DOWN, you dork! Jerk! Half-wit! This is assault!' she screamed, at the open-jawed clientele, as Ben finally got to the door with her. 'You can all see this! PUT ME DOWN, cretin!'

Someone had pressed a panic button: two security guards were running towards them.

The heavier one, probably more than a foot shorter than Ben but built like a small tank, plucked Leonie from Ben's arms and deposited her roughly on a nearby bench. 'You stay there, miss. Don't move! My friend here is trigger-happy, so he could jump the gun and somebody could get shot and it might be you. Don't think he won't. He eats kids like you for snacks.

'Sir,' he turned to Ben, 'what were you doing with that girl?'

'May I speak, Officer?' Grace, weak with shame, anxiety

and from lack of sleep, intervened. 'I'm her mother. Leonie suffers from her nerves and something upset her. I'm very sorry on her behalf. You're sorry, too, for the trouble you've caused to all sorts of people, Leonie, aren't you?'

But her daughter ignored her and there followed a small shemozzle as the various roles were sorted out, Tank telling Leonie she was coming with him, no arguments, 'and your mother can come too so we can figure out what's what. That OK with you, ma'am?'

Leonie opened her mouth to object but he noticed: 'Quiet, miss, if you please. If you want to give your opinion, you'll get your chance!' She subsided and then it was Ben's turn. 'So what's your connection, if I may ask, sir? Are you a relative of this young lady and her mother?'

'I'm not a relative,' Ben avoided looking at Grace, 'just a fellow passenger. The three of us met on boarding. But,' he glanced at the sizeable crowd now gathered around the five of them in the concourse, 'could you do something about the gapers, please, Officer? The young lady is upset enough. This isn't helping.'

'You got it,' and to the crowd: 'Show's over, folks. Go back inside. You three,' he took them in with a wave of his hand, 'you're comin' with me.'

'This isn't fair! This isn't my fault! They're hypocrites!' Leonie shouted and, pointing at Grace, 'She started it, and he assaulted me.' She indicated Ben. 'You saw the way he treated me. I might even sue. My daddy's rich and he'll pay for a good lawyer – I know my rights.' But the security man, putting a finger to his lips, silenced her with a glare that would have penetrated the bole of a California Redwood. 'This way, if you please, folks,' he beckoned, 'all three of you.'

As, shaken, she followed a little behind the others, the thought flashed through Grace's mind that she had just addressed her daughter as though she was a young child, demonstrating exactly what Maxine had always accused her of, and that she had, up to very recently, always resisted.

22

There were four of them in the room: Grace, the sleeve of her sweatshirt encrusted with some of her uneaten breakfast, Ben, whose collar was stained with his, Leonie, looking somewhat dazed, and, behind a desk, a woman in a white uniform, obviously a ship's officer.

The only nod to décor in this room was a black-and-white photograph of the *Magyar Bla* on the wall behind the desk. The only sounds, apart from the faint rhythmic engine noise from the bowels of the vessel, were of the officer clearing her throat and the soft clicking of her computer keys as she transcribed what seemed to be, in Grace's eyes, a written report. She was too far from it to read anything, and that was just as well, she thought. She didn't care to imagine what horrors it contained.

They'd all been sitting there for a long, *long* fifty minutes. Grace was now trying to ignore the gurgling of her stomach, her growing discomfort on the unyielding seat of her chair and her strong need for the bathroom. On his seat Ben, having taken a small journal from the pocket of his sweatshirt, was scribbling in it; Leonie had turned hers to face a blank wall.

As always in such circumstances, few of them as grave as this one, Grace was struggling to come up with some form of words she could use with the authorities to get Leonie out of this. For example, she and her daughter were embarrassed and ashamed and she, as a responsible mother, would personally make sure nothing like this could recur; or she would say they were sincerely sorry and ask for clemency, even mercy . . .

Although the silence that hung over the room like a foul mist was pregnant with words, she was finding it hard to come up with *any* that might work as an appeal for understanding: her daughter's conduct both yesterday and an hour ago had been indefensible, except, she suspected, in Leonie's own mind, because Leonie usually found a way to blame her mother. This time there had been cause, although, as yet, she could not possibly have any evidence and, in some ways, her behaviour might even have been a godsend. Who would believe what someone like her would allege?

That thought, though, raised a little geyser of guilt. It

had been cruel but her brain wasn't working properly, partly from lack of sleep, partly from shock at the events in the dining room.

And her imagination was playing tricks, putting up a scenario where she was living inside a room-sized TV screen; at the bottom a news ticker repeating, with excruciating exactitude and in quotes, the torrent of invective and swear words her daughter had hurled at herself and Ben.

The ticker's accompanying graphics, in full colour, were flipping between different perspectives: that vividly surreal art installation on the dining room's blue carpet; Ben lifting a flailing Leonie away from the table and out of the room; a wide-shot of the confounded restaurant guests, along with close-ups of her own agonised features.

She was furious with Leonie, but anger would be of no help in any case she might put forward on her daughter's behalf.

More immediately, her need for the bathroom was at crisis point. She stood and approached the officer to ask for directions to the nearest Ladies. 'Certainly.' The woman rose to accompany her to the door, but then Leonie asked, voice and expression fearful: 'Where are you going, Mum?'

'To the Ladies.' Grace tried to strike a balance between answering the ordinary question ordinarily, while simultaneously letting her daughter know how angry she was.

But Leonie's fear had been authentic. One counsellor had

said that her 'acting out', as she'd called it, was a symptom of terror that she would be abandoned. 'At some level,' she'd said, 'she's testing you, a familiar phenomenon in young children, but not only in children,' and she had gone on to label Leonie, who had been sixteen at the time, as suffering from anxiety about her father's sudden departure. Equally, however, she had felt that the girl could be exhibiting the classic signs of arrested development. 'Like a two-year-old, Grace, she's driving you to the limits to see how much you'll bear before you behave as she'd feared and abandon her. "My mother too" is how she'd see that, "I was right all along" and would feel justified.

'And, from what you've told me, Grace, her sisters too come into play. From Leonie's point of view, they seem to have moved away from her almost entirely and to pay only lip-service to her as a sister.'

At the time Grace had listened carefully while maintaining what she called 'healthy scepticism' about all this. Cautiously, though, she had started framing her daughter's behaviour in what the counsellor had outlined and began to see that, at some level, without a more compelling explanation from somebody else, the woman had possibly been on the right track.

On a practical level it didn't mean all that much. Having a possible 'why' might contribute to empathy with Leonie but had little or no effect on the daily frustration of dealing with her.

Anyhow, Grace had difficulty in knowing when Leonie's fear was real and when it was faked – because everyone who'd dealt with her at close quarters had agreed that she was a skilled manipulator.

At the door, the officer directed her to the nearest bathroom, but before she left, Grace asked her what was to happen and how soon. She received nothing helpful in return, only that the officer was there as liaison. 'There'll be someone here very soon. Please don't worry.'

'I am worried. My daughter is officially classed as vulnerable and this is all very hard on her.'

'I'm sure it's hard on all of you.' The officer's tone remained noncommittal.

Grace tried again: 'She has an appointment this morning with a psychiatrist in the ship's medical facility. Would it be possible for you to get word to someone there that she's been held up?'

'I'll do that. Certainly.'

As she hurried towards the Ladies, Grace thought she might have managed to stitch into officialdom *something* relevant about Leonie's behaviour not being intrinsically evil.

In the bathroom, after washing her hands, she pulled out her phone to find that, strangely, although they were still at sea there was network coverage. She saw Harry's message from the previous night – but it was not quite seven o'clock in the morning at home. If she rang now he'd be asleep and she'd get Cherry – and Grace would not be responsible for what she'd say to that woman right now.

She switched off the phone and made her way back to the room, building herself up to hear what fate awaited her daughter.

She couldn't help but be sad that her heightened sense of self, engendered by events of the previous night, hadn't survived even twenty-four hours and, in fact, seemed to be travelling backwards as Leonie once again dominated. Like a captive wild horse that had managed to escape its corral for a night, she had tasted the sweetness of freedom, and its loss made her feel even worse than she did before.

She wondered how Ben was feeling. He was the only person who was completely blameless and didn't deserve to be implicated in all this – but, in Leonie's presence, she didn't dare communicate with him in any way.

In fairness, she hadn't expected that she and Ben could romp their way ecstatically through the rest of this voyage, or that, somehow, she could have divested herself of responsibility for her daughter by sending her off in her lifeboat to a hypothetical Shangri-la. But she did wish that the wave of lust that had carried her away, and that she was now paying for, could have been allowed more gently to pass.

When she got back into the room, it had three additional occupants. The woman behind the desk had moved to one side, leaving her seat to be taken by a man Grace assumed to be the captain of the *Magyar Bla* because of his gold braid. He was stocky, with a thick neck, his upper arms straining the fabric of his sleeves. The other two were the security men they had already met, standing at each side of the room's door, as though primed to deal with escapees.

The woman officer introduced the captain and he got straight down to business. In a more deeply accented

English than Grace had so far encountered on the ship, he told everyone in the room that he'd had access to the transcription of the reports on what had happened yesterday and earlier that morning and that, as 'sole authority' on board, he'd made an 'irreversible' decision since he had to have regard for the comfort and safety of all on board, passengers and crew.

He looked at his watch before addressing Leonie directly: 'We dock just before eleven o'clock at Longyearbyen Pier, Miss McGee. Between now and then, you should have enough time to pack your belongings to leave the ship. You will be glad to know that we have decided, given what I hear from our hospital, not to charge you for your overnight stay there, the damage to the restaurant, or for the costs incurred yesterday by turning the ship around and diverting most of the crew to the search for you.'

He turned to Grace: 'You are Mrs McGee?' he asked.

Chastened by hearing such a precise summary of events surrounding Leonie in such an unemotional voice – the captain had seemed neither angry nor judgemental, his decision valid – she responded quietly, 'Yes, I am.' Having more than half expected the expulsion, she had been ready with a few counter-arguments but now knew that he would not entertain any promises of reform or requests for clemency. And she couldn't blame him. 'Whether you disembark with your daughter or not is a matter for yourself, of course, madam,' he continued, 'but we have been in touch with the airport and have booked Miss McGee on a flight to Oslo this afternoon. If you decide to accompany her, we need to know now since those on our main desk are waiting for further instructions – for instance, preparing your final account and booking you onto the flight. Do you think you will stay with us or go home?'

The speed at which this was happening was mesmerising Grace, whose sleep-deprived brain was barely keeping up. 'I shall have to speak with my daughter,' she said.

'Of course,' he replied, then, to Ben: 'And may I ask about yourself, Mr Brady? We find no reason to disembark you. In fact, the contrary is the case, since you were part of yesterday's successful search for the young lady, but I understand you are friends.'

'Like Mrs McGee, I will need to have a conversation.' Ben's voice was steady.

Grace had already gone over to Leonie, who was trembling, her eyes, wide as saucers, darting from face to face. Covering her own emotions, Grace asked gently, 'Did you understand that, Leonie?'

'What? Did I understand what?'

'We have only an hour or so, if that, to get packed. We're going home.'

'What?' Leonie repeated.

'Come on, darling.' Firmly, Grace took her daughter's arm. 'We have to go back to our cabins. Thank you,' she said to the room in general while leading Leonie towards the door. 'I apologise, truly, for all the disruption. *We* are truly sorry, isn't that right, Leonie?'

This elicited no response so Grace again addressed the table: 'Yes, Captain, I will be going home too.' But then she noticed Ben take a step forward. 'No, Ben.' She put up her free hand as though to stop him but with her eyes signalled, or tried to, her competing emotions – remorse, grief, empathy, shame, regret, sadness and, yes, affection. 'You stay and complete the trip.'

'But, Grace . . .'

He took another couple of steps, but Grace, continuing to apply pressure on Leonie's arm to keep her moving, shook her head emphatically, mouthing a very succinct '*No.*'

He froze.

One of the security men opened the door and, as she led Leonie through it, Grace understood that, with her 'No', she had chosen sides and had sealed her tomb.

23

J udgement having been handed down, Grace and her daughter walked, in disgrace, at some distance from each other to their cabins, the air between them teeming with accusations and emotions. Leonie, no doubt, had recovered her sense of grievance, while on Grace's part, guilt, grief and embarrassment swirled around her as turbulently as the ocean outside. Again she feared how Jacqueline and Adeline would see it when they were informed of what had happened, as they would be, from Leonie's point of view.

Harry? Harry's reaction didn't bear thinking about – and Cherry's?

Dear God! Cherry! *What did I tell you, Harry? Thank God I rescued you from that house of horrors!*

Still silent, they parted at their cabin doors to let themselves into their respective staterooms. In hers, Grace (whose talents, by dint of her very frequent travel when she was with Aer Lingus, ran to neat packing) accomplished her task in less than twenty minutes. The discarding of her laundry helped, with all toiletries, except shampoo and toothpaste, all cosmetics, except moisturiser, lipstick and eyebrow pencil, all of which she'd bought in Dublin airport: the displays had been so colourful and inviting, the lighting so kind.

Her skin was good – she didn't know why because she'd always been neglectful of it, if the beauty writers were to be trusted. Good genes, maybe.

Sadly, she couldn't remember the texture or even the appearance of her daddy's skin and, in memory, had never got close enough to her mother's face to examine hers (maybe when she was a baby). So, rather than the skin, she remembered her mother's habitual expression as pinched.

Oddly, when she had attended her mother's deathbed, the tense face seemed to have relaxed. She had very rarely brought that picture into her mind because it reawakened too many painful areas of their relationship and she certainly wasn't going to reactivate it right now.

So, her good skin wasn't from heritage, she decided. More likely she had lucked out because she wasn't outdoorsy.

She dumped the bulkiest of the new clothes she'd expected to wear during what the shipping line had promised as the highlight of the trip: a guided excursion whereby the two of them could take a walk on an ice floe 'in the footsteps of the polar bears'. She would hardly get the opportunity to wear these in Baldoyle, she thought. Also saddening was the missed opportunity to view the Northern Lights, which hadn't shown up. Maybe from Oslo?

Ironically for herself and Leonie, the captain had announced via his Tannoy that this evening and tonight conditions for viewing should be ideal.

It was these basic, mundane thoughts that were sustaining her now, keeping at bay, she assumed temporarily, the horror of what was happening, and now, having checked she'd packed everything else, she turned out all the lights in the cabin, wheeled her case into the corridor, closed her door and knocked on Leonie's. 'Are you ready, Leonie?'

'Go away! Leave me alone.'

This time she was having none of it. Instead of calling out again or cajoling, she used her key and let herself into the stateroom to find her daughter, back facing the door, humped in the foetal position on the bed, the floor strewn with her belongings, her suitcase open but empty. Grace got to work, picking up and folding, dropping items into the case, then went into the bathroom to gather up everything there.

Then she went back to the bedside and grasped Leonie's arm. 'Come on. We don't have all that much time before the ship docks and there's a bit of formality to go through.'

No response.

'Leonie? We have to go. I've packed your stuff. All you

have to do is make a final check to make sure you have everything.'

'I'm not going anywhere.'

'Yes, you are.' Grace's patience was wearing thin.

She pulled on the arm she held, but Leonie snatched it away. 'Take your filthy hands off me. You're not a mother. You don't know how to be a mother!'

'Whatever you say.' But Grace experienced the tell-tale tugging on the safety restraints she kept permanently fastened around her temper and, although she took a deep breath and retreated from the side of the bed to cool down, they gave way. Her frustration, speaking for her at first in a low, intense monotone, rose gradually in volume, unleashing on Leonie what she should have been saying to Harry and her other two daughters for years, certainly for the past seven.

She left nothing unsaid. How trapped she felt. How she had been left without any meaningful life of her own, no existence outside the house except for grocery shopping and the occasional trip into Dublin on the Dart to relieve the monotony – but even then never leaving without the thought that she couldn't count on coming back to the same house as the one she'd left.

How she was sick and tired of her non-life, 'just existing and minding you, pussyfooting around you, testing the temperature, worrying about Princess Leonie's moods and feelings from dawn to dusk. Putting out the fires you start . . .'

At one point during this impassioned monologue, Leonie, pale and wide-eyed, had turned in the bed and, still lying there, gazed at her in horror. 'Stop! Please, Mum, stop!' she cried.

It was too late: Grace couldn't stop. 'I'm your prisoner, Leonie, condemned to hard labour. And you know what?'

'Mum, don't!' Her daughter was hiccuping. 'You're scaring me!'

But Grace had gone far beyond caring about Leonie's sensitivities. 'Prisoners get parole or eventually get released altogether, Leonie,' she said. 'Some even manage to escape but not me – I'm stuck! For me, "life" means life. All of it. Until I die. Sometimes, Leonie . . .'

But anger at that pitch can rarely be sustained for very long. Grace felt it weakening, but she hadn't finished and, like the sudden re-ignition of a log or a piece of coal when you thought you'd put out the fire, she got a second wind: 'Sometimes,' she repeated, 'I think I hate you, Leonie, but don't worry, I hate myself even more.'

She was moving closer and closer to the bed, leading Leonie to recoil as though fearful of being struck, an action that, terribly, resounded in Grace's soul.

She did stop and Leonie jumped out of the far side of the bed, bolting for the bathroom while her mother, overcome with remorse, shouted after her, 'Wait! Wait, Leonie! I'm sorry, I'm sorry – I didn't mean all that!' She attempted to follow but tripping on her daughter's now redundant new boots, she almost fell. In the end, she managed to keep her balance and reached the bathroom door just as Leonie slammed it. 'I didn't mean all that! Please, Leonie, let me in.' She splayed herself against the door, trying to push it open. 'I'm sorry. Please . . .'

The door gave maybe a millimetre but, with a click, her daughter activated the lock.

Grace, her knees threatening to give way, barely made it back to Leonie's bed. To save herself from collapse, she sat on the edge.

So much for *no expressed emotion.*

What now?

24

Back in her own stateroom, Grace was trying to avoid lying down, although her body, craving sleep, was plaguing her to do so. She was afraid if she closed her eyes she wouldn't wake up until the following day.

And since she'd had only a couple of mouthfuls of breakfast before Leonie had done her thing in the dining room, she was also in dire need of food. Now she realised there would be a couple of hours before the ship sailed again after docking so perhaps she should make the most of the time they had left by availing herself of its facilities one last time.

It was hard to leave the safety of her cabin, showing her face to what had to be a judgemental public, but in any event she had to visit the desk to settle her bill and collect information about flight timings, boarding passes and so on. She would get through it by reminding herself that she would never see *any* of these people again. Let them have their fun, she and Leonie would be gone in a couple of hours and so, walking tall and looking neither right nor left, she took the stairs rather than the lift on her way down to the concourse where, standing in the queue for service, she stared straight ahead.

When it was her turn, she found she was expected, but the clerk gave no indication that he knew the reason for their early departure.

Her account wasn't ready yet, he told her, but there was some news, about which he was quite apologetic: she and Leonie would be waiting at Longyearbyen airport for at least five hours for their flight to Oslo – there were no longer any international flights from Svalbard. And because they would be too late for onward flights to Amsterdam when they landed at Oslo, they would have to stay the night in the city.

Grace didn't know which was worse, breaking this news to Leonie or living it with her. Whichever, she was in for a rocky ride.

The young man behind the desk was watching her and, clearly recognising the dismay written all over her face, offered to organise the onward flights next day, and to book a hotel for them, adding that there were at least two he could recommend because he was himself from Oslo.

'Thank you,' she said faintly. 'You're very kind. And please add the additional costs to my account.'

She found no satisfaction in the thought of having to present the receipts to Harry when she eventually managed to get the two of them home. The trip had been ill-conceived from the start, foisted on her and Leonie for reasons bordering on cruelty. She was angry with herself for not resisting it more strongly. Her relationship with Leonie might never recover from it, not least because of the unleashing of her frustrations.

Rather than hang around on the concourse until the account was ready, she decided to go to the Marine for a quick coffee and a sandwich. She'd bring something back for Leonie. And if her daughter wouldn't let her in, she'd eat it herself. When she walked into the restaurant or, rather, trudged, her feet as heavy as kettle bells, she instantly spotted Ben. He was sitting at a window table (disconsolately, it seemed, to judge by his slumped body), a beer and his open journal in front of him, staring out at Longyearbyen Pier. Grace was near despair. She and Leonie had created havoc around this young man who shouldn't have had to give either of them a second thought but should be out there celebrating his life and enjoying his holiday.

Her impulse was to back out of the restaurant but that would be absurd. They had enjoyed each other intimately (had that been as lately as last night?) and now she was chary of greeting him with a simple 'Hello'?

Hunger, however, overruled hesitations. While instinctively casting around for Leonie in the vicinity, she felt confident for once that her daughter wouldn't appear.

She wasn't thick-skinned enough to present herself as a focus of negative gossip.

Grace took a deep breath and walked around Ben to sit in the chair opposite. 'Hi,' she said quietly. 'Mind if I join you for a few minutes? I need to eat.'

Swiftly, he closed his journal, placed it in his pocket and stood up. 'Let me get something for you. What would you like?'

'Thank you, Ben,' she said. 'A Danish and a coffee would help.' She amended that: 'Two Danish, please. I need the sugar.'

'I didn't know how you take your coffee,' he said when he came back, bearing a large plateful of Danish pastries and two mugs of black coffee, then unloaded them onto the table and sat down. 'I do feel a little weird that I don't know how you take it.'

'That's modern life, I suppose,' she said, falling on the Danish. 'But I get the context.'

He was staring at her. 'I get the context of what you didn't say. One-night stand, ships passing in the night et cetera – hey! Get me? My funny, ha ha!' But he didn't look amused.

'Oh, Ben, I didn't mean it like that.'

'Yes, you did.'

But Grace didn't have the energy to argue, even about this. She had done enough fighting for one day.

She drank some of her coffee. 'This is good, thank you. Did you manage to eat – breakfast being such a non-event and so on?'

'Grace! This is rubbish. This is not you. Who cares about coffee?'

'I for one, right now.'

But he wasn't really listening. 'What time are you going? Is Leonie already off the ship?'

She told him about the row, about what she'd flung at her daughter, who was now in self-imposed lockdown and refusing to disembark.

'I'll go and talk to her. She'll listen to me and, looking at it logically, I'm the cause of all this pain for both of you. I certainly didn't mean to be . . . and please know that, for me, last night wasn't a fling, Grace. Maybe it started like that, a little bit, but it sure hasn't finished that way, not for me at least.

'I accept, although I don't want to, that there are too many odds stacked against anything more. You are a powerful woman, Grace, and it's not just the sex – although that was completely wonderful. I think you have no idea how powerful you are, which is another thing that makes you so attractive.'

'I'm sorry,' she said automatically, but it galvanised him.

'Dammit, Grace, what for? Why are you apologising? Is it an Irish thing?'

'I don't know why I said that. Habit, I suppose, but I'm not sorry. I want you to know that.'

They stared at each other, some residue of the previous night shimmering between them but just beyond their reach.

Abruptly, not caring who saw, or what they thought, she

reached across the table to touch his face softly, a butterfly kiss with her hand. Then: 'I'd better go back to the desk. I'll take another of these pastries with me. My bill should be ready.'

'I'll come with you.'

'Please don't, Ben. Let's say goodbye here – God, what a cliché, it's like we're stand-ins for the finale of *Brief Encounter* or *Casablanca* and acting it out.'

'Aren't we?' There were tears in his eyes now.

'Don't, please,' she begged. 'I really have to go. You're a lovely man, and that's how I'll think of you. I'm very glad we had last night. I'm very glad to have known you. It's unlikely that we'll meet again, but . . . ' Her voice started to fail her. Then, with an attempt at levity: 'We'll always have the Arctic.'

She stood and turned to go, but before she could walk away, he had moved quickly around the table and taken her in his arms. She stood on tiptoe and kissed his mouth, not passionately as last night but as gently and meaningfully as she could.

From the doorway, she glanced back. He was still standing and made as though to give her a small wave but then thought better of it, letting his hand drop. She turned away and, hurrying to the concourse, shook her head, hard, to discourage her own tears.

25

On board the flight to Oslo, Grace was barely able to keep her eyes open. Whenever the lids drooped, her head fell to her chest, jerking her awake again.

She looked across at Leonie, who was sleeping peacefully (but who knew what abominations she saw in her dreams?). Her head, fallen sideways, had been caught inside the curved headrest. Had she been a standard-sized adult it might have lolled right out into the aisle.

From where she sat, most of her daughter's face was visible, the plane's overhead reading light catching a faint, silvery trace of saliva running from her slightly open mouth to her chin. It also illuminated the tip of the little cowlick that, since early childhood, she had professed to hate, but was now cultivating with scissors and comb.

Grace's eyes welled (she'd wept more in and around this trip than she had in decades, she thought) and her heart seemed to expand. Although it was so hard to take, Leonie's trigger-happy, pugnacious veneer was just that, a veneer, tempered by polishing to be strong enough to survive all that life threw at her.

Or, more accurately, what she *believed* it threw at her.

Sleeping like this, nakedly defenceless, to her mother she seemed more indicative of the real Leonie and, despite everything, all the heartache, frustration, justifiable anger and worry she'd caused, Grace loved her third daughter more than she loved anyone or anything else in the world.

By confirming this once again, she was reminded that putting Leonie first in her concern and love was unfair to the other two, who were in joint second place. She had rationalised this many times, telling herself that Adeline and Jackie were now self-sufficient and, in the phrase of previous generations, 'done for' by their parents.

But did that mean she was short-changing them? She'd glanced off this conversation, they'd all danced around it, but had never got to its core.

She had made the same vow to all three when they'd been born, promising to love them fiercely and for ever and that she would never, no matter the circumstances, desert them either physically or emotionally.

But the outcome had been not what she'd expected. That promise had been, and still was, of greatest relevance to her youngest because she had shown the greatest need for it. Maybe, Grace thought, she had avoided the issue about the other two because she hadn't wanted to hear the answer. Something else to add to her faults as a mother.

But it would be natural for Jackie and Adeline to resent all the attention paid to their sister and to believe it had been at their expense, that Leonie had been rewarded for her 'difficulties' (which they might believe to be egomania) while neither of them had caused their parents any sleepless nights.

She now added this lapse to the sequence of her own misbehaviours, simplifying it in the manner of the nursery rhyme they'd been taught to chant in High Babies – Senior Infants, as it was now.

For want of a nail the shoe was lost.
For want of a shoe the horse was lost.
For want of a horse the rider was lost.
For want of a rider the battle was lost.
For want of a battle the kingdom was lost.
And all for the want of a horseshoe nail.

If she hadn't thrown that punch in the playground, her mother wouldn't have bought a cane that day. The physical blisters and welts of the beating had healed but the mental and emotional scars of the humiliation, and notice of abandonment that her mother had inflicted along with the lashing, had cut much deeper than the bamboo and were permanent, no matter how hard she'd tried to plaster them over.

If she hadn't thrown that punch, her daddy wouldn't have died.

If she hadn't thrown that punch, she mightn't have been blanked by her mother for the rest of her mother's life – or might not have married, at the age of nineteen, the first man who had asked her, offering her the opportunity to get away from home.

If none of that had happened, she might have been a better and more joyful wife to a husband who wouldn't have left her for a younger, more amusing, far more confident and prettier model. Petite too.

And – whisper it – she wouldn't have given birth to these particular daughters or had these particular dilemmas.

All because of a single punch.

And now, on a ship, as a result of her lust, which was, she recalled, one of the seven deadly sins, she'd abandoned Leonie so that she could indulge herself with Ben, stamping on her daughter's dreams however unlikely of fulfilment they'd been.

What would the other two think of her night of passion? Leonie was sure to give them her version of events, which, looking back, had been pretty close to the truth: she had correctly read the runes.

There was no point in making excuses for herself.

She had a hard life. She *deserved* a bit of relaxation and fun.

She *deserved* validation that she still had something to offer a man.

She was starved of physical contact: she had *needed* it.

And, anyway, she and Ben were two unattached adults who'd had a mutually satisfying encounter and for one night only – a fling, meaningless in the long term, as far as she was concerned. So where was the harm?

It all came back to Leonie. As a mother, Grace's betrayal of her daughter had been real. She knew it – and so would Jackie and Adeline.

That silent walk back to their respective staterooms that morning from their 'trial', sentenced to expulsion, had been torture. It had teemed with accusations – Leonie's no doubt born of her general sense of grievance. But while she had maintained a face of stone, Grace had felt obligated to field all the smiling good-mornings when they'd passed cleaners or other staff who had clearly not been apprised of their disgrace. How she envied them their lives of hard work and simplicity, although she did acknowledge that behind closed doors, they, too, might have been living a 'life less ordinary'.

But that morning, she had thought that, in a heartbeat, she'd swap with any of them.

26

Grace turned on her phone in the taxi on the way to the Oslo hotel and saw that Harry had called her. Twice? This had to be about more than his golf club – and having glanced at Leonie, whose eyes were closed, she'd sent him a message: *Sorry I missed your calls. Will ring you in an hour. Unable to talk now.*

'Who's that to?'

Although her position in the back seat of the vehicle hadn't changed, her daughter's eyes were open. 'It was Arnotts. Another offer, new women's dresses. Just in. We're on their radar, Leonie!'

'You're lying. You can't text Arnotts.'

'I have an app. You have too, don't you?'

'Whatever!' Leonie closed her eyes again.

Grace's heart thumped. She had always been a bad liar and, tied together as they were, Leonie always read her well. But with her listening to every word, she couldn't face Harry just now.

Their check-in went smoothly and they were in their rooms within ten minutes of arrival. This hotel, the Thief, ultra-modern and very obviously expensive, faced the waterfront. The rooms were huge, maybe seven or eight times the size of the cabins on the *Magyar Bla*, and from the fourth-floor window of hers Grace could see several flashy cruisers moored at a dock, a sort of adjunct to the hotel's ground floor, probably, she thought, belonging to it.

Prices were huge, too, but, of course, the helpful clerk on the ship had made the booking, and in her state of mind at the time she hadn't asked him how much she'd have to pay. She hadn't cared.

She turned on her phone again and, to block any possibility that Leonie would hear her from her room next door, switched on the TV, which, surprisingly to her, was showing both Sky News and CNN. She turned up the volume and tapped out Harry's mobile number.

'Hi Grace, oh! Hang on, there's a call coming in from Leonie too. Let me answer it. I'll tell her I'll call her back.'

'No! No!' Grace yelled. 'You need to hear what I have to say first.'

She hadn't been prepared for this eventuality but, of course, it made sense that Leonie would try to get her version of events in before she did.

'All right, Gracie, no panic! She'll probably leave a message. But what's going on?'

'You called me twice.' She stalled. 'I'm ringing you because I thought it must be urgent – we were out of coverage most of the time.'

'Were?' He picked it up. 'Has something happened? Is Leonie okay?'

'She's fine. No change, though, unfortunately. But you go first.'

He'd had a call from Dieter, who had given him a rundown on what was happening with his wife – 'You never told me about Maxine, Grace.'

'We were in a rush to get to the airport. I did speak to her that morning and we made an arrangement to talk again. She's not dead?' Her throat constricted.

'No. But apparently she's anxious for the two of you to meet face to face as soon as possible, so with her in Galway, I took the initiative and booked lunch for you both at the Radisson in Athlone on the fifteenth – Dieter will bring Maxine. That's pretty easy for both of you, sort of midway. Is that OK? It's a Thursday, the day after you come back.'

'It's fine, thanks. Actually,' she cleared her throat, 'as it happens, we're off the boat so we'll be home earlier than planned. We're in an Oslo hotel.' Winging it, she gave him a synopsis of what had happened over the past few days. 'She thought she was in love with one of the other guests – it was another Jaden situation, Harry, we'd met him together on the first night on board, and somehow or other, she'd got it into her head that he and I were, um, close and that I was robbing him from her. This, Harry, was on the basis of two sightings of me in a public place where he happened to be sitting with me. The first was in a crowded bar, the second was early in the morning in the public dining room. This guy, Ben, was an American – youngish, around thirty, I'd say. Sounds familiar, Harry?

'Leonie was in the ship's hospital overnight – I'll tell you about that in a minute – presumably asleep, so I went without her for breakfast in the dining room and I'd just started eating when this Ben came in and joined me.' She related the rest of the story, then went on to outline what had happened the previous day with the lifeboats and the ship being turned around and so on, and how Leonie had ended up in the hospital for observation.

'Anyway,' she concluded, 'it all finished with us being asked to pack our bags. The sad thing is that she was to see a psychiatrist today. I wish she had but we were thrown off, and here we are.'

'Jesus! What a nightmare.'

'How did Cherry's event go?'

He didn't respond and she let it lie, feeling that she had made her point, had distilled the story sufficiently so that it was her word against Leonie's and, given Leonie's history . . .

She didn't feel good about this – since when had she become so devious? While her description of the two encounters had been truthful, if missing a couple of little details, like, first, the handholding and then the sex, she was determined that her glorious night with Ben would never be anyone's business but her own and his.

And if she never went to bed with anyone else, its memory would, she hoped, be within reach to sustain her through the bleak years to come.

After they'd hung up, it was worth noting, she thought wryly, that it hadn't occurred to him that she might have been an object of interest to the young American.

Her next task was to call Maxine, a task she didn't relish because, despite Max's apologies being heartfelt and genuine, as Grace believed, she wondered if she really had changed her views so comprehensively. Her arguments, so stridently reiterated, had always seemed utterly entrenched. It might be legitimate to wonder if a person's convictions, deeply held, could perform a U-turn on foot of a cancer diagnosis.

She bit the bullet but Max's mobile number went straight to voicemail. It was impossible not to react to the sound of her friend's voice, as strong, as *commanding* as it had always been. Not the voice she'd used during their phone conversation of a few days previously. She steadied herself. 'Hi, Max,' she told the machine, 'sorry for the delay in getting back to you. Will tell you all when I see you. I know we're meeting in Athlone, but since I'll be home a bit sooner than I thought originally, if you'd prefer to meet earlier, that's fine with me. I'll call again tomorrow morning and, if it suits, we can make plans. Thinking about you.' She clicked off.

That night she slept soundly, but woke with tears flowing in the midst of a very vivid but unfinished dream.

She was driving in the gloaming, that final fade of the

light before darkness falls, when she saw a very tiny baby elephant coming towards her. She slammed on the brakes, got out of the car and the little animal ran closer until it touched her hand with its trunk, which was surprisingly warm and dry. Then, slowly, it curled its trunk around her fingers and its eyes met hers.

She woke abruptly, overwhelmed with an outpouring of mixed emotions: love, gratitude for the privilege of the little animal's trust, pity for its predicament. Not altogether a believer in dream analysis for psychological purposes, when she'd controlled herself sufficiently, she took out her phone, googling.

Combining information from all sites, Buddhists, Hindus, dream interpreters and 'elephant experts', she learned that since elephants are hugely family- and community-oriented, with the group cooperating in parenting tasks, to dream about them signifies loyalty, parent care, empathy and intelligence.

Elephants are also very big and powerful and, in dreams, could signify something major you have to deal with in your waking life.

But to dream about an infant of the species is significant in that a problem with something or someone you're passionate about will grow until it becomes too big for you to manage.

27

Days later, while Grace was having an emotional meeting in an Athlone hotel with Maxine Smith, Marcus Brady was sitting in a coffee shop at Hamburg airport with his nephew.

When he had seen Ben come through Customs, his first thought was that the holiday had not been a barrel of laughs: Ben looked drawn, tired, even haunted, as he headed for the terminal's exit, walking so fast that Marcus had had to move swiftly to intercept him. 'Hi there!'

'What are you doing here?' He'd clearly caught Ben unawares.

'What am I doing here?' said Marcus. 'Waiting for you. I thought I'd surprise you!'

'Well, you certainly have,' said Ben. My flight to Chicago isn't until late this evening and I was going to take a cab into Hamburg and have a look around.'

'So you have plenty of time for a cup of coffee.'

Ben was still mystified. 'Seriously, Marcus, why *are* you here? Does this have something to do with future plans to retire?'

'All in good time – we'll talk over the coffee. I need it anyway. The coffee on the plane from Chicago was disgusting, even in first class. There's a Starbucks here.'

'You flew first class? That's a departure for you – no pun intended!' Ben knew his uncle always travelled economy.

'Yeah, I did.' Marcus grimaced. 'An eye-opener. How the other half lives – but the only real benefit is that you get a flat bed to sleep on. I'm not one for the champagne and the rare-breed beef, as you know. It's a fantasy world, and a huge waste of money that could be used for something real. I won't be doing it again.'

'So the money came through, then.' Ben grinned as they took their seats in the franchise.

'Yeah. That's what I want to talk to you about.'

'And you came all this way to do it! Intriguing. Will I be happy, d'you think?'

'All will be revealed. What kind of coffee?'

'Cappuccino. With chocolate sprinkles. And real milk, please.'

*

In Athlone the conversation between Grace and Maxine was intense but, in a sense, meaningless. Max, whose appearance, Grace saw gratefully, had not yet changed all that much – although she was a little thinner since when last they'd met in December of the previous year – had ordered only a green salad with a glass of water, while she herself was pushing hake around her plate. It had come with one of those little tin buckets of chips and she was now absently picking them up with her fingers, dipping them in her little pyramid of salt on the side of her plate, before popping them one-by-one into her mouth.

They had hugged when they'd met, holding on to one another a little longer than usual. There hadn't been tears because, Grace thought, they had both been nervy about this meeting – certainly she was.

At first they'd talked neutrally, about the housing crisis and the shocking difference in Irish rain: agreeing that it used to fall gently or was violently blown about on a storm but now it came in straight, harsh lines, flooding driveways and flattening vegetation, the kind of downpours Irish people had seen, on TV, only in the South China Sea, the Indian Ocean regions or Malaysia and Bangladesh during the monsoon season. They further agreed it was due to climate change.

They had reminisced about school, about the nuns, many of whom were now dead or very aged in nursing homes; about their indignation about the position of the 'lay' nuns, who had cooked, cleaned and done the laundry.

(Although those women themselves believed this work in service was a vocational equal to that of the choir nuns.)

'Remember when you decided to join the order after the Leaving?' Maxine chuckled.

'How could I forget? The trip to Clery's for the trousseau, the trunk and the writing case! The fountain pen! In a sense, though, that convent was a haven, wasn't it? Off the planet in its own little bubble.'

'Especially when you developed lifelong friends.' Maxine invested this with many meanings. Grace got them because 'lifelong' might be pretty short in this case.

Their conversation was conducted, therefore, under a toxic cloud, infected by a mass of words, said and unsaid, on the two matters that had actually brought them there: Maxine's cancer, and Leonie McGee.

It was Grace who brought them into play. 'This is all very fine, Max, and it's horrible that we're meeting again in such difficult circumstances, but shouldn't we deal with the two elephants in the room?' She hadn't meant to use that expression, but clearly, after that dream, elephants were still in her mind. 'First, darling Max, I'm really upset about your cancer. I wish I could take it away from you. Dieter says you're both full of hope, though, and that the treatment is really good.'

'It is, that's for sure,' her friend said slowly. 'But, Grace – and please don't try to talk me out of this – I know what he wants, but it's not what I want. It didn't take me long to decide not to take the treatment. I've had all the tests, and while surgery is an option, along with all the usual chemo and radiotherapy, there would be a lot of side issues, not least a permanent colostomy bag.

'Why would I put myself through it all – treatments, more than likely, repeat treatments, losing my hair, gaining a colostomy bag *for life*, knowing there's no guarantee that any of it will work? I won't ask if you'd do it – because I know you would, for Leonie and your other children. What do I have to live for?'

'Dieter? And me, Max. I can't tell you how much I regret my part in our falling-out. What a waste of precious time. Twenty times I went to pick up the phone, but twenty times I didn't. I'm so sorry.'

Maxine looked at her plate. 'That's because you were dodging one of my lectures. I've had a lot of time to think. Oddly, a death sentence throws up a great deal of proper thinking' – she smiled, small, inward-looking – 'proper ways of looking at serious subjects, seeing what's truly important. Who'd have thought?'

'What does Dieter think about this? It's too soon to make these decisions, Max. You were diagnosed only — what – a couple of week ago? You could get a second opinion.'

'When you take scans and MRIs and biopsies all together they don't lie, Grace. The rest is magical thinking. All the hope and praying for miracles, it serves only to torture you. My mind is made up, and while Dieter will be upset – I've yet to talk to him in full – at rock bottom, he'll agree with me. I'm not going to die tomorrow. Without treatment, I'll have three to six months, they say.

But apparently they say that to everyone. But who really

knows, Grace? With treatment, they say they can't tell – they're afraid to in case you sue them – but when they're pushed they'll say something optimistic. So it's a bummer, yes, but my plan is not to have any pain and to fade away quietly and – eh – Gracefully! And if optimism is justified, I'll enjoy the extension!'

Grace's vocal cords were paralysed. Now was certainly not the time to bring up her objections to Maxine's nagging about her daughter.

'I know what you're thinking, Grace,' Maxine said then. 'I'm abandoning you like your mother did, but you have three children who, whatever their age, will always need you, and however difficult Leonie has been, she's still there, isn't she? And you love her. You've made that perfectly clear. You also love Adeline and Jackie. And they love you.'

'Dieter loves you. And don't forget me, I love you, Max.' She grasped her friend's hand, now feeling very fragile in her own. Maxine looked at her plate.

She looked up then, with that expression in her eyes Grace knew so well, that look of determination, bossiness, *doughtiness*. 'You, me, Dieter and "everyone what knows me"' – here she grimaced – 'we're *all* going to make the most of the time we have left together. Afterwards, my guess is he'll sell the house and go back to Mainz. He never really settled here. He stayed for me. He's shown his love for me that way.'

'Oh, Max . . .' Grace was so emotional now that she felt she couldn't continue in this vein, didn't want to either, but Maxine hadn't finished.

'The reason I needed to see you so urgently is that I want to talk to you about Leonie. Don't worry, not the way I used to, I promise! And I'm very, very sorry for the other stuff – it could even be called a campaign, couldn't it? I'd no right. I know you don't like people saying you're marvellous, but you are. A wonderful mother, a powerful mother.'

'I'm not!' The use of that particular adjective hit her like a runaway horse, or an elephant . . .

Maxine was brooking no argument. 'For God's sake, girl, take the compliment! So here's what I want to say.'

But before she could continue, she was overcome with nausea and had to dash to the bathroom. Dieter, who'd been keeping a watching brief from another table, came across to Grace.

Although she'd met him many times, Grace couldn't say she really knew him. He was several years older than Maxine and although, like Harry, he kept himself fit, his face showed the strain. 'I am sorry, Grace,' he said, 'but this is too much for her and I must take her away. Do you mind?'

'Of course not, Dieter,' she said. 'I'm very grateful that you've both made the effort to travel. She's told me about her decision but we haven't had time yet to discuss it – and of course I want to see her as much as possible until . . .'

'Can you come to us in Galway, perhaps? We are planning that she should go into the Galway Hospice as soon as we can get her a bed. She will be comfortable there and they are very experienced. We have been good patrons there for many years. They are very nice too. And they are willing to have her while she is having the treatments.' His gaze slipped to the floor.

He *knows*! thought Grace. 'But that's the end game, Dieter – surely she's not there yet?'

'Not necessarily "end game"', he said. 'You do not have to be at death's door to receive hospice care, just to need care and comfort and to be surrounded by people who can offer both. They don't throw you out because you don't die on schedule! My own mother had two very peaceful months in a hospice. And, to be truthful, Grace, while I am willing, I have no skills as a nurse.'

'Three to six months?'

'We do not know how long for Maxine, just like you do not know how long for you. They try to tell you the truth, but also good news to keep you strong. That is how I think of it. The plan is to be as happy and comfortable as you can be for as long— Ah – here she is!' He stood up, went across to take Maxine's arm and brought her to the table, quietly talking to her as they came.

Grace, struggling for control, got up to embrace her friend. Close-up, the borders of Maxine's heavy foundation and blusher were starkly delineated against the ashen skin at her hairline. 'Dieter's just told me you'll come to Galway. We never really got to talk about Leonie – and I hate the phone now. I've decided recently that face to face is the only way to communicate. See the whites of their eyes, kind of thing. I've decided a lot of things since I got this diagnosis.' She smiled.

'I'll come.' Grace was finding it hard to speak. 'You won't

be able to get rid of me – you'll be sick of the sight of me soon because we do have a lot of time to make up. We'll meet again in a couple of days, promise, wherever you are.'

That brought a flash of the old Maxine. 'You told her?' she said angrily to her husband. 'I said not to talk about the hospice.' The effort made her cough.

'It's all right,' Grace said. 'Don't be cross with him. Did you think I wouldn't find out?' Instead of hugging her again, because Dieter seemed to be propping her up, she touched her friend's cheek, which, under the make-up, was as dry as salt. 'See you soon, Max,' she whispered.

*

In equally deep discussion in the Hamburg airport Starbucks, Marcus and Ben were on their second cups of coffee, Marcus having managed to draw his nephew into a conversation he'd clearly been reluctant to have.

They were talking about the plans Ben's uncle had already outlined before the trip to Norway. At least Marcus was while Ben listened, or pretended to. Marcus wasn't sure whether he was taking anything in, as he regularly interjected with anecdotes from his trip. Ben's uncle, who knew his nephew inside out, had already divined that, unusually, Ben wasn't being totally open.

Something had happened on that ship, something Ben didn't yet care to reveal, and Marcus shelved his own concerns to ask about the voyage.

'Not all that exciting, but still very interesting,' Ben had his uncle, while they were walking to the café. But despite all the hype in the brochure, the Northern Lights had appeared for the first time only when they'd been well into the voyage, and had then vanished again. Something to do with the atmospherics not being right.

He had photos, he told Marcus, but they were just tourist snaps. If Marcus wanted to see pictures of the Arctic, he should buy postcards or illustrated books by professional photographers. 'Or watch David Attenborough,' he added. He hadn't seen any polar bears, but during the ice walk he had glimpsed a walrus, sitting quite near his group, unfazed by the clicking and all the attention, until it had slipped nonchalantly back into the water.

He had described the ship, in particular the Koselig. 'You'd love it, Marcus. It's the Norwegian version of your *hygge* hotel in Gary.'

'Speaking of which,' Marcus again took his opportunity, 'I know you've only just got back and all . . .' Ben had lowered his gaze. 'Are you listening to me, kid?'

'Of course I am, Marcus. I'm listening to every word.'

'That's good because I need us to have a serious talk. That's why I'm here. More coffee?'

'I'm going to turn into the Coffee Monster! But okay, go ahead, one more. I guess I'll live.'

*

The two discussions that took place that afternoon, more than 1,000 miles apart, in Athlone and Hamburg, were jointly, and relatively soon, to have a profound effect on the life of Grace McGee.

28

Having come back from Norway and seen Maxine in Athlone, Grace had to pick up the reins of her life in Baldoyle. In many ways, going to Norway had made no difference to her daughter: she had merely brought along her own world of illusions, delusions and recriminations.

As a result of their expulsion from the *Magyar Bla*, she was in the customary, silent sulk phase that occurred after such events, so at least she wasn't ranting and, for as long as it lasted, Grace could pretend she had some form of the normal life that could be expected of a middle-class, middle-aged woman with adequate means.

She hadn't even tried to talk to Leonie about what

had happened on the ship, knowing it would lead to an immediate eruption and accusations of her own perfidy. That Leonie had guessed correctly about that single night off from the roster of care served only to complicate matters: Grace had had to stand sentry on her words in case she dropped one to reignite the fire.

She didn't regret the event – or told herself repeatedly that she didn't – although there was no denying the aftermath. Her skin still remembered every touch of his hands and lips, the male strength of him, and if she could have cut Leonie out of the equation she might have allowed herself the freedom to engage a sculptor to cast her memories in bronze, a reminder that, for one night, she had been a free woman.

Maxine, frail and sick as she'd been, had recognised during their conversation something was up. 'Grace, what's happened to you?'

'Nothing! Why would you think anything happened? I was on a trip, got thrown off because of Leonie, back early, that's all.' Grace had rehearsed her look of baffled innocence because she and Maxine had known each other for so long, it was difficult successfully to dissemble.

'Come off it, Grace Lennon!' Since Harry had left, Maxine had insisted on using Grace's maiden name. 'I know you! Tell all.'

But Grace had promised Ben she wouldn't talk about it, foolishly perhaps – what harm could it do for her to tell her friend she had bedded a man half her age and it had been great? He'd promised to keep schtum too, but would he tell his uncle? He'd said more than once during their brief friendship that he could talk to Marcus about *anything*. And how much difference would it make to Grace Lennon McGee if Ben's uncle knew when the two men were four thousand miles away?

She wouldn't break the promise, though, and had stared blankly across the table at Maxine. 'Really don't know what you're talking about, Max.'

'Sure sign,' Maxine said. 'All your life you've used that phrase when you've something to hide. Hope you enjoyed yourself and that he was a sexy beast. You deserved it. Don't worry, I'll take it with me to the grave!' Then, seeing Grace's look of dismay: 'Gallows humour is part of the condition, I'm told. It feels good to be able to say things like that, shocking everyone. Kind of releases the fear.'

'Are you afraid, Max?'

'Truly not now. I did dread the pain, but it's the hospice's job to take care of that side of things so that's what they'll do when I get there. I'm sorry it's happening before my sixtieth. We'd planned on taking a round-the-world cruise, but I've learned that there are no entitlements in this world and how lucky I've been in some respects.'

'Not in others?'

'No children. Not like you.'

'I wouldn't be without them but sometimes, Max . . . '

'Just having them is a bonus, isn't it?'

'Sometimes.' Grace's tone had been rueful. 'Depending.'

*

But the next day Grace, tired to her core, found she was dragging herself around and, no matter in what direction she looked, there was some sort of wall or hurdle. She was running out of the energy necessary to get around the walls or leap the hurdles, and although she would never disclose it to a soul, she felt a tinge of envy in thinking of Maxine. Wouldn't it be nice to close your eyes and just slip away, quietly, knowing that all the turmoil and pain and fighting would be over?

She caught the thought before it could develop. Ask Jenny. Ask Harriet what it's like for those left behind.

But then she couldn't completely quash a gleam of envy for Maxine, whose course was now plotted. She'd have many kind, helpful pilots and navigators to carry her on her way and the destination was certain and peaceful. There would be no surprises, no traps set, no axes permanently poised to come down on her head should she stray, however inadvertently. And everyone would be onside to help her get through.

Grace and Leonie had been home for only a couple of days and, superficially, it was like coming into *Groundhog Day*. Leonie was still behaving erratically and unpredictably, sometimes fulminating at her mother, at others speaking on her phone calmly and professionally, in a way that suggested she might be applying for jobs.

So, she thought, looking around the kitchen, her royal domain, it's *status quo ante*. She'd loved Latin at school but not much had stuck. That was one phrase that had.

Yet not quite *status quo*. Something had changed

infinitesimally, not just because she'd been speaking to Maxine, but because of events in Ben Brady's stateroom. She couldn't yet describe it succinctly and had no one else to whom she could say this, apart from Maxine (if she ever decided to break her promise).

But a little lock had been sprung, allowing a torch-beam of light to shine through. Sitting in her silent house, she'd discovered she was a little less resigned to her fate, a little more willing to find a way of insisting that something *could* be done to help her daughter – and consequently herself.

If she could figure out how to say 'no' with conviction to Harry and Cherry, Adeline and Jackie, the situation would improve. If she'd made up her mind to say a firm 'no', it should be reliable and there was no chance she could be persuaded in any other direction. Cherry had seemingly perfected this dark art. She should be more like Cherry.

She sat in her TV room in front of her bright bay window, the TV black, her crossword still missing an answer to one clue. Up to that ill-fated cruise she had been more or less resigned to her domestic and caring role, managing it and the strictures it imposed with the best face she could construct.

But she now knew that she was no longer happy to carry on regardless, taking all of Leonie's insults and tantrums on the chin, excusing her behaviour on the basis that she was ill, but not ill enough for the state to help her meaningfully.

Harriet, the second of her two bereaved friends, had told Grace of how she'd found herself on the side of a motorway, on her mobile, arguing with a registrar — the consultant wouldn't come to the phone – about whether or not he would take her daughter into hospital. 'He said no, Grace, because, would you believe, her behaviour wasn't bad enough.'

After ten or fifteen minutes of increasingly heated argument, Harriet had found herself yelling, as lorries and trucks trundled past in long convoys, 'You're telling me, Doctor, that if she isn't standing behind me with a Samurai sword over my head, or rampaging around a shopping centre with a machine gun, she wouldn't be sick *enough* for you to take her into your psychiatric hospital?'

'And the reply was,' she'd said bitterly, '"I'm afraid that, yes, that's the consultant's decision."'

Her daughter had died two and a half months later.

Grace was still relatively young, but every second day on Joe Duffy's *Liveline*, she listened to horror stories of parents in their eighties being terrorised by offspring in their fifties or even sixties and being given very little help. She corrected herself: Leonie wasn't terrorising her, of course she wasn't, but sometimes . . .

There was a strange anomaly in her case and in those of thousands of others: she and Harry were comfortably off and willing to take care of their daughter so it seemed that the medical and mental-health systems were taking advantage of them as carers, no matter how much they suffered from the demeanour and behaviour of their charges. No official respite was offered to people like them, probably because they were seen as flush enough to afford it for themselves.

But mental illness and the chaos it engenders shows no fear or favour to those it affects, no mercy to any group, rich or poor. The psychological damage caused is the same whether you can afford fancy treatment or have to wait your turn to get any at all.

Thinking about this, Grace decided that, in a rather perverse way, the system leaves those with the fortitude and willingness not to abandon their mentally ill charges, to get on with it, sometimes for the whole of their lives, no matter how grave the effect on their own health.

But this wasn't getting her anywhere. Leonie wasn't up yet, or if she was, she wasn't playing her music. Grace decided she had better things to do than wait for her to emerge in order to judge whether it might be safe to say something as simple as 'Hello, Leonie. Sleep well?' In the past, that had indicated to Leonie that her mother was not only spying on her but invading her space. She had her three-monthly appointment with her psychiatrist this afternoon so Grace would try to make sure she wasn't in the house when she returned. Because after each session of, usually, between three and eight minutes, Leonie's mood was never good and when she came in she usually stomped straight up the stairs to her room.

She rang Maxine, and although the call went, again, straight to voicemail, she left a message to say she was on her way to Galway. Then she scribbled a note and left it beside the kettle:

Have to go to Galway for the day, back tonight. Good luck with your appointment and there's plenty of food and sandwich material in the fridge. Should be home before nine.

Love, M.

Her spirits lifted as she closed the door behind her and headed for the car. Depending on traffic, it would take approximately three hours to drive to where Maxine and Dieter lived on the shores of Galway Bay, on the outskirts of Clarinbridge.

Maxine was dying but, strangely, Grace was looking forward to the journey. Her car was more than transport: it was peace. A peaceful cocoon. And, most importantly of all, it was freedom.

29

For years, traffic had been permanently snarled when passing through the environs of Clarinbridge bound for Galway City, but the recent advent of a new bypass helped significantly, at least if Clarinbridge was your destination. Grace saw she'd made good time from Dublin when she peeled off to take a narrow rural road to where the couple lived in some splendour.

The impressive entrance to their house was fronted by a pair of high, wrought-iron electric gates with discreet CCTV cameras embedded in the pillars. They parted silently as Grace drove up. She had phoned again when driving through Dublin, to let them know when to expect her, so they must have been watching out. Maxine had been pleased she was coming, urging her to stay at least for a night. 'We need to have a long talk about something,' she'd said, but wouldn't discuss it on the phone.

Loath to leave Leonie alone in the house, Grace said she'd see about staying the night but hadn't said no. Whatever it was Maxine wanted to talk about must be important to her, so who was Grace to deny her request?

She passed through the gates, hoping that their differences were now buried for good.

Bad analogy, she said to herself.

In the meantime, she was in a beautiful location, going into a beautiful house to visit old friends. That was how she'd look at the next couple of hours. Maxine and Dieter had always been superb hosts and this felt like a real visit of the kind she and Harry used to enjoy way back. And as she drove over the gravel up to the house, the gates closing behind her and the sun dancing on the waters of Galway Bay, she experienced something unusual, a feeling of calm, not least because she'd switched off her phone, to remain within the law but primarily, to enjoy the peace.

Dieter was at the front door by the time she had parked between his big Beemer and Max's little VW Golf. 'We tried to call you, Grace, but your phone went to voicemail.'

'Hello again, Dieter. Hope I'm not barging in on the two of you.' She hugged him, explained about the phone, then, suddenly alarmed, extricated herself. 'I hope that call wasn't urgent. Is she all right?'

He glanced into the house. 'Nothing we didn't expect,

but it's come sooner than we thought. The hospice rang about an hour ago. They have a bed for her. She's packing.'

'Oh, Dieter . . .' She caught him to her again and he dissolved on her shoulder.

'I'm not ready.' He sobbed. 'I thought I was, but I'm not. You know what she's like when she wants to do something. She wants to take the burden off me, is what she said. I'll see her every day, of course. And I'm so glad you're here, Grace. You have arrived at the right time, like an angel, thank you. She'll be delighted!' He attempted to steady himself. 'You can help her pack – she'd like that. I – I . . .'

'Come on, let's go inside.' Grace was holding herself together, just about.

He wiped his eyes. 'I'm sorry, Grace. It's just that seeing you and remembering all the fun we used to have . . . We Germans are supposed to be stiff and stoic, but that is a travesty in my case. I am like a sponge, these days, or a jelly.

'She'll be delighted you're here to help her,' he repeated, 'and don't worry, she's not the one behaving like a big baby. She's still very positive, bossing me around, telling me I'm fetching the wrong cardigans. Same old Maxine, yes?'

But he couldn't keep this up and again the tears came. He bolted for the hall cloakroom, managing to say, just before he closed the door, 'You know where to go, Grace.'

Grace knew that the sad thing about hospices was that usually, although not always, someone had to die before a bed became available. Dieter was not the only one grieving on this cold but gorgeous November afternoon.

She went upstairs and along a corridor to their bedroom, normally as fresh and tidy as if it was marketing itself to a potential buyer. While not chaotic, all of the drawers were open and the bed was piled rainbow-high with nightdresses, blouses, jumpers, underwear and a few comfortable-looking pairs of sweatpants.

Maxine saw Grace straight away as she came into the room. 'Well, look what the cat's dragged in! Twice in two days! Sorry about my little turn yesterday. It turned out to be nothing, Dieter overreacting as usual, removing me from the scene.'

'He's desperately upset, Max.'

'I can hear him. It's new for him. Grace, it's worse for him than for me. I'm off to be pampered, amn't I? My every wish gratified. I only have to lift my little finger from now on and handmaids will come running. There are advantages, you know.'

'Shut up, Max!' As she had with Dieter, she pulled Maxine to her.

'I'm so scared, Grace.' Her friend wept. 'It's all too real too soon.'

'Come on over to the window seat with me and we'll watch the sun on the water. It's gorgeous outside But freezing. We've always loved this view, haven't we?'

'Oh, that's lovely, that is, really great. Talk about tact – come and enjoy the last sunny day you'll see through these windows before you go into the hospice to die! Lovely!'

The window seat was plush, constructed like two large

commas end to end, the curly, fatter tops fitting into the corners of the window so two people could snuggle into them and face each other.

'So that's the gallows humour done for this evening, eh, Max?' Grace managed a smile. 'What time do you have to be in?'

'Dieter took the call and they said this evening or tonight but neither of us was expecting it to be so soon because that hospice is always jammed. They're applying for planning permission to build a much bigger one. To tell you the truth, I'm so scared now I'm wondering if I'm doing the right thing, going in there. Was it the right move in the first place to refuse the medication? It's all very well to be brave in theory but have I made the right decisions?'

'First things first, Max.' Grace kicked off her loafers and placed one of her feet on both of Maxine's, stroking them with her toes. (How many times in the past had she and her friend done this, discussing their lives while Harry and Dieter, still in the dining room, talked finance and politics?) This discussion, however, had to be unique in the memory of both. 'Although it probably came on you like a ton of bricks,' she said gently, 'I think that going into the hospice is certainly the right decision. I don't know, but I'm sure that if you decided to change your mind about the treatment, you could still start it, using the hospice as a base?'

Her friend considered this in silence, looking out over the lawns and clipped hedges towards the sea. The sun had already lost some of its brightness, and the hollows beneath Maxine's cheekbones seemed to have deepened even since the day before, the skin of her face and neck slacker. Her make-up in the Athlone hotel had concealed some of the depredations of cancer, but it seemed to Grace that even since yesterday she had deteriorated. Maybe it was the stress. And, knowing Max as she did, she was quite sure her friend must have noticed too.

Although she knew little of how fast or slowly different cancers could progress, she was reminded of her own bedside vigil during her mother's last days, and although hers had been a cancer of the bowel, she now accepted that Maxine's three-to-six-month prognosis had been optimistic, as she believed Maxine herself had intuited. It was not the kind of thing to be argued about at present, though, was it?

Maxine's head was still turned away from her and on the horizon, Grace could see a front – an advancing line of black cloud. A storm was approaching, or at least serious rain of the new monsoon variety.

She wondered what Maxine's thoughts were as she stared through her bedroom window. She loved her house and was very proud of her garden. 'I know it's a ridiculous question to ask in these circumstances,' she said gently, 'but how are you feeling, Max? You do look tired. Would you like me to stay with Dieter tonight after you've gone, just to keep him company? I can do a bit of a tidy-up here, too, so you can save your strength. And maybe I could take him out to dinner later? It'll be lonely for him coming back on his own after settling you in. I can leave a message for Leonie.'

'I've made a mistake, haven't I?' Maxine's expression was suddenly piteous.

'Only you can decide that, darling. I don't think you have. If you want my opinion?' Her friend nodded and Grace went ahead. 'No matter how much you're told that the modern treatments are much less invasive than they used to be, they're still very tough, although they affect each person differently. So, no, I don't think you've made a mistake. If it was me, I'd opt for comfort and gentle care at every turn, and that's what the hospice offers, as far as I know. I wish I could have got my mother in to a hospice.'

At mention of her mother, Maxine seemed to be about to say something, but to change her mind. She again looked out. The rain had started and was already gurgling along the gutters into the downpipes, hopping off the patio outside the window to rebound halfway up Maxine's ceramic pots, their contents dormant now.

Even discussing this most awful subject, Grace realised that she and Maxine were now talking as they used to, with ease, not hiding anything, no subject taboo because of their long history together. And as the rain pummelled the Dutch gable roof over the bay window, she too looked again out over the garden to the sea, grey now under the accumulating cloud and only barely visible through the sheets of rain.

The room was warm and quiet, despite the racket on its roof, and as Maxine dealt with her own thoughts, Grace tried to imagine them so she could choose the right things to say.

Then she realised that whatever she said would probably be of little comfort. It wasn't talk that was appropriate: the best thing she could do was what she was doing – to sit there with her friend, inhabiting the same space as supportively as she could.

The rain stopped as suddenly as it had started and, in the silence, Maxine turned back to her. 'Sorry about the mess here, but would you mind asking Dieter to come in, please, Grace? It's lucky you decided to drive here today because we have something serious we want to talk to you about and, in a way, it's urgent so we need to do it now.'

30

Grace made sure her Bluetooth was connected and active before she drove away from Maxine's house just after eight o'clock that evening, having said a mutually tearful goodbye to Maxine while Dieter was loading his car with her suitcase and a series of carefully boxed photographs, including a formal portrait of them after their wedding.

She'd tried to get in touch with Leonie a couple of times, but although her daughter's phone had been ringing, she wasn't picking up so she had decided not to spend the night at Dieter and Maxine's home. Although she felt bad about Dieter being alone in his otherwise empty mansion for the first night after his wife's departure, she was chary of not going home, especially as she'd said in her note that she would be home by nine o'clock.

She'd helped with Maxine's packing, one of her specialities, and had done most of it as her friend had had to stop and rest every few minutes. She also helped make the decisions as to what, and how much, to take: 'It'll all be still here, won't it, Max? Our job now is to make it easy for Dieter to find things, blouses all together in this drawer, cardigans and sweaters there, trousers in the wardrobe on hangers. You'll have your basics with you in that suitcase for the first week and from then on you can tell him whatever you want him to bring in when he visits.'

They had decided to put in just one dress, a beautiful maxi in heavy red silk – Maxine's choice. 'I've had that dress for years,' she said. 'Always loved it, and Dieter did too.'

Maxine's pragmatism had come to the fore as she made her choices, and while neither woman had put words on it, Grace had known that the red silk was Maxine's choice for her final outfit. 'Where's your jewellery box?' She'd forced herself to turn away.

'Over there.' She seemed to be indicating an ornate mirror, ormolu, encrusted with curlicues, and hanging over her dressing-table. 'Count the sticking-out bits from the bottom right side. Eight from the top, grab that one and turn it a full hundred and eighty degrees.' Grace did so and, to her astonishment, the mirror swung out and a large square hole in the wall opened to reveal a metal box.

'Gas, isn't it?' Maxine was watching Grace's reaction.

'Leave it to Dieter. He engineered the mechanism, even constructed that horrible box. But it's safe! That's all that counts!'

With some difficulty, Grace lifted out the box. 'God, this is heavy, you won't want to take all of this, will you, Max?' She was astonished at how much it held. Nothing at all in the costume line that she could see. 'I had no idea you had so much.' She dumped the box on the bed.

'I've worn only a small percentage of it but Dieter kept buying me things, lovely things. He never seemed to notice that I wore the same pieces over and over again. I'd be willing to guess that more than half of it was never worn at all. Now that it's too late, I'm sorry. What a waste.'

She sorted through the compartments and took out her pearls. 'Just these. They go with everything, including the red dress. And a couple of brooches, maybe – could you find the little cloisonné bluebird that his mother gave me?' She pushed the box in Grace's direction. 'And the diamond spray? The one he gave me for my fiftieth? Also my good watch. It's Cartier – you'll see the name written on the face and it has diamonds all around it. More diamonds – he likes diamonds. I'll wear that every week to Sunday Mass!' She smiled sardonically. Then, suddenly, looking bleak: 'You'd wonder now why I amassed it all, wouldn't you?'

'Oh, Max...' Grace rushed to hug her. 'Don't cry – please. You'll set me off. He bought you all this stuff to ... to *adorn* you.'

'To make up for no children, you mean? Sorry, that sounded bitchy. But please, Grace, take whatever you like, and as much of it as you want. I've no further use for it, for obvious reasons.' She blew her nose. 'He drives me mad sometimes, but he's a good, honourable man . . . for a German!'

'Maxine!'

'One more thing, I'm putting you in charge of something.' She blew her nose a second time.

'Anything, darling. What is it?'

'No feckin' rosary beads entwined in my fingers. D'you hear me?'

*

Of the two, poor Dieter had been the more upset, inconsolable when he saw their official wedding portrait being taken down from its place on their mantelpiece and placed in its box, she in a white lace wedding dress handed down through generations of his family, with the string of pearls he had given her as a wedding present. It wasn't surprising to Grace that this was the first piece of jewellery she'd chosen to take with her.

Maxine's suitcase and vanity, with the chosen jewellery safely pouched inside, were in the boot of Dieter's car when the three of them went into the kitchen to have a valedictory cup of coffee, and the discussion about Leonie the couple had wanted to have with Grace when they'd been in Athlone.

*

The two cars, hers and Dieter's, left in convoy, following what had turned out to be an extraordinary offer on the parts of Maxine and Dieter during which they had pressed their case until she had reluctantly had to accept the American brochure now lying on the passenger seat. It caught her eye every time she turned the car, even slightly, to the left.

Having gone through the security gates she drove slowly towards the motorway to let Dieter's car get ahead, but about a hundred metres from the house, she pulled into a farm gate, took the phone from its holder and, in her settings, turned off Show My Caller ID and again called her daughter.

After just two rings, Leonie answered with her best 'journalistic' voice. 'Hello? This is Leonie McGee.'

'Leonie, it's me.'

'What do you want?' The change in tone was marked but Grace was accustomed to this and it didn't faze her. 'I'm letting you know that I'm on the way home from Galway,' she said. 'I've eaten so I won't have to stop and I'll come straight home. At this stage, about eleven or so?'

'Don't knock yourself out, Mother dearest. Your scuzzy note with the "plenty in the fridge" remark? Guess what? Most of it is either disgusting or rancid.'

'Sorry about that,' Grace said levelly. 'I don't think that's accurate, though. I'm nearly sure that there's a new pack of cheese in that fridge, salad stuff I bought only yesterday, yoghurt, fresh fruit in the fruit bowl and good bananas on the stand, cereals in the press, eggs on the counter, and lots of milk. Oh – and a pizza in the freezer.' She carried with her a mental picture of the contents of her fridge and freezer and where each item lay. 'Enough to keep you going anyhow,' she added mildly. 'I'll be doing a shop tomorrow. Things will improve.'

'Stop pretending you're a mother – *skank*!' Her daughter hung up. Leonie hadn't taken much joy, obviously, from that three-monthly three-minute appointment with her psychiatrist.

She told herself that Leonie hadn't upset her, but she had. Again.

Slowly, delicately, as if she was de-wiring a time bomb, she pressed End Call, reset Show My Caller ID and stashed the phone, then picked up the American brochure and placed it in the glove compartment.

As she shifted into gear, her skull didn't feel big enough to hold the contents of her brain. For the last hour or so they had been spinning in confusion, crashing into each other and wheeling away again: Maxine. Dieter. BrochureHospiceBrochure. Now Leonie. Then Maxine again. Brochurebrochurebrochure . . .

To distract herself, she turned on the car radio, tuning it to John Creedon's music programme on RTÉ Radio 1, a nightly offering of his infectious good humour and an eclectic selection of music. But tonight it didn't work to divert her focus from the literature in the glove compartment.

She gave in, put the car into neutral, again applied the handbrake, then turned on the car's map light and took out the brochure. From the discussion in Maxine's kitchen, she already knew what it was selling but she was intrigued to read it for herself and to see in pictures what its proprietors *claimed* it offered.

It seemed to be exactly as Maxine and Dieter had described.

She had turned down their offer straight up and, despite their persistence and efforts to persuade her differently, she'd stuck to her guns, although very moved, naturally, and grateful that they should have made such a proposition. In the end, while continuing to insist that she was grateful and humbled, but that she couldn't accept, she had agreed to take the brochure off their hands. The offer was far too generous and, anyway, she believed Harry wouldn't stand for it.

As for her ex, when she'd spoken to him from Oslo, he'd told her he was sorry, but he wouldn't be in Dublin when she and Leonie got home because he, Cherry and Jasmine would be away for a few days from the following morning. They were taking a short break on the Orient Express.

Grace put the brochure back into the glove compartment, out of her sight, turned on John Creedon again and pulled out onto the road.

The journey to Dublin was uneventful until, when she was about five minutes from the exit for Leixlip, her phone rang.

She didn't recognise the number on the car's display screen — it seemed very long, perhaps foreign. She had been damned with calls recently about her computer being broken and needing service, but this wasn't one of the numbers she had got to know and didn't answer, so she clicked on it.

'Hello?'

'Who's this, please?'

'Who are you looking for?'

'I'm looking for Grace McGee.'

'That's me, who's this?'

'Sorry, Grace, are you driving at the moment? I didn't recognise your voice. Sorry.'

Her stomach turned over. 'Ben? Where are you?'

'We're in Dublin.'

She panicked. 'I wonder would you mind calling me back, Ben, please? You're coming and going, breaking up a bit.' He wasn't. 'Coverage is bad in this section of the motorway.' It wasn't. 'Could you give me, say, ten minutes? I should be clear then.'

'Talk to you in ten. Looking forward to it.'

She saw she wasn't far from the Leixlip exit now and when the slip road arrived she took it and parked at a small row of shops, including a Spar grocery and an Insomnia coffee shop, with parking. Her hands were shaking.

Why? Why the panic? He was in Dublin. So what? He wasn't in Baldoyle, was he? He certainly wasn't in Leixlip, but why had he rung her? Her understanding, *their* understanding, she thought she'd made clear, was that their entanglement on the ship had been a lovely episode but nothing more.

And where did he get her mobile number? She hadn't given him either of her numbers, mobile or landline.

And what was he doing in Dublin?

31

Grace had been parked at the Spar in Leixlip for a couple of minutes and she was nervous. She was tired too, emotionally drained because it had been quite a day, lots of tears, but also lots of love, she believed.

The love bit had been genuine but not easy because both she and Maxine had been out of practice, and love needs practice. What a waste of time and energy on her part – all that deliberate blanking of a decades-long friendship, time neither of them would be granted again. With her boycott, Grace might as well have ripped up a precious tapestry and thrown it into a sewer.

An outsider seeing them together today, crying on each other's shoulders, hugging, probably wouldn't have guessed that this was a friendship that had been holed under the water. Grace hadn't realised it herself until now, in the car park, when she had thought it through. That didn't negate the genuine feelings they'd both expressed, but Maxine's cancer and the time pressure it exerted had distorted the situation because, knowing there was a hurry, they'd patched the holes without first clipping out the ragged bits. Before she'd left their beautiful house, Maxine couldn't resist having one last try: 'I don't want to open up old wounds, Grace, but there is one thing I need to say in case I snuff it before we meet again.'

'Don't *say* things like that, Maxine!' Grace cried.

'Then just indulge me one last time. I do want you to remember something I said with an open heart and no agenda. I went completely over the top into a pool that was none of my business, really, and was pontificating on a topic I didn't understand because I'd never lived it. But I really do want you to remember something – and please don't be angry with me. I'm not opening up the whole thing again.

'Remember I used to ask you how you put up with the situation, especially after Harry's departure, and you used to say to me that you had to because you'd no choice?'

'You said you weren't going to go into it again, Max . . .'

'I'm not. Because here's the thing. You *do* have a choice. You *can* live your own life. It's a matter of adjustment and taking a few crucial steps. You don't have to abandon her, as you would probably see it. But at the risk of sounding like one of our lovely nuns, you have an obligation to look after and value your own life too, Grace. God gave it to you and you're letting Him down. Take it back from Leonie.'

'God almighty, Max! Is this what cancer is doing to you? Are you going religious on me?'

She smiled. 'When I heard you were coming down today, I worked out how I'd say this to you without you re-imposing your fatwah. I thought bringing in God might help, since I failed so significantly.

'I've a selfish motive anyway, because I'll need you in my corner for the next little while. Dieter's great and all, but he's already living his loss. You're like a big old oak tree, Grace, just there. Immovable for ever. And you have the height!'

Sitting in front of the shuttered Spar, rain on a gusty wind assaulting her car, Grace thought about the oak-tree image. She didn't know how to react to it because in the same week two people had come up with something similar: one who couldn't know her but had been intimate with her, the other who'd known her intimately for decades but had tried to change her and had pushed too hard for her own reasons, which were probably deeply complex.

It was now too late to get back to where they'd been before Maxine had taken it on herself to be judge and jury on Grace's mothering. They would never get back to those schooldays when Maxine had been Grace's defender in all things, and Grace had loved her above all others.

But an oak tree?

Her phone rang. The same international sequence of numbers. 'Hi there!'

'You still driving, Grace?'

'No. I found a sweet spot so I parked. Fire ahead! You say you're in Dublin?' She was determined to keep this bright and casual, although even to hear his voice brought back the sensations of the night they had shared. She wondered if he felt the same. This conversation was sort of preposterous, neither of them referring to the event, while it hung between them.

'Yeah,' he said, 'with Marcus. Remember I told you my uncle was trying to coax me to change careers? Well, he flew first class from Chicago to Hamburg to nab me and continue the campaign.'

'He obviously has a very high opinion of you!'

'Looking for cheap labour, I'd say.'

'Oh, I doubt that, Ben. Given what you've told me about him, it might have something to do with love and wanting you close. Am I right?' As soon as she said it, she realised she'd landed in dangerous territory.

'You might be,' he admitted, 'and speaking of which, how are you, Grace?'

He'd lowered his voice but she fielded it: 'How am I? Well, I'm on my way from the west of Ireland, or I was until I stopped to take your call – because today I helped my best friend, who's dying, to move into a hospice. A couple of hours ago my youngest daughter called me a skank, whatever that is, and my ex-husband is travelling on the Orient Express with his wife and seven-year-old daughter. So that's how I am. Aren't you glad you asked?'

'That's challenging, all right.'

'Listen, Ben, did you call just to catch up? How're you by the way?'

'Confused. I sure hadn't expected to find myself in Dublin doing the rounds of financial institutions with my uncle!'

'So it looks like he's serious about this plan of his. How long will you be in the city?'

'Another three days. Then we're going down to Cork. You know Cork, Grace?'

''Fraid not. Not well, anyway. Listen, Ben, why don't we meet for coffee or lunch or something? I can come into the city tomorrow. We can figure out who's the more confused!' She'd discovered she wanted to see him again.

'Sure, I'd like that. Marcus too? That okay?'

She got it. He was 'normalising' their friendship. 'That'd be great,' she said. 'I'd love to meet him.'

'We're staying at the Westin, which is pretty central, I guess, so I'm sure we'll find somewhere good. Twelve thirty?'

'I'll meet you in the lobby at about twelve fifteen. By the way, I should have asked you earlier, where did you get my number? I don't think I gave it to you.'

He hesitated and she could almost hear his thoughts. 'I found a note from Leonie in my jacket pocket after that first night in the singing bar. It was on a beer mat and she'd written me both the number of her cell and your home. I called that. It's your voice on the answerphone, Grace, and you give your cell number and ask us to call it if our call is urgent.'

'I'll kill that girl one of these days! Sorry about that.' But she laughed, not wholly from amusement. 'Hardly anyone in Ireland uses landlines now and I'd completely forgotten that message. Bye, Ben, see you tomorrow!'

'Looking forward to it. Cheers!'

She peered at the screen of her phone for a few seconds, then put it away, not knowing whether she was sad or happy about the tenor of the call – glad, probably, because she was the one who had imposed the friendship thing in case he'd had expectations.

But perversely, she was sad that now he didn't. She accepted that what had happened between them had been of its time and place, an unexpected and undeniable flare of desire for its own sake. Not to speak of two Black Russians. Now, she thought, for them both the episode was definitively yesterday's news.

She started the car and resumed her journey, but the nearer she got to Dublin, the more the tension grew. This always happened when she left the house for more than half an hour.

So far, she'd had a largely Leonie-free day and evening, but who knew what faced her when she got home? Each time she left, worry came too, stalking her, a black cat mewing for attention.

She tried to put Leonie to the back of her mind, taking advantage of the last twenty minutes of freedom, but the mewing got louder.

Since her daughter had become an adult at the age of eighteen, it had been nigh on impossible to get any specific information about her condition from anyone she'd tried to consult, even their family GP (who'd treated Leonie since she was born), without Leonie's specific authorisation.

Her condition had gradually worsened at around the age of sixteen. Instead of being thought of by teachers as a 'difficult' child and then an 'undisciplined' or 'ungovernable' teenager, her reputation had morphed into a generalised 'There's something wrong here. Something has to be done about her.'

The nearest Grace had got to understanding Leonie's illness had been some time ago when meeting one of the three-member WhatsApp group Grace belonged to, the third being away on holiday.

Shortly before her death, Jenny's daughter had been diagnosed with borderline personality disorder. The mother had read so much about the condition and had consulted so widely about it – with people who would talk in theory but not specifically about her daughter – that while she couldn't have been designated 'expert' without formal training and qualifications, to Grace she was as good as.

She'd said recently that there'd evidently been some sort of tweak in BPD characterisation. For reasons she couldn't figure out, because the symptoms were so similar, it was now tagged as 'emotionally unstable personality disorder'.

Sufferers from EUPD, she said, behaved just as it said on the tin, being highly anxious, forming unstable relationships, flirting inappropriately, misreading social signals – and, most visibly, flying off the handle, subject to uncontrollable bursts of anger.

There was a lot more — sufferers were unable to sustain friendships, were suspicious of others' motivations, and misread offers of help from friends and families as a ploy to dominate them.

But permanently flowing under all of that was a deep river of profound loneliness. 'I kind of see it as the Styx,' Jenny said, shyly, that day, 'because it carried her off.'

There were no lights on in the house when Grace pulled into her driveway. It was two minutes after midnight. She'd said she'd be there at eleven.

32

At twelve fifteen the next day, Grace was walking into the lobby of the Westin Hotel in Westmoreland Street. It was a hotel she'd always liked, and its staff were efficient and friendly.

Also, the concierge, whose name she seemed to recall was Dara, remembered her from previous visits. 'Good afternoon, Mrs McGee,' he said now. 'Long time no see, but it's nice to have you here again! Let me take the umbrella for you.'

It was bucketing outside.

'Thank you, Dara.' She smiled to herself, thinking he probably didn't remember her for her personality or beauty and she shouldn't rest on her laurels: as a woman, it was probably her height that made her somewhat memorable.

She saw Ben immediately. Head bent over his journal, he was scribbling intently – lifetime habit of an author, she supposed. He was sitting in a large armchair, one of a pair on either side of the lobby fireplace, its flames brightening the brasses and highlighting the red in his hair. He sensed someone approaching and looked up. 'Grace! Dead on time!'

'So are you, Ben! For me it's boarding school and airline roster training, what's your excuse?' He laughed and there was a tiny hesitation before, simultaneously, they reached out to hug each other, albeit a little awkwardly.

They smiled. 'Bound to happen,' he said. 'After all, together we make up one big octopus!' An image she didn't want to think about too much right now. And, to judge by his reddening face, he didn't either.

He stepped back a little. 'That was a bit unfortunate – it just popped out of my mouth. I don't know about you, Grace, but I feel sorta weird about this – maybe I shouldn't have called last night. It was just a whim.'

She didn't answer. She couldn't. Even the smell of him was disturbing her. He was wearing a white Aran-knitted turtle-neck sweater and tan slacks and looked like someone straight off a catwalk in Milan. 'Shall we go?' she suggested. 'Are we staying here or going further afield?'

'Here, if that's okay?' He gazed up the stairs. 'Marcus is protecting a table up there in the Atrium – it's very busy.'

Deirdre Purcell

'That's terrific. I love the Westin Atrium.' She was ultra-conscious of how stilted the exchange had been and as they headed towards the staircase, before mounting the first step, she clutched his arm. 'Ben? You haven't told your uncle?'

'Of course I did.' He frowned. 'Did you not want me to tell him?'

'We promised each other to keep it private, Ben!' She was aghast.

'But me and Marcus, we tell each other *everything*! You must have known that promise didn't cover *Marcus*, Grace. He can't wait to meet you!'

But he couldn't hold the straight face. 'Course I didn't! What do you think I am? Get a grip, Grace! We're two men, for God's sake! Come on.' He put an arm around her shoulders, buddy-style. 'He's waiting, having heart attacks no doubt because there's a line waiting for tables at the counter up there. He's afraid we'll be shifted to a smaller one because we're only three. It's what he'd do.'

She followed him up the stairs, which ran through the tables on either side, and saw a man rise from behind a table on the right. In fairness to the management, it could have seated six.

First impressions were that Ben's uncle was taller than the Irish average, but only slightly, with dark hair going grey. He had Ben's brown eyes, in a face more weather-beaten than chiselled, and today, mirroring his nephew, wore a white turtleneck (looking at the two of them she was reminded of the Clancy Brothers) although his slacks were dark green. Ben made the introductions and both men stayed standing until she had slid in beside Marcus.

'Shall we order immediately?' Ben's uncle asked. 'Get that bit out of the way? Then we can get acquainted.' He had one of those chocolate-brown voices Grace had always admired on PBS, the public broadcasting service in the States. She didn't have an internet radio but, like last night when she couldn't sleep after the day's events, she occasionally tuned in to RTÉ Radio 1 Extra, offering documentaries and other 'good' radio from the BBC and other broadcasters around the world. They were great company, especially during a sleepless winter night with the rain lashing and the wind howling outside.

A waiter, doing his best not to show he was harassed, stopped at their table, and the three of them ordered. Grace decided on an open prosciutto and fig sandwich. She'd had it there before, but its main advantage in the present circumstances was that it was easy to manipulate. No sawing with your knife.

'Are you driving, Grace?' Marcus asked. 'If not shall we have a drink?'

'Marcus is a vintner. He touts alcohol,' Ben explained.

Under all the smiles and graciousness, the tinge of awkwardness was still there between herself and Ben. It was early, however, and maybe this event and the lovely venue would iron things out. 'Why not?' she said. 'I took the

Dart – that's the commuter train, Marcus. If you're lucky enough in Dublin to live on the coast it's a great service.'

'What'll we all have?' Ben's uncle looked from one to the other of them.

'Let's celebrate your deal, Marcus. And being in Ireland for the first time.' Ben picked up the wine list and handed it to his uncle. 'Why don't we have champagne?'

'Sure!' Marcus took it. 'Don't drink it myself normally. It's just fizzy wine, in my opinion, but, hey, why not?' He ordered a bottle of Veuve Clicquot Grande Dame.

The waiter brought the champagne quickly, opened it with some ceremony, then went through the usual palaver of handing it to the host for tasting.

Grace was not an expert – although she did like champagne and had been to lots of wedding, anniversary and birthday celebrations where it was served. Occasionally she had suspected that the 'champagne' wasn't quite as billed.

But she instantly took to this one, deciding on first taste that it was gorgeous and that she could detect the money spent on it.

Maxine was – had been – the expert, not on vintages but on the kind of champagne she liked. She had adored it along with sparkling wine and a 'good' Prosecco, and would use any excuse – the rain stopping, it was a Friday, she had a new pair of high heels – to open a bottle.

Any time Grace (or Grace and Harry) had visited, there had always been at least two bottles in the main fridge, with a store of replacements in a second.

Maxine. She didn't want to think of her right now, but

as the conversation stumbled on while they waited for the food, she was wondering how her friend's first night in the hospice had gone. Had she been afraid? Had reality dawned in the middle of the night that this was *real*?

And how had poor Dieter got through it? In case he was asleep, she'd deliberately held off ringing him this morning although she'd had ample opportunity, even on the Dart coming in. Her plan now was that as soon as this elegant torture was over, she would ring him, and Maxine, if he gave her the green light.

What had possessed her to agree to this lunch? A clean break from her lover – if you could call Ben that on the basis of one night – had been the plan. But when she'd heard his voice she just hadn't been able to resist. The time to sever the rope had been immediately when he'd contacted her the first time last night.

Marcus seemed nice, for sure, but he was clearly a man of few words. Why didn't Ben say something to cover this? Even though he'd already ordered, he was reading his menu again as though to learn it off by heart.

She took another deep swig from her glass, emptying it. *Slow down, Grace. Remember, you haven't had anything to eat since yesterday* – but Marcus immediately took the bottle from the silver bucket beside him and refilled her flute.

'Thank you, Marcus.' She smiled at him. 'I've always loved this place. You chose well.' She added, 'During the Christmas season they put up what they call a Champagne Tree in here – this is lovely by the way, thank you again!' She held up her glass to toast him. 'Right in the middle of the room. They take advantage of the height, you see. It's five storeys up to that glass roof, believe it or not!' She glanced up. 'But will you just look at that rain, bashing away on it! It's great to be indoors when the weather's like this, snug and warm, isn't it?'

Both men nodded obediently and she realised she was making an idiot of herself. 'I'm sorry, both of you,' she said. 'I haven't eaten since yesterday. I had a lot on my mind.'

'How is Leonie?' Ben at last came in, then addressed his uncle: 'I gave you the gist of what happened with Grace's daughter on the cruise, Marcus, and why Grace had to take her home early. The two of us had just met for breakfast and she freaked out, reading stuff into the situation that just wasn't there.' He nodded at Grace then, with an over-to-you expression. 'Want to fill Marcus in, Grace?'

'Oh, I'm sure your uncle's not interested in my domestic woes, Ben!'

'Try me.' Marcus looked from one to the other, and she wondered how much he actually knew, or had guessed. To hell with it. She'd never see him again and she was relieved to have something real to discuss so she told Marcus a little of what was involved in minding her daughter. 'Ben behaved wonderfully. If he hadn't read the situation so quickly and taken charge of it, God knows what would have happened in that dining room.'

'Has it been going on for a long time?'

'Probably since she was born,' she said, with some feeling. 'Although we didn't realise at the time that there was anything intrinsically wrong.'

The food came then, but as they ate, he continued to ask questions about her daughter's diagnosis and prognosis, about both of which (she had to profess) she was largely in the dark. She described the symptoms of what she believed, without firm confirmation, to be EUPD, which had led to her friend's daughter's suicide.

'Does that remind you of anyone?' Marcus asked Ben quietly.

'Not totally, but a lot of it.'

This was clearly something between uncle and nephew and Grace didn't ask any questions. She continued to eat.

But then Marcus explained that his ex-wife had displayed at least some of that behaviour. 'I won't go on about it but it was a nightmare for the last year or so of our marriage, wasn't it, Ben?'

'Mmm.' His nephew's mouth was full but he nodded.

'There's been no contact, except through lawyers during the divorce.' Again he glanced at Ben. 'And that was so messy and angry that I don't want any. Is your daughter having any treatment?'

'Not really. Quarterly visits to a psychiatrist, medication adjusted – or not.'

'Does she take it?'

'Possibly, possibly not. Perhaps some of it, but not at the right dosage. It's the first question anyone asks, even doctors, but I simply don't know. I'm not privy to it, or to any significant information, really. Leonie has to agree before *any* information can be relayed to me, and she won't do that. I'm just expected to deal with the consequences and shut up!

'Sorry. I didn't mean that. I don't do well with alcohol, obviously.' She smiled ruefully. 'Even champagne as delicious as this – particularly champagne as delicious as this, it turns out! Sorry for rabbiting on and, truly, I'm not as bitter or resentful as that sounded just now. Long ago, Marcus, I decided on a phrase that I use every day to keep my own sanity. *Acceptance is key.* There are those who think differently, that you have to fight, fight, fight, but in this country, everyone is fighting or lobbying for something, particularly in the mental-health service. There's competition for everything, including psychiatry and even basic care.'

'Is there not someplace she can go? I'm not talking about locking her up or anything like that, but some sort of shelter, or retreat or sanctuary that will take time to understand her needs, just talk therapy if she can't be sorted out medically.'

'I've searched for years but haven't found anything suitable – or that she'd be willing to consider. I've come to terms with my lot – but to tell you the truth, Marcus, I'm wondering now if this is how I want to spend the rest of my life. I'm not sure why now in particular . . .' She concentrated on what remained of her food to avoid eye-contact with Ben. 'It's probably my age.'

'How old are you?' he asked, in that very direct American way.

'Fifty-three.'

He didn't react, concentrating on his own food. 'So it seems you've tried everything. There's nothing to be done?'

Grace hesitated, then improvised: 'Not in this country, as far as I can tell.' But then, impulsively, she went to her handbag and pulled out Maxine and Dieter's brochure. 'I was given this yesterday by a friend and her husband. She's dying, they're rich – he runs a number of successful businesses in the west of Ireland. They have no children and, as it happens, Leonie is their goddaughter.

'They made me an offer yesterday, insisting they won't take no for an answer. She's been my best friend for more than forty years, and says she wants to know this plan for their goddaughter,' she tapped the brochure, 'is in train *before* she dies, which could be a matter of weeks, maybe a few months at most.'

'Sounds intriguing!' Marcus finished his meal and placed his cutlery neatly on his plate.

'Are you sure you want me to go on with this, Marcus? I've said no so it's no longer germane to anything.'

'Tell me anyway.' He was leafing through the brochure. 'It looks pretty okay, this place. Where is it?'

'Near Boston.'

As succinctly as she could, Grace outlined what Maxine and Dieter had proposed: they'd agreed that after Maxine's death he would sell everything, including the house, and go back to Germany where he still had relatives ('He can't stand any of them,' Maxine had offered), and he still owned the family home in Mainz, which was actually two houses, the main one and a cottage in the grounds.

Before she died, which made this urgent, they wanted to have signed over enough of their money – from the proceeds of their home in Clarinbridge and all of the interrelated little companies Dieter ran – to fund at least three years' residential therapeutic care for Leonie at this place, with reserves in the bank as a sort of trust for her should more be needed.

Marcus was still paging through the glossy brochure. 'So why did you say no, Grace? Sounds like a good deal for your daughter.'

'It's huge money, three hundred and fifty dollars a day plus ancillary charges. We don't have that kind of money, unless I sell my house, and that's too risky for me, but her father and I aren't charity cases.'

'So you *might* do this for her if you could afford it? Could you take some of the money? Is it a matter of pride or something else?'

Suddenly she felt on the defensive. 'She probably wouldn't go. A residency involves, as you can see, menial work on the farm there that she'd consider beneath her – milking cows, working in the kitchens and the café, in the fields and the tractor barns. And she'd need a special kind of visa – my friends have investigated that, but it would be very tricky. Mental illness? Going into Trumpland for three years? Not possible, I'd say.'

'Have you asked Leonie about this, Grace? Offered it to her?' He'd stopped turning the pages of the brochure and was looking directly at her, the light in those brown eyes challenging.

'No. And I won't. This would probably be proof to her that I want to get rid of her altogether. She's not a fan! And she's quite paranoid.'

'But isn't it really her choice?' he persisted quietly. 'Isn't it about her, not you? Where's the money going if not to Leonie?'

'No idea. Charities, I suppose.'

That wasn't strictly true. What she hadn't mentioned was that if she continued to refuse the offer the money would go to Gould Farm anyway, in Leonie's name, as a benefactor. 'In her name.' Maxine, clearly frustrated, had repeated this the previous evening just before Grace had left. 'So you've a choice to make here, Grace. Remember we talked about choice? Do you want some other kid, probably American, to benefit from our money or would you accept it for your daughter? Our goddaughter, Dieter's and mine?'

'Added to which you've always claimed you wanted less hassle, more freedom from your caring role. Are you turning down three years of that too?'

That was what had kept her awake all last night while, via RTÉ, the BBC had relayed a documentary on the origins of the viola, something she would have thought wouldn't interest her, but it had included wars, faction fights, Shakespearean sonnets, personal tragedies of the instrument's makers and its solo music. She couldn't turn it off.

In the shower that morning, she had postponed thinking about the proposal. Had she the *right* to refuse it since it was for Leonie? During the argument in her kitchen, Maxine had questioned this.

And now, she thought, staring at the American stranger, he had put it up to her too.

Perhaps because he had detected her unease, he dropped the subject and ordered dessert, although they had to relinquish their table at two o'clock. Also, he and Ben had booked a slot to see the Book of Kells in Trinity at half past.

At about a quarter past two, she said goodbye and left them. Each gave her his phone number and, although she had presumed this was a once-off meeting, she found herself agreeing that they'd meet again, all three before both men left either for Scotland, to go home, or to explore rural Ireland, with the search to acquire a possible fishing lodge ('Or whatever,' Ben had said) in mind. They had decided nothing, Marcus told her, 'but we know absolutely no one here except you, Grace, so you'll just have to take us on. Okay?

'Anyway,' he chuckled, 'I've still a few meetings to take with your financial institutions. They seem to want the fillings out of my teeth as proof of identity, not to speak of my soul, before they'll accept that my money is legitimate, and I am who I say I am. My passport and other papers aren't proof enough, apparently! Even the big cheque isn't enough.

'It's lucky I have all the time in the world now so I'm finding it amusing – and the two of us are going to make the most of our time here. We have an appointment with a genealogist tomorrow morning to find out if it's worth going over to County Mayo to see if there's any trace of the old homestead. This is fun, Grace. Something I haven't had for a very long time. So, we'll be around for a few days anyhow. It was great to meet you.'

'You too,' she said.

33

Next morning, her breakfast over and the kitchen tidy, it was still only five past nine. For forty or forty-five minutes, Grace had been sitting in her TV room, thinking about Maxine and Dieter's proposal.

And what Ben's uncle had said about it.

About those who had expressed opinions on her relationship with her third daughter – even what Jenny had so gently suggested, that to look after herself, maybe she should take more extended breaks, rather than the short ones she seemed to favour.

Rumbling away under all of this was the memory of having for one night, during that ill-fated cruise, stood on the threshold of freedom. The recklessness of it, the joy . . .

How fanciful! she thought ruefully. *What a pop-psychological TV mini-series! What a way to clothe the nakedness of what had been essentially a one-night stand.*

To an outsider parachuting unexpectedly into this room, what would she look like, sitting like a lump of basalt in the dark, with a silent TV, staring into space?

Regardless of such self-scorn, the stream of thoughts continued as she took stock of where she was in her life. For years she had been a competent employee at Aer Lingus, with lots of colleagues and friends, had been at the top of her game, successfully managing the work/domestic life conundrum. All the while she'd also managed to have a social life, much of it with Harry, but also with her colleagues, with Maxine and Dieter and her two older children when they were young. Visits to Dublin Zoo, to the Phoenix Park, to Portmarnock and Dollymount beaches.

Even after Leonie's unexpected arrival, the first seven years or so of her third daughter's life had been enjoyable although, even then unlike the other two, who'd been (mostly) biddable, she'd been a handful. A 'live wire' was how Grace, somewhat defensively, would have described her at the time.

With money not a problem, she was able, solo, to take them on holiday abroad when Harry was too busy. With him, they took houses and cottages in places like Connemara, Sligo and Achill Island. One winter, when Leonie had just turned four, they had had a weekend, all five of them, in the magnificent Slieve Donard Spa Hotel in County Down, where the two older girls had taught their little sister to swim in the pool.

Looking on fondly as Leonie screamed in delight and the other two laughed, Grace could never have suspected what lay ahead, that eighteen years later, on many days and nights, she would be sitting in a dark room in winter, alone, and waiting for the sound of her daughter's key in the lock if she was late coming home, sensing her mood before she ventured to greet her, cooking for the two of them and wondering if she'd eat, and pretending to herself and others that Leonie's insults flowed off her, like water from a duck's back.

And having to make excuses for herself to those who had decided it was her own doing that she and her daughter had become trapped in toxic symbiosis in this nice house with its barbed-wire walls.

Maxine and Dieter had now offered her the wire-cutters to get both of them out – but Grace McGee had said, in effect, that she preferred to keep them imprisoned. What had she been thinking? That had been nonsensical.

If it hadn't been for the clear disbelief in the eyes of Ben's uncle as she'd tried to explain why she was rejecting Maxine's offer, she would never have asked herself why she'd done that. He had been straight out incredulous. That's because he's an American, she'd told herself. An Irish person would have danced around the subject, paying lip service to the notion that the offer was, perhaps, a fifty-fifty bet.

But, she had tried to assure herself, she couldn't let herself be influenced by someone she'd never see again, except perhaps for another short lunch before these two men left Dublin.

She got up from the chair to fetch a notebook and pencil – even the back of an envelope would do because the first thing in this case was to make a list. Pros. Cons. Feasibility of getting Leonie through US immigration. Visas: should she just take her in for a 'holiday' and overstay?

No.

Eligibility: would Gould Farm take her? That had to be a priority. She'd call them.

She'd have to get the pending court case adjourned: a conviction, and it was curtains to the idea.

The kicker would be Leonie's attitude – whether she would agree to go. That would have to be at the bottom of the list, last item to be negotiated when everything else was either in place or in train. It wouldn't, couldn't, happen overnight.

Suddenly she was busy. Instead of sitting around worrying and thinking about the past (or a dismal future) she had a project. A research project with possibly a real outcome.

Trying to keep all these details – which continued to generate more – in her head, she found some yellowing paper in the bottom of a kitchen cupboard and a pen in her handbag. Standing at the kitchen table, she wrote down as many of the tasks as she could envisage:

1. *Call Dieter and Max mid-morning.*
2. *Buy one of those project notebooks with different-*

coloured dividers.
3. *Call Gould Farm (availability/costs/eligibility).*
4. *Ring GP/Psych.*
5. *Ring American Embassy.*
6. *Ring solicitor (ask Harry if it's okay to use his, mine's dead).*
7. *Guards re court case.*
8. *Google re court case adjournment/Probation Act. Find out if Probation Act in criminal cases counts as crim conviction?*
9. *Harry/Adeline/Jackie.*

Because, of course, the rest of Leonie's family had to be included in the planning. No doubt Harry would vehemently oppose the move for all kinds of reasons. She'd have to be strong there. Strong but understanding of the complexities.

The faster she wrote, the more possible obstacles occurred to her.

She had made the decision to take the money (she'd argued her case with Marcus – an outsider with his straight-as-a-die approach, with no stake in the issue, and logic on his side – and she could now see he'd run her out of reasons to refuse). Now she couldn't wait to tell her benefactors. Leonie's benefactors.

It was getting bright outside. She checked her watch: twenty past nine. She'd wait till half past. Dieter would probably be up: Maxine had always said he was an early riser.

*

'This is good!' Marcus Brady looked down at his Irish stew, with the accompanying bowl of vegetables and potatoes. They were in the Canal Bar of Creightons Hotel in Clones, County Monaghan, not too far from Newbliss.

On the advice of Ben's new buddy, Dara, the Westin's concierge, they'd left Dublin after an early breakfast and had visited the Writers and Artists Retreat at Annaghmakerrig, 'on spec', stopping for lunch on their way back to Dublin in their newly rented car.

They were now discussing whether it might be possible to locate another Annaghmakerrig-type premises, not necessarily confined to artists, but to include them in a polyglot retreat, incorporating yoga, Ayurvedic healers and, of course, Marcus's own dream, fishing, even a dive school.

If it were to attract Americans and other international clients, it would have to be reasonably close to decent golf courses. Say a radius of eighty miles and there would need to be ways to get the golfers to the courses quickly – not helicopters, too disturbing of the serenity he was going for.

He had been online the previous evening, he told Ben now, putting in a search for 'castles and mansions for sale in the Irish countryside' and had been deluged instantly with dozens of offers from estate agents all over Ireland – and from abroad.

At least half were wrecks with barely one standing wall, but there were quite a few that could be restored with relative speed, and three that were fully intact, two inhabited and one restored as a six-star hotel but now in financial difficulties.

He finished his meal and pulled out his phone. 'There are two here incorporating lodges with the main house – this one is a going concern but fighting off the banks and bailiffs. How do you feel about us owning a castle?'

They'd both been very impressed with Annaghmakerrig. Ben had known about it – most writers did – although it offered just eleven bedrooms for resident artists of all kinds, writers, painters, musicians, composers, choreographers, circus artists and dancers. For a time they had the space and comfort to work in serenity while interacting with other artists from diverse disciplines and nationalities.

Situated beside a lake, it had been bequeathed to the Irish state by the late Sir Tyrone Guthrie, an eminent theatre director and BBC broadcaster, great-grandson of the Irish stage actor Tyrone Power and second cousin of the Hollywood star, another Tyrone Power.

It was dry today, even sunny, and although the trees were bare, the shrubs and lawns had been beautiful.

'Hushed but not silent is how I'd describe the atmosphere back there,' Ben had said, after they were again in the car.

'Yeah, that place was the real deal, wasn't it, Ben?' In the restaurant, Marcus was forking pieces of lamb into his mouth. 'It's exactly the kind of place I'd like to have as my fishing lodge or some other kind of retreat – just the right size. Those grounds! That lake! Those extra studios and accommodations – pity it's already taken!'

To his own surprise, Marcus had rarely felt as relaxed as he'd been over the past couple of days. On Day One, having arrived in Dublin too early to check into their hotel, they'd 'done' the National Art Gallery, the Little Museum of Dublin, the Dead Zoo, as Dubliners have named the Victorian 'cabinet' Natural History Museum. On Day Two there'd been lunch with Grace, and after they'd seen the Book of Kells, they'd boarded the Viking Splash, a trip through Dublin streets on an amphibian vehicle where, with other tourists, they wore Viking horned helmets and were encouraged to yell like, well, Viking invaders at passers-by before driving straight into the River Liffey.

Then, with their concierge having secured them a bag of stale bread and umbrellas, they'd fed the ducks in St Stephen's Green. Everything seemed to be within walking distance of their hotel.

And here they were, on Day Three, in Monaghan, having seen what could possibly be the retreat to end all retreats. And it was now sunny!

'This is a lovely country, Ben. You can get anywhere in it within a few hours. I think we'll forget Scotland!'

'You mean *you*'ll forget Scotland, Marcus. I'm going back to Chicago.'

'We'll see.'

They'd discussed their lunch with Grace in the car on the way up, Marcus opining that she could be suffering from a version of Stockholm Syndrome where the captive becomes tied to the captor and stays put, even if offered the opportunity to escape. 'I suppose it's another version of the devil you know and all that. Why else would she turn down an incredible offer that'd surely help them both?'

'I'm with you on that one,' Ben said, but something in his tone brought Marcus sharply to look at him.

His nephew, however, was assiduously cleaning around the inside of his ice-cream bowl with a sponge cake fragment, concentrating, it appeared.

34

Grace, in the shower in preparation for her second lunch with the Bradys, was mentally reviewing her telephone adventures of the previous day, at the end of which she was almost hoarse and definitely frustrated.

Working from her list, she had started by tapping out Dieter's number, then changed her mind and tapped Maxine's instead. She knew her friend, and even if she was not yet up, she'd have her mobile on or near her hospice bed, certainly not far from arm's length.

She'd thought about what she would say. While she was writing her list (which had got longer as she scribbled), one of Maxine's most frequently uttered exhortations during their exchanges about Leonie had been uppermost in her mind: 'You keep saying you've no choices, Grace, but you do. Most people have choices in life. It's a matter of exercising them fairly and I think you've more than fulfilled your responsibilities, don't you?'

As far as Grace remembered, her friend hadn't used that particular mantra during their last Arnotts meeting but, then, she hadn't had the chance because Grace had truncated the event.

Well, thanks to Maxine and Dieter, she was exercising her right to choose now. The fallout would be considerable on many fronts, but she'd just have to find a way to manage it. Maybe she could seek professional counselling for herself if dealing with it proved overwhelming. Another thing to add to the list, she thought, hoping she'd remember it on top of everything else swirling in her brain.

When Maxine answered, after just one night at the hospice, her voice already sounded stronger, less tight. 'Grace! What can I do for you this morning?'

'A lot, Max. Sorry to ring so early but I thought you wouldn't mind. If it's not too late, and I haven't burned my boats, I've decided to take the advice you gave me.'

'I don't believe it! After all that arguing yesterday?' but to Grace's ears, she sounded delighted. 'What made you change your mind?

'Long story. I've had time to reflect, though, and I think there's a good chance this will help Leonie, but . . . this is for her – and you can never know how much I appreciate it – and . . . I don't want to say this . . .'

'Say it!'

'It will help me too. It'll help both of us to be out of each other's hair for a while. And you never know, it might even work!'

'Hallelujah! Thank the Lord! At *last*, Grace.'

'But of course it's dependent on whether I can get Leonie into Gould Farm and if she'll agree to go. I'll refund the money if all this doesn't work out.'

'For God's sake, darling, I certainly won't need it! And Dieter will have so much money in Germany he won't be able to spend it all unless he does something really stupid, like take to the casinos and that's hardly likely – you've met my husband, haven't you? No, you use it for yourself. Forget the feckin' Arctic. Find yourself a toyboy and the two of you go on a round-the-world cruise in a fancy suite on one of the really big ships like the *Queen Mary 2*. A different cruise every year for three years!' Grace, rattled by the 'toyboy' reference, had been glad they weren't speaking face to face, but Maxine was now talking on: 'The only thing I ask is that you might stay in touch with Dieter. He's going to be lonely.' Her voice shook.

'You don't have to ask, Max, of course I will – and I can't emphasise enough how grateful—'

'I want you to shut up now, Grace. Just take the money and run! I'll talk to Dieter later this morning and we'll sort out the details. This is as much for me as for you, you know. I couldn't die with a clear conscience if—'

'Now *you* shut up!' Grace had been close to tears. 'If necessary, Max, I'll drug her, roll her up in a carpet and take her as extra-large luggage in the hold of the plane! I already have a call in to her psychiatrist to see if he'll refer her – one of a long, *long* list of calls I have to make.'

'I really wish I could help you with that. But, you know, giving Leonie – and you – a break, because we can, means there's a big load off my mind. I might even get better! That'd be cats and pigeons, eh? I'll get Dieter to call you about the money transfers and all the rest of it. Better add to the list that you'll have to warn your bank. Some people will believe that you're involved in something nefarious! Talk to an accountant too. You'll have to argue Leonie's case with the Revenue or you'll be charged Gift Tax.'

Another line for the list, Grace thought. *Ring Rev Commrs.*

After they'd discussed Gould Farm, they'd talked about how Maxine was finding life at the hospice ('Too early to tell, but so far so good') and how she was coping with her new situation. 'Maybe it hasn't fully sunk in yet, Grace, but it isn't too bad. Once I stopped thinking I was the unluckiest person in the world, I looked at the life I've had – no financial worries, more diamond jewellery than I can possibly wear, a beautiful place to live in an amazing location and a husband who loves me to bits – and I wondered what I had to complain about. Who said I was *entitled* to live to be a hundred?

'I am one of a minority in this world, where so many people, so many populations, are starving, suffering horrible diseases, being tortured, denied any rights – dear God, that all sounded so preachy! Preachiness is one of my faults, Grace! Did you find that, by any chance?'

Grace could *hear* the twinkle in her friend's eye. 'Never

spotted it, darling, not for a minute!' Although she'd played along, she thought it so sad that it had taken cancer to bring about her rapprochement with the friend who'd had her back through her youth and early adulthood, her marriage and her divorce.

'There's just one more thing before we say goodbye for now, Grace – and that's another apology. Please let me. I mentioned it before, but I want to be succinct. I believed you had a choice on how to handle Leonie, but I was wrong. You didn't. Because you had to defend her with all your might. And the reason behind the money and stuff is that I hope things will work out and that now, at last, you'll have a stab at freedom.'

After they had hung up, Grace had sat for a couple of minutes at her kitchen table, staring at the list, then got up to brew herself a strong coffee. Instead of a sensible piece of toast to go with it, she had raided the freezer for a container of chocolate-brownie ice cream.

For most of the rest of the day she had barrelled methodically through her list, or had tried to, but very quickly had come up against all the usual obstacles to be endured when dealing with officialdom.

The Bradys' invitation to lunch had come late yesterday afternoon at a time when she was so fed up she was contemplating giving up on the idea of taking Leonie to Boston. She had just been talking to a woman in the American Embassy where she had been offered, and had accepted, an appointment to come in to Ballsbridge on 2 January next year, but that was perilously close to the

February date for Leonie's court case. She tried to bring it forward but the woman had politely insisted that this was the first date available.

At least, she thought, an actual appointment was tangible progress and she had gained some satisfaction from writing the date beside the embassy's name on her list, then in next year's diary as well.

Minutes later, her phone had rung and she'd hoped it was someone returning one of the calls she'd made earlier. She'd grabbed it and heard Marcus Brady's unmistakable voice, asking her to meet him and Ben for lunch the next day, this time in Chez Max, a French restaurant on Baggot Street. 'We went in there to have a look. It's real casual, Grace. You okay with that?'

'Just a second, Marcus.' She covered the mouthpiece and took a few seconds to think: she still had plenty of calls to make, most of them follow-ups, and she was anxious to be available in case anyone called her back. On the other hand, why the hell would she pass up on a pleasant invitation like this? Again she was behaving as a slave to Leonie's needs, not her own. She liked Chez Max, it had been on their circuit along with the Troc and Chapter One when she and Harry had been married.

'Sorry for the delay, Marcus,' she'd said then. 'That'd be wonderful. I'll look forward to it and I do know the place.'

But now, in the shower an hour before she had to be there, she regretted accepting: lunch might add to the complexities she'd suffered when being around Ben at the previous date. Nothing terribly serious, but it had been awkward.

Why had she bloody accepted? She didn't need lunch. And she certainly didn't relish the idea of tiptoeing around Ben, minding how she looked at him, watching what she said in case Marcus detected something. She assumed Ben would feel similarly.

They'd got away with it at the first lunch, probably, but a second? She slammed angrily around the shower, upending the shampoo bottle, hitting her head on the wall tiles when she bent to pick it up – and then the hot water ran out and douched her with cold. She'd forgotten to switch on the immersion heater.

Rubbing what she was sure would be a bump on the top of her head, she actually laughed. 'That'll teach you! Ingrate!'

*

In her bedroom half an hour later, she opened her wardrobe and, without thinking, pulled out a stylish but sober navy dress in light wool, knee-length, warm without being heavy, a reliable staple that she knew looked good on her. She unzipped it from its hanger and was about to put it on, but then paused . . .

Many years ago at a dinner party in the home of one of the directors of Harry's bank, she'd been sitting near the director's wife who was adept at making small-talk. From the usual chat, politics, religion, the weather, conversation had switched to psychology and habitual behaviour, and this woman had advised her that to shake yourself out of a rut you should start small, moving deliberately out of your comfort zone.

For instance, if you wear your wristwatch on your left arm you change it to your right; when you fold your arms, pay attention to which arm goes where and switch them so it feels slightly odd, even a little uncomfortable. Or if, when you sit down you habitually cross your legs – don't! And if they automatically cross themselves, uncross them immediately and attempt to keep them that way.

Even these small physical acts can affect your brain patterns, she had explained, guiding you to see things differently.

Why had that come to her now? She looked at the navy dress, at its safeness and warm comfort, then put it back in the wardrobe and, although it was winter, pulled out a jumpsuit in heavy white linen, which she had bought on a whim from the clearance rail in a TK Maxx store several years previously, not bothering to try it on – she could take it back if it didn't fit. In her mirror at home, she saw it fitted.

She glanced through the bedroom window now to see that the early-morning drizzle seemed to have stopped, with the sun attempting to make an appearance. The hell with it, she thought, and wriggled into the garment – people wore whatever they wanted to wear year-round, these days, but in clothing as in a lot of other areas, she had become a rut-creature.

Why shouldn't she wear this if she wanted to? She checked it out in the mirror and yes, it still fitted well. It had a Stella McCartney label and had probably been on that clearance rail because you'd need to be as tall as she was to do it justice.

It was one of only two designer pieces in her wardrobe. The other, from Jaeger and also bought in TK Maxx as recently as the previous winter, was a three-quarter-length car coat in royal blue cashmere. She fetched it from the spare room, put it on over the jumpsuit and, paying homage to the season, slipped into an ancient pair of tan ankle boots. At least they matched her handbag.

Before leaving, she stopped briefly in the hallway and listened for Leonie: she could hear rhythmic music emanating from her daughter's room and the thumping of feet on the floor.

Should she go up and say she was leaving for a couple of hours?

No, she thought. She wouldn't be out all that long: why let herself in for a possible reaction and go out in a bad humour? But then she realised that the thumps were coming from different parts of the floor – her daughter was dancing. Dancing on her own.

Before she could allow her brain to access its habitual response (*This is so poignant. Let me do something to try to help*) she checked that her customary note to Leonie about when she'd be home was in its usual space, opened the front door, closed it quietly behind her and set off for the Dart to Dublin.

35

Grace wasn't the only person in Dublin making lists that day. Marcus Brady, using the online facility on his phone to check out realtors with large Irish country houses on offer, was compiling a shortlist – an intriguing castle in west Cork still at its head – beside his plate in Chez Max on a piece of Westin Hotel stationery.

His was one of a handful of tables occupied. It was only twenty past twelve and the place, although ready for business, was not yet fully up to speed as staff moved around quietly, adjusting place settings and chatting easily among themselves.

Ben had called to say he would be late. He'd gone to the National Library early that morning, hoping for help with researching the Brady origins and ancestry in County Mayo. So far, he'd said in his call, he'd had limited success with the genealogy, but had met a fellow writer from the States. She'd been in Dublin for a while and had offered to take him to the Writers Museum and the Irish Writers Union adjacent to each other in Parnell Square on the north side of the city: 'And there's a terrific restaurant up here, too, called Chapter One, Marcus – it has a Michelin star. Shall I try to get us in for tonight?'

'Sure, since you're up there – but try not to be too late getting to the restaurant where we're to meet Grace. I don't mind holding the fort but it would be rude to be too late. Take a cab.'

Ben had promised he would and Marcus had set off to be early, not wanting their guest to arrive on time with neither of them there.

His seat was facing the door, and each time someone came in, he lifted his head from the phone.

At precisely twelve thirty, he saw a tall, very beautiful woman handing her coat to one of the waiters and revealing a white outfit, top to toe. She seemed, then, to be making straight for his table but it took him a few seconds to recognise her as Grace.

He scrambled to his feet to greet her, nothing coming to mind about what she'd worn on their previous encounter, except 'nondescript'. Her hair had been loose, but today she had scooped it into a sort of unstructured topknot, which accentuated her cheekbones. This time there was no other word for her but 'spectacular' and he noticed he wasn't the only man watching her progress towards him. 'Grace!' he said. 'Lovely to see you again.'

'Likewise, Marcus.' She smiled. 'Thank you so much for inviting me.'

They sat. Then he explained that Ben would be late, told her why, and offered her a drink. She accepted a glass of white wine.

He realised that, unusually for him, he felt quite awkward now, even a little shy. Normally sociable – you had to be in the hospitality trade – he was somehow off balance.

Could it be because of the disparity in how they'd dressed for the occasion? His chinos and sweatshirt epitomised the gauche Yank, while she was the elegant European. This was not something he generally cared about, and in sweltering Chicago summers he had even been known to attend crucial financial meetings wearing his Bermudas.

Or perhaps it was because there were just the two of them, however temporarily. Where the hell was Ben when he was needed?

Marcus had rarely been intimidated by this kind of meeting but now, for whatever reason, he found himself lost for words.

Luckily, her wine came (*thank the Lord*) and he signalled to the waiter for another beer. 'This place is nice, isn't it?' he asked. 'Food good? You said you'd been here before.'

'Food good,' she responded. 'Just French enough!' She smiled at him and took a sip from her glass.

It just popped out: 'Sorry for being so casually dressed. Obviously, when I see the way you—'

'Oh, for goodness' sake, don't worry. Anything goes, these days, unless you're trying to make an impression as a petitioner with your bank! I won't protest, "This old thing?" but it's certainly inappropriate for November. I just felt like making an effort and brightening myself up. I spend so much time cooped up at home, and there have been lots of times when I haven't even bothered to change out of my pyjamas and dressing-gown all day because no one would see me except Leonie. And it always perks me up a little when I'm wearing white – could be a throwback to First Communion!'

'But it's not just the clothes – you look different today, Grace.'

'Thanks,' she said simply.

He was recovering. Beginning to relax.

The waiter came again then, declaiming the specials and handing them menus, which gave Marcus a little breathing space. He castigated himself for behaving like a wet-faced juvenile. He'd encountered lots of beautiful women over the years in his pubs and hotels. He'd made love with beautiful women. His wife had been beautiful . . .

But there had been none he'd had any truck with since she'd left him. He'd closed down that area of his life and yet, for some reason, he'd been knocked for six today by Grace McGee. 'How's your friend with the cancer?'

'Funny you should ask.' She averted her eyes as though in pain. 'She's doing as well as can be expected and remarkably calm about her immediate prospects.' Then, after a short pause, she looked across the table at him and told him she had accepted the offer to send her daughter to the Boston facility. 'I thought you should know because it occurred to me that you might have helped change my mind when we last met.

'You were the objective outsider, Marcus, not worrying about my sensitivities or how I might react. Made me see sense when I couldn't. I was too wound into my normal view of Leonie, and what I finally grasped was that my sense of loyalty to her had paralysed my thinking. It overshadowed everything else, even something that may help her.

'You weren't the first to say what you did but you got through to me because you saw that offer for what it was. Probably because you're a businessman and know how to cut deals without causing offence. Misplaced offence. I'll let you know if it works out. Now,' she consulted her menu, 'what shall we order? Should we wait for Ben?'

Marcus knew when to push for more information and when not to. This time it was 'not to'.

'No,' his confidence had found its niche again and was clicking back into place, 'let's not wait. Apparently he's met an Irish colleague and they've gone to a writers' museum or something like that. He'll turn up eventually. I told him to take a cab, but in the meantime it's his loss, so let's go ahead. How much time have you? I don't want to delay you – have you plans for later?'

'My time is yours!' She smiled. 'I'm out of the house and I'm going to enjoy it!'

*

It was a quarter to three. Marcus couldn't believe it when Grace looked at her watch and told him, but Chez Max had been gradually emptying for about half an hour. He marvelled at how long the Irish, even workers, took over lunch. 'If I get half an hour, that's classed as leisurely! I much prefer this!'

He had relaxed, and so had she, he believed. Ben had called sometime around one thirty to say that, on entering the museum, he and his colleague had met a third writer, known to his new friend, and they had decided to have a snack in the café there. 'He sends his apologies to you, Grace,' he said, on finishing the call, 'but says, and I quote, he knows you're in good hands and will call you later to apologise in person. Are you, Grace?' He'd grinned. 'In good hands?'

'Never better!' She smiled, and searching for a word to characterise the mood at the table, Marcus came up with 'mellow'.

*

Grace, thinking subsequently about that lunch and its conversations, had been genuinely impressed by this man's enthusiasm for finding a base in Ireland. Marcus kept emphasising that this was for Ben but she had her doubts about whether that would work. Ben didn't seem to be a manager-type, no matter whether he was given a writers' retreat, a fishing lodge, a dive school (which Marcus had said was on the list, depending on location) or anything else. To her it seemed Ben's bent was naturally to participate in such endeavours rather than manage them.

He told her then about how the visit to Annaghmakerrig had affected both himself and his nephew, but again, although she listened, encouragingly she hoped, his tone led her to believe that, again, he had been the enthusiast.

In thinking about it, Grace decided they had got into the discussion about failed marriages because he had asked quietly about Leonie's current status, diagnosis and symptoms.

At first she'd been reluctant to go there. But as he continued gently to prod, the details of her daughter's behaviour, insults and invective, and how devastating she found all this, had rushed out, despite her normal stoicism in public. Although she'd been far from drunk, her tongue, she thought in retrospect, must have been loosened by wine. And Marcus had certainly proved to be a good listener.

In the course of her revelations, she had told him about her daughter's disastrous and short-lived Las Vegas marriage, which had led on to the subject of failed marriages in general and then their own.

For a time, she had told Marcus, she had resented Harry's lack of courage – that he didn't have the guts simply to walk away honestly because he found life too hard in their home, but had had to find a compelling reason to escape. But she'd got over that, she'd said, and it was fine that he seemed happy now, although, she confided, he seemed more than a little afraid to stand up to his wife.

She continued, though, to take issue with two aspects of the current situation: his continued evasion of major responsibility where Leonie was concerned ('Handing out money is easy!'), and his having replaced Leonie in his affections with his new little daughter, Jasmine ('Not her fault of course').

In general, though, she'd told Marcus, she now wished her ex-husband well.

'I wish I could say the same,' Marcus had replied, and went on to tell her, which she already knew, that his wife had left abruptly, without mentioning a valid reason, but that it had been with another man and he had never heard from her again, their divorce being conducted by their respective lawyers.

'Mine was just as sudden,' she said, 'but at least I knew why Harry left me, even if it wrecked my confidence and left me feeling like a female version of Tom Thumb. And we are in touch, uneasily sometimes. It can't be easy for you. It must be like looking into a void.'

'Something like that,' he said. Suddenly, he had raised his hand to signal for the bill. This conversation was over, she knew, and she didn't push it any further.

But then, almost diffidently, he'd asked, 'If you're sure you have the time, shall we go somewhere else? My dance card is clear for the afternoon!'

36

Grace, with Marcus, was leaving the Shelbourne Hotel when, at around five o'clock, Ben, full of apologies and excuses, had turned up. They had crossed paths in the hotel's lobby.

Marcus, she knew, had texted his nephew from the hotel's Horseshoe Bar to let him know where they were, but that had been shortly after three o'clock and Ben's uncle was, she saw, quietly angry about the no-show at the lunch: 'If you've booked that restaurant,' he'd said, 'call and cancel it unless you want to eat there by yourself. I'm not hungry.'

'Sorry,' Ben repeated. 'We just got carried away. We didn't feel the time passing.'

Grace, not wishing to get involved in a family row, or to stay away from home any longer – for the past fifteen minutes she had reverted to wondering what Leonie had got up to in her absence – took her leave and, despite both men offering to walk her to her train, declined their offer.

She thanked Marcus, told him she'd had a wonderful afternoon, wished him well in his search, and promised that if she could help in any way, he had only to ask, although she knew hardly anything useful about castles or country mansions, even about west Cork. Then she left as quickly as she could.

This carelessness was a side of Ben she hadn't seen, although to make judgements on his behaviour when she'd known him for a couple of days and one flaming night was not only presumptuous but silly.

And, a little shamefacedly, she acknowledged that, on seeing him come through the Shelbourne's famous revolving doors, she had experienced a (very brief) glimmer of chagrin that, clearly, he had moved on to his next 'thing' and was no longer interested in her company.

But as she hurried along the teeming pathway, the air filled with languages from all over the world, she scolded herself for that stinging thought, fleeting though it had been. What had she expected?

Their farewell to each other in the crowded lobby of the Shelbourne, self-consciously chaste, would have made it hard for an onlooker to believe what those two bodies had been up to just ten days previously. On her part, she could still, at will, recreate the sensation of each kiss of that night but, in the cool afternoon of a winter's day in Dublin, it now seemed a million miles away, especially with Ben left behind to argue with his uncle about his apparent disrespect to her, as their guest.

This, of course, was to make another leap into surface judgement of a person's character. But she already believed Marcus was the type to advocate courtesy and good manners.

The jury was still out, however, as to whether Ben's uncle suspected there'd been more to the history between his nephew and Grace than the handling of Leonie during the two crises she had caused on that ship.

None of that was important any longer, she told herself. The two men were now on a mission that had nothing to do with her. She'd had an extraordinary encounter with the younger, and a very pleasant afternoon with the elder, who had proved to be excellent company – and, despite her offer of help, she didn't expect to hear from either again.

*

She barely managed to squeeze into her carriage on the Dart and had to stand all the way to her station. A woman near her, she saw, bore a striking resemblance to Adeline, the stooped shoulders, the cramped expression.

Poor Adeline. Although she had tried to love all three of her daughters equally, she'd always felt sorry for Adeline and not just because, as the eldest, she'd borne the brunt of her young parents' inexperience. In fact, she had always felt that her first child had been born unhappy – she'd cried a lot – and had remained so despite proclaiming fulfilment in her job. There had been a few desultory attempts at relationships among colleagues, but male primary teachers had been in very short supply in recent years – there were many more women.

As Adeline's mother she had tried to encourage her daughter to expand her horizons, to take courses unrelated to teaching, or even to go on solo package holidays, but she had brushed off these suggestions with protestations that Grace should look to her own situation and stop interfering in hers. 'I'm absolutely fine,' she'd reiterate. 'Stop fussing about me. There're lots of unhappily married women I know in my profession and I'd prefer my situation to theirs. I can't be bullied or hindered with anything I choose to do in my life. So, as politely as possible, Mum, I know you mean well, but would you ever butt out!'

Although he hadn't said it outright, an implication from Marcus that both older girls had been somehow obscured by the smoke from Leonie's blaze had been disturbing. It had been phrased as a question, but it had stuck in her mind.

Had she short-changed Adeline and Jackie? Could she make it up to them if she succeeded in getting Leonie into Gould Farm? *There you go again,* she thought. *Your attention to the other two still hinges on what happens with their sister.*

Grace had never had to worry about Jackie. She was one of those people who woke up every morning looking forward to her day. She loved managing her little household, comprised of her beloved easy-going Mick and little Tommy.

Jackie rightly felt lucky that, with Mick's salary from a successful development company, known for treating its staff decently, enhanced with a few private commissions – putting in fitted wardrobes and kitchens, for instance – they could well afford the mortgage on their little house, holidays to places like Lanzarote, and even save for rainy days. 'Carpenters will never be out of work, Grace,' Mick had said to her, when she'd been worried about the price of their house. They'd bought it near the peak of the Celtic Tiger years when homes the size of sheds were selling for silly money. 'Look at Jesus. He's still workin'!'

Marcus had brought up the topic of Leonie versus the other two girls, when they'd been chatting at the bar in the Shelbourne. 'It'll be quite a void in your life, won't it,' he'd asked, 'if you do manage to get Leonie into that place? How are you going to fill it, Grace? With your other two daughters? Or do you have hobbies?'

'Do you, Marcus?'

'No.' He'd grinned. 'Watching baseball on TV. Watching the Cubs live at Wrigley Field. That's about it.'

'Then why are you looking at me like that?' she challenged.

'How am I looking at you?'

'You're just *looking* at me. You're intimidating me because I have no hobbies.'

'I suppose I should say something nice.' He'd chuckled.

'Let's see . . . Something nice about the way the light from this lamp in the corner of this bar falls on your face? Would that help soothe the intimidation you feel?'

'Well said!' She'd smiled back, the subject of her family safely averted, and they'd both had another drink, one last white wine for her, a final beer for him.

Now, as the Dart swayed along the tracks, she realised that, surprisingly, she didn't feel in the least tipsy, despite all the wine over the course of the afternoon. Perhaps it was because most of it had been spaced around food. And there had been that little hiatus, a bracing shot of cold fresh air while they'd walked between venues.

However, to the strangers jammed in around her, everyone studiously avoiding everyone else's eyes, her breath probably betrayed her so she kept her mouth shut and breathed through her nose.

*

It was a nice evening, clear and crisp, the sea calm in the bay, and as she walked home, Grace rang Maxine. Her call went to voicemail so she left a message, sending her love, and saying she'd ring again tonight to arrange another trip to Galway during the next couple of days.

As she walked up her driveway, glancing automatically towards the window of Leonie's room, she saw that, while the rest of the house was dark, her daughter's light was on. She braced herself for a reaction to her being late home.

Although Leonie always professed indifference as to

whether her mother was in the house or not, Grace knew instinctively that wasn't the case: when she was going out, she always left that note beside the kettle as to what time she would be back, stretching it a little to allow for delays on the Dart.

If she was going to be properly late, as she was this evening, her practice was to ring Leonie, but the afternoon's events had been so different from her usual routines that she'd forgotten and, with her head so unusually full of distractions, she hadn't remembered until after the call to Maxine.

By then she was only five minutes away from home and there'd been no point.

She couldn't remember precisely what time she'd indicated on today's note. Having calculated that the lunch with Marcus and Ben would take two and a half hours at most and not having included the unplanned extension with Marcus, she'd probably have said she'd be home between four and four thirty. It was now six twenty-five.

As she let herself in, the house was silent, no radio or TV – or, indeed, music coming from Leonie's room. Had her daughter fallen asleep while working up a grudge?

Oddly, she could smell something sweet, quite sickly – a vanilla-scented candle? That wasn't usually Leonie's bag. What point was she making now?

Grace sighed, turned on the hall and landing lights, then, still wearing her coat, trudged slowly upstairs and opened her daughter's door.

She screamed.

Her daughter, clad in the wonderful gold gown they'd bought together for Cherry's awards event, was lying on her neatly made bed, arms folded across her chest, candles flickering on the bedside tables at either side of her head. Her eyes were closed.

At first glance Grace was so panicked she didn't catch anything else about the staging. She rushed over to the bed and bent to her daughter's face to see if she was breathing. At first she thought she wasn't but then caught a very small but discernible movement of air for what might have been only a millisecond.

She raced down to the hall to fetch her mobile, then remembered she'd placed it in her coat pocket and, still panicking, pulled it out, blanking briefly. *Call nine one one!* rang around her brain – but then she remembered that was from TV. It was American. There was definitely a special number for mobiles – 112? 221? Hands shaking, she stabbed out 999 and was answered instantly: 'Emergency. Which service do you require?'

'Ambulance! Ambulance! *Ambulance*!' she yelled. 'My daughter's unconscious!'

Calmly, the operator took her address and Eircode, asked for her daughter's name and age, Grace's name and other details – crucially, if Leonie was breathing. In response to Grace's repeated requests to know how long the ambulance would take to get to them, the operator, who told her his name was Leonard, reassured her, saying the dispatch had been made and it wouldn't be long. 'And I'll stay on the line with you, Grace. Are you with Leonie now?'

'No. She's upstairs in her bedroom.'

'Would you mind going up there, please? Bring your phone with you if you can, Grace, and I'll guide you on how to turn her into the recovery position.' He reminded her that the ambulance was on its way and that he would be with her until that help arrived.

'But it's rush-hour!' she quavered.

'Don't worry, they have your Eircode and they've found where you are – seven Winslow Close in Baldoyle, isn't that it? And they always know the fastest route.

'When you get back to Leonie's room, Grace, could you have a look around to see if she might have taken pills? Are there empty pill bottles or boxes around the place?'

By now, Grace was in the room and noticing what she'd previously missed. There were pill boxes and empty blister packs, neatly arranged, by size, in a pyramid. 'Do you know what they are or were? Are there labels on them?' he asked.

'I can't read them without my glasses.' Grace again panicked. 'I'll have to go downstairs and get them – but one of them seems to be paracetamol.' She'd recognised the box from what she termed the medicine drawer in one of the kitchen cabinets.

'Let's turn her first,' Leonard said, 'and when you're doing that, ask yourself if you can smell alcohol off her clothing or her breath. Is there an empty bottle somewhere? Maybe vodka. You ready, Grace?'

She said she was. 'So here we go, Grace. Is she heavy?'

'Very small and slight.' The man's demeanour and low-key delivery – and having something practical to do – had calmed Grace down. But tears sprang into her eyes as she realised how accurate her description of Leonie had been – lying so peacefully on her white counterpane in the exact centre of her bed, wearing the gorgeous gold dress bought so joyfully and with such rare optimism. It had seemed such a shame to disturb her. Like destroying a perfect religious painting or icon.

But as she followed Leonard's quiet instructions on how safely to reframe the picture, she heard the distant but urgent siren of an approaching ambulance.

37

During the long hours she spent in the Accident and Emergency waiting room, Grace – grasping at the last fibre of positivity in her body – refused to contemplate anything other than that her daughter would survive. In desperation, she had reverted to her 'holy' years of being first down to Mass each morning at school.

They had all been encouraged to find a name for their guardian angels. Grace had named hers Joseph Ignatius after St Joseph and St Ignatius of Loyola because her English and music teachers, Mothers Joseph and Loyola, were so nice and she had nothing but happy memories of them. She hadn't thought of him for decades but now she called on Joseph Ignatius, in her mind begging him and Leonie's angel to get together to pull her daughter through.

By tradition (hers), she had to promise something in return and so, extravagantly, she promised the angel perpetual acknowledgement of his presence in her life – and that she'd go on a pilgrimage to Knock. More prosaically, she promised that if Jackie had another baby, very much on the cards she'd thought recently, she'd try to persuade her to call it Joseph or Josephine.

She and Harry, who had been sitting beside her for the last couple of hours, barely spoke. They'd had no updates or information since Leonie had been rushed into a treatment room directly from the ambulance.

Harry, whom she'd called while their daughter was being loaded into the ambulance, had dashed straight to the hospital but, coming from Ranelagh, had been caught in the tail-end of cross-city rush-hour traffic. Leonie had been taken away for treatment by the time he'd arrived.

It was just as well, Grace thought. He would probably have broken down if he'd seen his waif-like little girl, seeming no bigger than a child of ten or eleven, being handled carefully enough, but as easily lifted and manoeuvred as though she was a piece of cloth.

In that waiting room, both parents simmered with repressed emotion. In Grace a bubbling mélange of love, fear, horror, loneliness and guilt continually rose to the top. There were puffs of resentment also. Every bone in her body was bent on rescuing Leonie; it was, however, still only days since the debacle on the cruise. If she came through this, how many more such episodes had she, Grace, to face?

But each time that unworthy thought came to the surface, she pushed it down. This was not about her. It was about marshalling all forces, physical, mental, emotional and, yes, even spiritual, to bring Leonie back to life.

She knew that guilt had to be one of Harry's predominant feelings but, up to now, he'd always had a way of decanting it onto her. Right now, she was glad of the silence between them. In any case, she felt she had nothing relevant to say to him in the circumstances. They were surrounded by the injured, drunk, bleeding and aggressive, some with long-suffering relatives or friends, some so desperate for attention that they kept going to the glass-fronted desk and demanding it.

Some were resigned. The elderly woman sitting beside her, noticing that Grace had been glancing covertly at her ruined face, said she had been sitting there for nearly nine hours. On one side, her face was marred by parallel streams of blackened blood that, when fresh, had oozed from under her eye-patch, a make-do with cotton wool and criss-crossed Elastoplast. 'I didn't wash it off,' she explained, 'because I was hoping that if they saw so much blood, they'd take me seriously and I might be able to jump the queue, but they haven't. And now it's all dried up and I'm worrying that when they see it's stopped bleeding, I'll be shoved to the back of the queue again. These chairs are fucking hard, aren't they? Me bum is as sore as me eye!'

'What happened to your eye?'

'Slashed!' the woman said. 'Me son had a skinful and I wouldn't give him any more money – couldn't because I hadn't any, except a few coppers. What can you do?' She shrugged.

All heads turned when a doctor or a nurse bearing a clipboard came out of the sanctum at the end of a little corridor and called a name. Someone then jumped out of a chair and, while everyone else watched with envy, went away with the saviour. Then everyone turned back to gaze up again at the small TV fixed high on the wall above a vending machine (Coca-Cola, Fanta, crisps, Snickers, fruit-and-nut chocolate), chirruping with a re-run of *The Good Life*.

'This is horrendous,' Harry murmured.

'This is real life in Dublin,' Grace whispered back, adding, 'although maybe not on your side of the tracks. Yes, it's horrible, but I'm not surprised and you shouldn't be either. Have you never listened to Joe Duffy? At least there's no one dead in one of these chairs.'

'Not yet,' he growled, then: 'I'm going in there.' And before she could blink, he was walking quickly down the little corridor, stopping at the door of a room, one of many along one side. It was slightly ajar. He opened it a bit further and peered in. 'She's in here!' he hissed back towards Grace, beckoning furiously. 'Come on!'

She got up quickly and half ran to the room. Through the half-open door she saw Leonie's gold dress bundled into a ball on the seat of a chair. All she could see of her daughter was her feet, sparkly pink nail polish glistening under the bright lights overhead.

Their backs to the door, two people were attending to her, both in overshoes, green scrubs, latex gloves, head coverings and face masks. Then a third person, similarly clad, rushed towards them to close the door, but Harry stuck his foot into the gap and, in a low, but authoritative voice, said, 'We're this young woman's parents and whatever your rules, or laws, or what you claim about privacy or GDPR regulations, in the name of decency we are entitled at least to an update. We want to know if, in the opinion of someone in there, our daughter will survive. We've had no contact with anyone since we arrived here,' he glanced at his watch, 'nearly three hours ago. While we appreciate that you're doing all you can for our daughter, and we're grateful, I'm not taking my foot out of this doorway until you tell us what's going on.'

Another of the men, obviously having heard all this, turned and approached them. He opened the door wide, came through, closed it behind him and took off his face mask. 'Your timing is good. We're just finishing with her here, tidying up, if you will. She'll be moved up to Intensive Care very shortly. They'll take a couple of hours to settle her, and if you want to hang around, I'm sure you could visit her for a minute or two. I don't recommend it – what you'll see won't be pretty.

'I apologise for the delay in talking to you, Mr and Mrs McGee, but while we know that your wait was agonising, your daughter was our priority. She'll be groggy for the rest of the night and probably won't recognise you so my advice to you is to go home and get a couple of hours' sleep.

It's almost eleven.'

He took off his gloves and dropped the formal tone: 'She's young and her vital signs are good. We got her back, I believe, and although I can't guarantee anything, I don't think there will be permanent damage – you got her here in time. We won't be discharging her until she's been seen by a psychiatrist — it's procedure in these cases.' He covered a yawn with a hand, then apologised: 'It's been a long day. Sorry.'

Grace followed a grim-faced Harry out to the car park. The night had turned cold and the air was filled with the kind of soft rain called 'wet drizzle' in her midlands village.

Harry stopped just outside the door and lit a cigarette.

'I thought you gave up long ago.' She was surprised.

'I did, but I started again recently,' he said gruffly. 'Look, can we go to a pub or something? There are a few matters we need to discuss.'

'The pubs are closing and, anyway, I've no car. I came with Leonie in the ambulance.'

'Well, she's in here, there's no one in your house and you'll need a lift.'

'I can get a taxi.'

'Don't be absurd, Grace. My car is over here.'

Once in the driving seat, however, rather than start the engine, he turned on only the wipers and sat staring for a few minutes into the darkness, the rain describing fuzzy yellow circles under the glare of sodium streetlights. 'Could we turn on a bit of heat, please, Harry? I came out in a bit of a rush.' She was still wearing the white linen jumpsuit, which was utterly inappropriate. She had ditched the blue coat in Leonie's bedroom at home when taking instructions on how to turn her daughter, who had seemed so perfectly placed, so peaceful and rested, a work of art: *In Repose, Girl in Gold Dress.*

It hit her again that this might have been her daughter's deathbed and she began to tremble so violently that the bracelet she was wearing rattled.

'I get it, I get it,' Harry said. 'No need to be so dramatic.' He started the car and snapped angrily at the heat controls, turning them up to full strength. 'Before we leave, are you absolutely sure you don't want to stay and visit her in a couple of hours?'

'Yes. It's a good reason to go home. If I change my mind, I'll have my own car and can come back in.'

'You've no bag with you. Have you got your keys?'

'No.' She was dismayed. In the rush to the ambulance, she had simply shut the front door behind her. She hadn't even turned on the alarm. 'It's okay,' she said. 'One of the neighbours keeps a spare for me but we'd better hurry or she'll be in bed.'

As he sped towards the security hut at the car park's gates, again the image of what *could* have happened was very vivid – even now she could have been calling undertakers, fighting over the formulation of a death notice. She glanced at Harry: how would they phrase their own relationship? Would he be the carefully worded 'Leonie's father'? Were Cherry, who had no time for Leonie, and Jasmine to be noted among the mourners as 'her loving stepmother and half-sister'?

She tried to force herself to penetrate the horror with at least a little light. The doctor had certainly seemed to think everything was going to be okay. They *didn't* have to cope with Leonie's death.

Which meant the shuttle was back at her door. Again she glanced at Harry, whose shock and grief had genuinely mirrored her own. There was a further shock in store for him. He didn't get to have equal rights in the sadness without taking equal responsibility – or as near as made no difference. Life, as Harry had known it for the past seven and a half years, was about to change.

38

Because Leonie was in good hands and in no position to pull more stunts, Grace had calmed down during the car journey to her house. She felt lighter. She had temporarily handed over custody.

She collected the spare key from her neighbour, who was full of sympathy because, like everyone else in the close, she had seen the ambulance and had watched Leonie's transfer into it. 'We all want you to know that if there's anything you need, Grace, or anything any of us can do, please don't forget to ask. The poor child! Poor you, too!'

Grace thanked her. She had asked Harry to stay in the car for fear of fuelling speculation about a reunion and waited until the neighbour had gone into her own house before she let the two of them into hers. He had immediately raced upstairs to Leonie's room.

She put on the kettle and, while it was coming to the boil, texted Maxine, copying Dieter in case her friend was resting, apologising for not making the contact she had promised earlier.

On getting home, found I had to deal with an unexpected crisis. Will definitely call tomorrow a.m. between 9 and 9.30 if that suits, and will explain everything. (Boston plan now crucial.) Gx

She was deploying crockery on the kitchen table when she heard her ex running down the stairs. 'I'm in the kitchen!' she called.

But instead of coming into the room, he stood in the doorway holding out two pieces of torn paper, the first being her note to Leonie, the second something in her handwriting. He was white-faced. 'Did you see these while you were performing your heroics with our daughter?'

'No – show me.' Grace refused to rise to the bait. 'What are they?'

'They're the prelude to Leonie showing us that she's prepared to kill herself. You were late home yesterday, from some junket, it appears, nearly too late.'

'What are you talking about? Give those to me. Where were they?'

'They were openly on her dressing-table. She meant for

them to be found. Look at it, Grace!' He handed her the piece of paper with Leonie's handwriting.

Grace, who had believed she'd been through so much horror in the last fortnight that she was now immune to it, was shattered once more as she read:

4.11 p.m. She's due home in 15 mins and I'll be out by then. The only sad thing about it is I won't be able to see her face when she finds me! What'll she do?

You'll have to call Dad, won't you, Mother?

I am a HUMAN BEING, with HUMAN RIGHTS to belong to FAMILY and to be RESPECTED!

I can't take your hostility any more or your trying to isolate me. You're trying to ruin my life and deliberately driving people away from me, even my dad.

You're completely selfish Grace. I can't take it any more!!!

Carefully, Grace put the note on the countertop, smoothing out the creases Harry had made. 'This makes no sense, Harry,' she said. 'You're saying she didn't want to kill herself, only to warn me, and that it was my doing she nearly died? Based on this?'

'She didn't *want* to complete it, that's the point. But because you were so late— Read it again, dammit!' he yelled. 'Look at the timing! What time did you get home?'

Grace resolved to stay calm. 'I'm not going to argue about this, Harry, because the thinking here is completely garbled. There's no thinking at all. The world is against

Leonie, nothing is ever her fault, and this is what she does. She pulls stunts and spectaculars. It's her way of getting attention.'

She glanced again at the note. 'I know how serious it is, Harry, but this note is not the problem. This is just warning us, me, really, that this will go on and on until she wins whatever weird game she's playing in her head.'

She slumped into one of the kitchen chairs. 'I'm tired of it all. I'm fed up living with Leonie in this house. Will you make the tea, please? You know where everything is, don't you? I'll get the milk.' She got to her feet again, crossed to the fridge and, against the whine of the kettle, heard him say, 'Where the hell were you yesterday, Grace?'

'I was having lunch with a friend, if you really want to know.'

'Until half six?'

Slowly, Grace closed the fridge door and, not bothering with a jug, put the carton of milk on the table. She walked to the sink where Harry was dropping a teabag into each of two mugs. 'What friend?' he asked, adding the boiling water.

Behind him, Grace stretched her neck and raised herself to her full height – something she'd rarely done in the latter years of their marriage, since he was shorter than she was. She used to do it for fun, teasing him as part of a mock-argument, but as he'd got older and crabbier, he'd started to push back, and she'd stopped. This, she figured now, was part of the self-inflicted near-obliteration of Grace Lennon.

As he turned, with a mug in each hand, to go to the table

he was startled to find her looming over him, blocking his route. 'Don't do that!' he barked. 'You know I've always hated it.'

She didn't move. 'I am the height I am, Harry, and I thank God for it. It helps me deal with bullies.' She eyeballed him, then, smiling pleasantly, backed off a few inches, turned and went to the table.

She breathed deeply. While he continued to stand near the sink, she said: 'The sad facts are, Harry, that it takes two to make a child and you're one of those fifty-percenters who made Leonie and who *should* be taking half of the responsibility for what you've created. Marrying someone else doesn't negate that. I'm tired of taking on your half as well as my own. We can discuss this, if you like, but only if you take it seriously and commit to some sort of meaningful action, not just playing the good guy leaving me as the witch.

'I have an idea that might help her, but today is not the day to tell you. It's an idea that's not in your gift and, if I can pull it off, I will tell you then and you won't stand in my way.

'You have no right to make decisions for me or Leonie – certainly to have anything to say about who I might have lunch with. Now, can we have our tea and a ten-minute moratorium on talking about Leonie?'

He came to sit opposite her, and put the mugs on the table. Then, with both hands to his face, shoulders shaking, he wept.

*

With her ex-husband sleeping in her spare room, Grace, driving back to the hospital at about three in the morning, too tired to maintain panic – and surprised at how that happens – considered the twists and turns of life.

She had spent seven ultra-quiet years (bar Leonie's regular upheavals and her annual spats with Maxine in Arnotts) sequestered in her nice Baldoyle house where the biggest event in the day had been the successful solving of a crossword. Or maybe the arrival of her key-holder neighbour in the spring with a sack of new potatoes she had dug from her vegetable patch.

By contrast, the past two weeks had blown through her life at hurricane speed.

And now here came Harry's news.

He and Cherry (Cherry had decided) were to take a break from each other for a couple of months around Christmas, the crux of the inevitable 'Why now?' being – who else? – Leonie.

With the festival now less than six weeks away and it being Ranelagh's job again to have Leonie for the day, Cherry had refused to countenance it. Her parents, a placid couple who ran a successful B&B in County Wexford, were not to be inconvenienced again by a repeat performance of Leonie's drunkenness at their table two years previously. And that was that.

Grace had been looking forward to her own Christmas Day this year: a whole day free from obligations. She was due to go to Jackie's, with Mick's parents, of whom she was very fond, and Adeline. Mick had been born in Dublin's

Liberties and his parents, ardent supporters of their area and their hordes of Liberties' friends and neighbours, were great company. Even Adeline lightened up in his presence, and Christmas at Jackie's was always fun.

The row between Harry and Cherry, he'd told her, arose after they'd disembarked from the Orient Express in Venice, when Jasmine, attracted by the wares of the quayside vendors near St Mark's Square, had wanted to buy some beautiful Christmas-tree baubles, made of real glass, to take home with them. The word 'Christmas', so tuneful and merry, had been the starting gun, but because Jasmine had been omnipresent with them that day, the subject of Leonie's Christmas visit had been put on hold. They'd waited until she was in bed to thrash it out. Cherry had been implacable: she was *not* having another Christmas Day ruined for her parents or, indeed, for Jazzy.

The problem had escalated when they were themselves in bed and she'd brought it up again, accusing Harry of caring more about his older daughter than he did about little Jasmine. (As she'd listened patiently to this section of Harry's outpourings, Grace thought it almost amusing: Leonie believed exactly the opposite. In her view, her dad had demoted her in favour of his youngest daughter.)

'I don't want to go back there tonight, Grace,' he implored. 'It's become a daily battle and I don't know how to manage it.'

She cut this short before it, too, became a long monologue. There was nothing she could do about his domestic woes: it was up to him and his wife to settle their differences.

Leonie was at her most vulnerable now, and despite Grace's growing anger at what she'd put her parents through, she felt that, at least for the moment, she had to play the hand she'd been dealt. Christmas was still far enough away for some kind of solution to be found and she was determined it wouldn't be at her expense. Not this year. 'Go on up to the spare room, Harry,' she said, 'but ring Cherry and say you're still in the hospital. Do *not* involve me in any way.'

He was suitably grateful.

She waited until he was in bed and settled – she could hear his snores from the kitchen – then took off the white jumpsuit, went to the laundry basket in the utility room and swapped it for jeans and a (fairly clean) sweatshirt. Then she picked up her keys, left the house and drove back to the hospital.

*

The kind doctor in A&E had warned her and Harry that if they did decide to visit their daughter what they'd see wouldn't be 'pretty'. How right he'd been.

The overall light in the facility was purposely dim. The main sounds were of beeps, compressed air and the squish of soft shoe-soles as nurses moved between the beds. In the one beside Leonie's, a middle-aged man, strung with multiple tubes, wires and drips, was clearly struggling to breathe under the oxygen mask covering most of his face.

Leonie lay in a high-sided hammock, presumably to

prevent her falling out because, moaning, she was rolling violently from side to side and the flimsy hospital garment she wore had twisted itself into ropes on her small body, much of it now exposed.

Worst of all, though, was the thick white foam that flowed from her nose, mouth, and elsewhere.

Grace endured these sights and sounds for several minutes until she couldn't take any more. She touched Leonie's forehead very gently and whispered, 'I love you, little baby. I love you.'

Then, looking neither right nor left, she fled.

39

It was five minutes to four when Grace got home from the hospital. Even though she had just left her daughter, it was a jolt to the system to see that her bedroom window was dark. Leonie always kept a lamp on at night.

When she opened the front door, she'd almost forgotten that Harry was in the house until she heard the male snoring from upstairs.

She was so tired and frazzled that her legs could barely carry her up the stairs so, without brushing her teeth, she kicked off her ballet flats and got into bed in her sweatshirt and jeans, set the alarm on her mobile for seven o'clock and was asleep within seconds.

Grace dreamed she was searching for Leonie in an

enormous ruined temple that resembled the Parthenon. The floor was littered with fallen columns, so numerous that in many areas she had to climb over them. On the northern side a line of trees backed a platform of living oak. Its leafless branches curved upwards around Leonie, making a cradle for her body, which was adorned with wide, twisted swathes of white lace, her hair studded with pearls. She'd been prepared, Grace knew, for sacrifice.

'Grace! Grace? Wake up, Grace!'

She opened her eyes.

A man was standing over her. She struggled up on one elbow. 'Harry? What are you doing here?'

'It's half six and I just came to tell you I'm leaving,' he said, and, with the dream fading, she remembered everything that had happened.

The image that wasn't dissolving was of her daughter in her spiny cradle. Abruptly, she was frightened, didn't want to be left alone in the house. 'Wait, please!' she said. 'Can we have a cup of tea before you go? Put on the kettle, and I'll be down by the time it boils. There are scones in the freezer – I'll warm them up in the microwave.' Then: 'I went back to the hospital last night, Harry. She was still unconscious but the good news is that she's going to survive.'

'Why didn't you wake me? I'd have gone with you.'

'You were fast asleep and, anyway, I needed to be alone. Just go down and put on the kettle, please, Harry, and I'll fill you in. That doctor warned us it wouldn't be pretty and it wasn't. But at least she's alive. We can ring the ICU, find out how she got through the night – you can do it, if you like.'

'We can discuss that. You know the whole story better than I do.'

Grace recognised avoidance when she saw it. 'Just go downstairs, Harry! I need to get out of this bed and into the bathroom.'

In the mirror, she was hollow-eyed and her hair was a mess, but this was only Harry. Why should she smarten up for him? She sluiced mouthwash into and around her mouth, then hurried down.

He'd already made the tea and the table was set for two. He'd found the scones and the microwave was defrosting them. 'Thanks for this,' he said. 'I didn't have anything to eat last evening and this is very welcome. So, tell me how exactly she was.'

She told him, not sparing him the graphic detail, and he was genuinely shocked. 'I'm sorry you had to go through that by yourself.'

There was a pause while she considered how to respond, whether or not to reveal her true feelings. Then, quietly: 'I've had to get through quite a lot by myself. There's something I want to say to you, Harry, and it's long overdue.'

'Go ahead,' he said, watching her, clearly expecting the worst.

'Don't get me wrong,' she carried on, determined not to place his feelings above her own, 'I don't want you to think that anything I say about our daughter means I want to get rid of her – or that I don't love her to bits. Although I get utterly frustrated with her, I'm not often angry. I will admit that sometimes I'm close to it. I had a terrible go at her when we were on that ship because of all the trouble she caused – it was *major*, Harry – but I truly regret that now. She may never forgive me for some of the things I said.

'But the thing is, I honestly believe that, however awful a situation becomes for me, it must be far worse for her. It must be terrible to be so alone in the world, all appearances to the contrary, and to be unable to control her impulses to act out or behave inappropriately with men. She's desperate to be liked, but she behaves in ways that either turn people off or open the door for shysters like Jaden to exploit her.' The microwave clicked off and, as though to block out the sound of her voice, he went to fetch the scones. She waited, until he was again seated, and carried on.

'She's far from stupid, but it's very upsetting to hear her fantasise about her so-called career and her non-existent CV. I get sad for her that she feels acting out is the only way to gain attention and can understand why frustration boils over when things don't go as she wants. She blames everyone else, especially me, because she can't find her place in the world. I'm the punchbag because I'm the only one in the yard, the only one who'll take it from her.'

She stopped briefly to gather the words she needed to say next. His head was low and he was staring at the uneaten scone on his plate and she asked him, as quietly as she could, to look at her. He did.

'She blames me for your departure, Harry, taunts me with Cherry's youth and beauty – and waist measurement, by the way. She hurls at me that I'm a failed wife whose jealous behaviour forced you to abandon me. In her book, I was jealous of the attention you paid her.

'I don't take credit for much, Harry, but I do think I've been honourable in that regard because I've never corrected her on it.' He flashed her a look, but then returned to contemplation of his plate.

During the silence that ensued, she picked up her cup to drink the tea, choosing her next words carefully. 'Where the bigger picture's concerned, Harry, it's time you stepped up to your responsibilities to our daughter.'

It had sounded firm. She had sounded firm, but her hands were shaking so much that the tea was slopping all over the tablecloth and she had to put down the cup.

Harry had sat silently. Always in the past, he had been argumentative, if not downright combative, when she had challenged him. Had she gone too far?

No! She had said nothing that wasn't true. Where Leonie was concerned, she had been letting him off the hook time and time again.

But across the table he looked so sad, so dismayed, that her need to apologise, long ingrained, was growing fast. But she pushed it away, forcing herself to concentrate on buttering her scone. For she wasn't sorry. She knew he was quite likely to dismiss at least some of what she'd said because of what they'd both been through with Leonie in the past twelve hours.

'Listen, Harry,' she said quietly. 'As I've explained, maybe not very well, I've been left alone to deal with Leonie, and the rest of our family, Adeline and Jackie too, but especially you, have had a free pass. I probably shouldn't blame any of the three of you for using it because I gave it to you. I made it easy.

'I hate to bring this up but, as you may remember, I told you how I was bullied as a child. Although that was a very long time ago, the effects have been long-lasting, and I know one of them is my tendency to avoid confrontation.'

He looked at her from under raised eyebrows. 'Nobody would ever guess!'

'Sor—' She stopped herself just in time. *Had it been Marcus or Ben who had asked her why she said 'sorry' all the time?* 'It actually feels good to get those things off my chest,' she said now, 'but it's been a waste of breath, Harry, if there's going to be no change for the better.'

'I'm shook,' he admitted. 'It wasn't that I was blind to all this but I guess that deep down I knew I was getting away with something I shouldn't. I think I always feared that this day would come.

'But there's a lot to take in all in one go. Can we talk again? You've made a string of points and you're right about some of them. Look, I have to get home,' adding bleakly, 'if I have a home to go to right now. Will you ring me if there's anything that needs doing Leonie-wise? And keep me in the loop about her progress?'

'Let's ring the ward now while you're here?' she suggested. When she got through, she was told that Leonie was awake, a little disoriented, although that was to be expected, and that she should call again, probably in a few hours for a further update.

*

After her ex had departed, Grace felt beyond exhaustion, in that realm where nothing seems real. It was still too early to ring Maxine with the news that she'd have to postpone the visit to Galway for a couple of days. She pulled herself upright and trudged through to the TV room to tidy it, picked up several old newspapers and brought them to the green bin.

One of the property supplements caught her eye. The front page showed a picture of a gorgeous Victorian house in a prosperous Dublin suburb, five bedrooms, seven bathrooms, on a two-acre site leading directly to the sea and despite all that had happened a stray thought intruded: Marcus's mansions-and-castles quest and his having sked for local input. He and Ben had presumably left Dublin by now.

She fetched the business card he'd given her, picked up her phone and texted:

Hi Marcus, Hope your search is going well. Just had an idea. Our newspapers all run property supplements: Irish Times on Thursdays, Irish Independent on Fridays, etc. Ask any newsagent. Saw a feature about a seaside Victorian mansion with landscaped gardens, for instance? That the kind of thing you're looking for? Hope the Irish weather's not letting us down. Grace

Funny how the brain works, she thought as she put down the phone, flipping from the tragic and into the mundane in the space of a millisecond. She sat in her armchair, picked up the TV remote and tuned to one of the sunrise shows. Twenty seconds later she was asleep.

*

The persistent shrilling of her phone woke her at almost eleven o'clock. It was the hospital. Leonie was discharged: could she come to collect her?

'She's discharged?' Grace, although instantly alert, thought she'd misheard. 'So soon? Wasn't she supposed to have a consultation with a psychiatrist?'

'He had a clinic this morning but he reviewed her notes and certified her as fit for discharge.'

'He didn't see her?' All traces of sleep had evaporated. Grace was furious.

'I'm afraid not.' The woman at the other end was not fazed by Grace's tone. 'She's fine, Mrs McGee, or she will be.'

'That suicide attempt wasn't a cry for help. It would have been the real deal, if I hadn't found her. Could you not keep her for one more night? Please? When I saw her at three o'clock this morning she certainly didn't look well enough.'

'This is an acute medical hospital, Mrs McGee, with scarce resources. I suggest you contact Pieta House or the community psychiatric services in your area.'

'But—'

'Mrs McGee,' the woman was clearly losing patience, 'someone is on his way up from A&E to take the bed. Your daughter's fine. And she's been certified as fit for discharge.'

'Is there nothing we can do? Someone I can talk to there? Some manager or other doctor? That psychiatrist?'

'I'm afraid not. Your daughter has been discharged, Mrs McGee— Oh, hi!' Her voice changed. 'Yes – that bed there. I'll be with you in a few seconds.' The woman came back to Grace. 'I have to go, Mrs McGee. I understand how you feel but, please believe me, as far as we're concerned here, Leonie's fine.'

This conversation, Grace thought, had fallen through a hole halfway between *Alice in Wonderland* and *Catch-22*. 'Thank you,' she said, and the line was immediately cut.

She still hadn't rung Maxine.

40

Marcus Brady already loved west Cork. Already loved Beara in particular – the people, their friendliness, lack of insularity, outwards-looking world view and acceptance of outsiders.

Just a day after his and Ben's arrival, the pain of the journey was now a distant memory, leavened by the extraordinary welcome they had received at their hotel in Castletownbere which had turned out to be a fishing port.

There'd been a similar open-arms policy towards visitors in a pub they'd gone to last night on the recommendation of the hotel. MacCarthy's Bar, quaint to say the least, had been buzzing with welcome, extending from the women behind the bar to the clientele. Although he and Ben had thought they were too tired from the journey to have more than one drink, they'd stayed until nearly midnight and had strolled back through the fog to the Beara Coast Hotel, right on the water, discussing their feelings about the place. But senses of humour differ from continent to continent, even country to country – pub landlords learn that quickly on their premises. And although Marcus had been dying to relate the details of a quirky encounter that had tickled him pink on the way down, he hadn't yet revealed it to anyone here: he didn't want to seem patronising.

But he was still chuckling fondly about it next day: 'I still can't stop thinking about that guy with his horse buddies,' he said to Ben, busy with his journal on their bench in MacCarthy's where they'd come again, this time to have lunch. By contrast with the day before, the weather did allow them to see beyond arm's length.

They'd spent the previous night in Cork City, and had driven here yesterday through sea-mist as visually impenetrable as milk. Google Maps had guided them along the type of route that neither of them, city bred, had imagined could still exist in any developed country.

On a relatively straight part of a twisting road, they'd passed the man in question when they believed they'd missed a turning. Marcus had stopped the car and reversed it into a little lay-by in front of a farm gate, on which the man had been resting folded arms to chat with two horses, all three heads close together.

Leaving the engine running, Marcus got out as the man

came to the car to meet him. 'Good morning,' he said. 'Americans? Ye're lost, are ye?'

'We're not sure.' Marcus swivelled to survey the dense grey mass all around them. 'We can't see even the sides of the road. The map says there's a mountain somewhere over there.' He'd pointed into the fog. 'And, yes, we are from the States.'

The man nodded, as though this explained everything. 'Where're ye bound?'

'The Beara Peninsula.'

'Well, the good news is, ye're facing in the right direction. Just keep going. But then,' he backed up, settling himself against the gate, 'we'd need to know *where* on Beara ye want to go? And, like, *which* Beara? The Cork Beara?' He held out his left hand. 'Or the Kerry Beara?' He indicated right.

'Is there a difference?'

'Dear God in Heaven, you'd want to be careful, now, not to say something like that down there! Cork and Kerry have been deadly rivals since Noah was a boy. They share the peninsula but that's pure geography. Would there be maybe a town ye're headed for?'

'Castletownbere.'

'Cork. Ah, sure that's no problem.' He had given a string of instructions at machine-gun speed.

At the request of Ben, who had been trying to transcribe all of this into his journal, he'd repeated what he'd said slowly and patiently, watching Ben write to make sure he was keeping up. At the end, Marcus shook the man's hand. 'Thank you very much, sir. What's your name?'

'Bartley.'

'Thank you, Bartley – and how did you know we were Americans?'

'Why wouldn't I? Are ye not?'

There was no answer to that so they had thanked him again and crawled on.

From where they'd stopped, it had taken more than two hours at that pace to get to the port and both men had been stressed, not just from fatigue but from what to them had been close shaves with giant container lorries, farm machinery and construction trucks, all of which had loomed without warning towards them out of the thick grey blanket. It had been a huge relief to get to the outskirts of Castletownbere. A relief to have arrived at all.

But today, Marcus thought happily, what a difference! At about nine fifteen, the sun had risen into an almost cloudless blue sky, combining with a stiff breeze to lift the fog. Before they'd come into the pub, they'd walked a little, visited the small library and the pier where, with many of the boats already gone, the trawler fleet was moving from its moorings, one by one, to head for open sea. And now, sitting here in MacCarthy's, he could see that the outside still sparkled with invitation.

He was ordering another beer when his phone pinged twice in succession with messages. 'They're both from Grace,' he said to Ben, his voice warm. 'Looks like they were sent separately, one much earlier this morning, but they're arriving together.'

'What's she saying?' Ben took a slug from his own beer glass, emptied it and added another to his uncle's re-order.

'Hang on.' Marcus was still reading. 'I'll tell you when I've gotten through the second. Quite interesting, actually. It involves you! The first is just advising me on how to widen and even shorten the search for my castle, and the second . . . Well, here, read them for yourself.' He passed the phone to his nephew. 'Tell me what you think.'

In her second message, Grace had apparently recalled reading a newspaper article about a writers' retreat on Beara a few miles from where they were sitting. She couldn't remember the name of the village but the name of the retreat was Anam Cara. Apparently it was intimate, friendly and very professionally run by an American woman.

> May be a good idea to check it out, see if it helps you define the market. I'm sure she could offer you a few tips! Also, don't mention this to Ben if you think I'm speaking out of turn, but he told me what happened with his third novel. Maybe the woman could help get it published here. She's an editor. Hope the mansions are throwing themselves at you! Grace

'What do you think, Ben? Worth following up?'

'Mmm. Maybe.'

So far during this visit to Ireland, even when they were in Dublin, Marcus had found that Ben's normally breezy personality had dimmed a little. Its only spark-up had been when, with his two new writing colleagues, he had come into the Shelbourne Hotel after his no-show at the lunch with Grace. And the more he thought about it, the more he suspected that Ben's non-appearance at the Chez Max might have been deliberate.

Thinking back, he had been quiet during the Westin Atrium lunch too. If Marcus had been a betting man, he'd have put a few dollars on the fact that Ben was avoiding Grace.

He knew, of course, what had happened with Grace's daughter, and how the two episodes had resulted in the women's premature departure from the ship, but it made no sense that the daughter's behaviour could have led to Ben's disassociating himself from the mother, who was clearly blameless. He didn't delve into the 'why' of this right now.

He had made the mistake of mentioning it to Ben shortly after the first lunch in the Westin but his nephew had been evasive and had, in effect, told him politely that it was none of his business. 'I am and will be perfectly civil to Grace as I try to do with everyone. She is a lovely woman and I do like her. I'm just preoccupied with something I'm writing and I don't expect you to understand. Okay?'

'So, shall we have a look at this writers' retreat?' he suggested now in MacCarthy's. 'It's apparently only a few minutes away.'

'You go. It's your thing.'

'I'd hoped it could be yours too. What's the matter with you, Ben?'

'Why is Grace poking her nose into my life?'

'All right, forget that. But you're going to come with me this afternoon to that castle, aren't you? We have to meet the guy there at a quarter to four. That's why we're here, after all, and it'll be too dark if we leave it any later. Although I hear it gets dark in these parts more than twenty minutes later than it does in Dublin. I really want to see the place, so I'll pick you up outside here at three thirty.'

41

At eleven twenty-five that morning, worn out from insufficient sleep, stress and worry, Grace stepped into her car and, using her Bluetooth while she was on her way to collect Leonie from the hospital, she finally rang Maxine and explained why she hadn't been in touch sooner.

At the beginning of the conversation, she could tell that her friend was miffed, but Maxine softened when she heard what had happened. 'Where is she now?'

'She's still in the hospital. I'm on the way up to collect her – I'm wrecked, Max. I don't want to complain to you when your situation is so much worse than mine but, honestly, I'm furious with that hospital and with the system in general.

'It's not even nine hours since I was standing by her bed in the ICU, seeing her lying there, unconscious, tossing and turning. And now she's discharged! I can't believe it. And she didn't even get to see the bloody psychiatrist. He "reviewed her notes" and that was enough. I've been advised to contact Pieta House.'

'The sooner you get her over to Gould Farm, darling, the better!'

'I've been working on it. I've a long list – you know me and lists, Max . . .'

She had barely time to tell her about Harry staying the night and his news concerning Cherry before she was pulling into the hospital car park. 'But that's all me, me, me, Max. I don't know exactly when I'll come to Galway but, on my sacred word of honour, I'll be there as soon as I can.'

She was speaking as she tried to slot her car into a parking space between two humongous SUVs encroaching on the white lines from both sides. 'Hold on, Max, don't hang up . . .'

It was done. She got out, locked the car and carried on talking on the way into the hospital, asking how Maxine was feeling.

Having threaded through the smokers outside, a few with oxygen tubes in their noses, she went through the hospital's entrance and looked around the reception area for Leonie. Her daughter didn't have her phone with her, of course, and had nothing to wear but her lamé dress, last seen as a small golden pile on a chair while the medics were working on her.

Grace couldn't see her at first, but when she did, she had to work hard not to burst into tears.

Her daughter had turned a chair to face a corner where two plate-glass windows intersected. She was practically invisible from where Grace stood. On the floor beside the chair was a large clear plastic bag. The sun was shining on something gold in the bottom. The dress. 'I see her, Max, I've to hang up. I'll ring you again tonight.'

She approached the chair from an oblique angle so she wouldn't startle Leonie, but stood off for a couple of seconds so she could make sure it was her daughter. It was, but as she had never seen her before.

Leonie's dark hair was greasy and stood in clumps. She was wearing a grey hoody far too large for her, and striped cotton pyjama bottoms, the legs rolled up. Her small bare feet were curled under her and a pair of white terry-towelling slippers, big enough for Grace, lay beside the bag.

Grace's first instinct was to rush over, scoop her daughter into her arms and run with her to the car, but Leonie's eyes were closed as though she was sleeping and she was reluctant to wake her, as much for her own sake as her daughter's: she'd had little respite since they had shopped for that damned dress in Arnott's.

She moved away a little but kept an eye on her chair while tapping out Harry's number.

He answered on the second ring. 'Grace? What's happening?'

'Can you talk?'

'Yes. I'm in my car.'

'I need you to come to my house immediately. Leonie's been discharged. I'm taking her home now but I'll drive slowly to give you the opportunity to get there first. I don't want to be alone with her in the house.' She ended the call and turned off her phone. Then she went to her daughter, hunkered down beside the chair and softly called her name.

*

Leonie, subdued, had refused to get into the front passenger seat beside Grace and had climbed into the back. When Grace got to her estate, she swung by her house to check if Harry was there. He wasn't. She continued to the turning circle, drove around it slowly, back past her house and out again onto the main road. She continued to the little row of shops about a kilometre away, then back again.

Three times she did this, always watching her mirror to see if Leonie was reacting to anything. The third time she approached her house, Harry's car was there. He was in the front seat, head resting on the steering wheel.

*

During these delaying tactics, tumblers were clicking in Grace's exhausted brain, and finally fell into place. Although she had skirted around this many times, she was accustomed to 'feeling' Leonie's emotions, disappointments and setbacks as if they were her own. And when she was feeling Leonie's pain and frustration, she wasn't rating her own.

She had long ago accepted that a symptom of her daughter's condition, described as lack of empathy, was not that at all: Leonie simply couldn't recognise other people's feelings. With her, there was no point in complaining, for instance, 'I'm upset by what you've done,' because to her that wouldn't make sense.

Immediately after Harry had left home because their daughter's behaviour worsened, Grace had managed to get her to agree to see an eminent Dublin psychiatrist. The woman said she could make no difference to Leonie's behaviour or offer a definitive diagnosis, but she had taken Grace aside to explain the situation in simple terms: 'You could go up to Leonie and tell her: "Hey, isn't this terrific, Leonie? All our troubles are over. We've won twenty-five million in the Lotto."

'Equally, you could say, "I'm so sad, Leonie. I've been diagnosed with terminal cancer. I'm very upset that I'll die soon and I'll have to leave you."

'Her reaction to both will be much the same. Reason will tell her she *should* be happy with A, and that she *should* feel upset on your behalf about B. She may even make appropriate noises of joy or sorrow but she won't feel those emotions. The "appropriate" reactions will have come from observation of others and learned experience – *This is what people say.* And whatever about winning the Lotto, all she has actually heard in B about your cancer is that you will have to leave her. That could trigger some quite profound reactions.'

Grace and Harry woke their now-sleeping daughter and all three went into the house. Leonie stumbled over the raised threshold, and would have fallen if Harry hadn't caught her and half carried her into the hall. 'Why is she wearing that ridiculous outfit?' he demanded.

'Bring her into the kitchen and stay there with her while I sort out her bed.'

Trying to keep at bay the image of what she'd seen the previous night on that bed, Grace stripped and remade it with clean sheets. To her relief, her daughter offered no resistance when Harry, having helped her upstairs, put her into the bed and pulled up the duvet. 'But she's still wearing those awful clothes,' he said, as the two of them left the room.

'Who'll see her?' *Typical!* Grace thought. *Cavil at the little things, why don't you! Paper over the big ones.*

Downstairs, she made tea for them both: *tea, tea, tea!* In her childhood, tea, for Mrs Kennedy, doyenne of the beloved radio soap *The Kennedys of Castleross*, had been the elixir to cure all ailments and solve all difficulties. 'What are you doing tomorrow, Harry?' she asked, as she handed him his mug.

'Why?'

'I hate it when you answer a question with a question. Are you free tomorrow?'

'Yes.'

'Remember when I did you a favour and you offered to return it? "Anything!" you said?'

'Yes.' He was watching her closely.

'I want to go to Galway to visit Maxine. She's in the hospice there now and although the original prognosis was three to six months, I fully believe that was highly optimistic. Despite what they say, looking at her, I don't think she'll last that long. I don't say this, of course, but I can't leave Leonie in the house on her own, especially after what happened yesterday. I couldn't go through that again.

'I want to leave immediately after the rush-hour tomorrow morning. Will you come and stay with her for the day?' She had been about to add that she'd make a casserole and leave it ready to be reheated, but immediately quashed the thought. 'She doesn't eat breakfast, and if she's here at lunchtime, she usually has cornflakes or Rice Krispies, and a proper meal at around six. Sound okay by you?'

'But what'll I give her for her dinner?'

'You'll be fine, Harry. You'll think of something, I'm sure! Thanks for doing this. Now, if you wouldn't mind excusing me for a few hours? I can't stay upright. I have to go to bed. And thanks, Harry, for tomorrow too.'

As she left the room, she glanced at him over her shoulder, to see a look on his face she could describe only as consternation.

42

The directions Marcus had been given to Anam Cara had been very simple. Just before going down into Eyeries, the retreat's home village with its cute little coloured houses, he turned left at a sign for Allihies, another village on the other side of a mountain.

The retreat, formerly a salmon smokehouse set on a small, tumbling river, was a couple of hundred yards along the road. At first glance, it looked like someone's home. He parked in the driveway, got out, and as he walked towards the front door, it opened. Astonishingly, he was expected. 'Come on in, Marcus,' said the woman standing there. 'I've been watching for you. Your timing is good. My writers are out temporarily, but when they come back I'll have to throw you out!'

'How did you know I was coming? I didn't make an appointment,' he said, having been installed at the kitchen table to eat homemade brown bread with local cheese and to drink what subsequently proved to be very good coffee.

'You're on Beara now.' She smiled. 'That's all that has to be said.' Then she gave in. 'Apparently you were asking around in the hotel and elsewhere. And if you do come to settle here, it's something you'll get used to. It's mostly of great benefit because we all look out for each other. Even blow-ins like me are included – once we've demonstrated that we're community-minded and not about to throw our weight around as the mighty know-alls coming in from outside.'

'You sound as though you love it here.'

'I do. I'd seen this wild, extraordinary landscape in a TV series and came on impulse. I saw the "For Sale" sign almost immediately and had bought this place before I could blink. I guess I was seeking respite and found it. Beara's like that. Something about it blows your mind, if you're a certain kind of person. If you're not, you'll find out sooner rather than later. So here I am, years and years later, very happy with my small but viable business, and doing something I love, maybe adding a bit of value to the world by trying to help the arts. I hear you're interested in setting up something similar on my doorstep.'

'I won't impinge, I promise.' He had detected the worry. 'I'm going to look at the Puxley Manor at Dunboy Castle this afternoon, with the idea that maybe I could make something of it.'

'Nobody told me that!' She laughed. 'That's amazing!'

'I'll be no competition for you. At first glance your business here would be far more intimate, certainly more homely and owner-driven. No contest. I'll be hiring managers.

'Well, lots of luck with that!' She laughed again. 'Many have tried – I hope you have deep pockets!'

'Pockets adequate,' he responded, 'for what I want and more importantly what I need!' He liked her. She was enthusiastic and vivid with a go-for-it attitude. 'But we're not talking just a writers' retreat. I'll need to see the place, but if I can manage what I *think* I want to do with it – I've only seen photos so far – my plan is that my business could lift others in the town and the hinterland. I'm hoping to offer some accommodation, the writers' thing, a dive school, deep-sea fishing, yoga, alternative therapies, art, pottery, music and dance studios. And, if I think it's warranted, a flexible conference centre that could double as a theatre and a wedding venue.'

'Wow! Wouldn't that be something? There's a lot of art practice down here, with individuals like myself involved, but compared to what you're talking about – *Field of Dreams*?' Seeing him look puzzled, she added, 'It's a film. Gave rise to a phrase you've certainly heard: "Build it and they will come."'

'Oh, yeah!' He knew the film because it was about baseball. 'I was nearly first in line to see that in Gary.'

'Indiana? You're the first person I've ever met from Gary, Indiana. It's interesting that you think you could pull all that together in one venue,' she said thoughtfully. 'Sort of a small university of the arts, information and the marine. Hey, there's a good name for you – Dunboy AIM! You think a cinema, too, maybe?' she added. 'People from here travel for miles to see a good film. Or *any* film.'

She came to the door with him as he left, and as she waved him off, 'You asked for a few tips and I don't know how helpful I've been in a practical sense, because the scale you have in mind is so different – so much bigger. But one thing I do know for sure and I thought I should tell you when I heard you were coming. Advise you, maybe. It's all about community on Beara. If you keep that in mind, you'll thrive. Never overlook it, never underrate it, never undermine it. And the best of luck with Dunboy.'

As he thanked her, he was already deciding that, if he could drag her away from her own little business, she'd be the first in line for a job in any he set up.

On his way back to Castletownbere, he felt nervous, unusual for him because, in this instance, he held all the cards. He had planned to look at Dunboy Castle as part of a much bigger search, but nothing else that interested him had come up on Beara so this viewing was far more crucial than he had thought it would be.

If Dunboy looked as though it wasn't viable (he had a good instinct for these things), he knew already he would simply try harder to *make* it viable, and if he couldn't, he would scour every nook and cranny of the Beara Peninsula to find an alternative.

Mad, he thought, but then so was the idea of making a

boutique hotel, *hygge*-style, in Gary, Indiana. And that had worked far better than anyone could have expected.

His was patently a daft way to do business but he was driven by heart and instinct. The business corset, in which profit was more important than anything else, had never attracted him.

They say that seventeen seconds is all it takes for a prospective house-buyer to decide whether or not to purchase. His equivalent was proportionally the same. Twenty-two hours he'd been on Beara and he already knew he was going to do everything possible to stay there, business established or not. He had more than enough money not to lift a business finger for the rest of his life and still leave Ben with more than he would need. Marcus was tired of the way daily life and news bulletins had developed in the USA, but not, he'd discovered, of business per se, which could actually be fun.

This area of Ireland had, in twenty-four hours, already exercised a mystical, almost spiritual pull on whatever was left of his soul. He wasn't in the least surprised that so many artists of all disciplines had come here to make their homes.

It would be very interesting to see how Ben would react to this nascent, insubstantial half-plan. His nephew was already mumbling about having to get back to work: his vacation time was running out.

Uncle Marcus could fix that for him, though. Money did talk occasionally in the most unusual of circumstances.

*

By any measure, the Dunboy estate, with its historic castle, was special.

Their guide had shown so many people around the place that he now knew to stand back, not to interfere with the shock-and-awe impact of Puxley Manor at first sight.

Its exterior had been beautifully restored and more or less remained so – and although the interior had once been brought back to a state resembling its former glory, it had now deteriorated so badly it would need a huge amount of work and re-investment, or so the guide had told them even before they'd driven through the entrance, flanked by a pair of crumbling gatehouses.

Yet as they drove towards the manor, now dismally enclosed with security fencing, to Marcus, the whole place pulsed.

After they'd absorbed the exterior of the manor, he and Ben were taken through the grounds to the historic ruins of the original Dunboy Castle, seat of the O'Sullivan clan who, after defeat at the battle of Kinsale in 1601, had gathered up their surviving fighters and families and fled to what they'd hoped was safety, but proved otherwise. Now, on a high, grassy mound at the mouth of Bantry Bay, the castle's walls and fundamental architecture, even its kitchen, could still be traced. The story of its abandonment by its lord, his family and all who had worked in it had been so vividly evoked by their guide that his words hung in the air and stirred something deep in the soul of Marcus Brady, businessman, more accustomed to the buzz and hustle of Chicago.

The name 'Dunboy', the guide said, as Marcus's brain teemed with plans and possibilities, had covered the entire estate, including the nineteenth-century manor, which, at one point, had been considered the most beautiful mansion in Ireland.

'What happened to it that it's left unfinished? The restoration of the manor's walls looks fine from outside,' Marcus asked, when they were walking back from the castle ruins. 'More than fine. It seems intact. The roof is good, those beautiful windows too.'

'What happened?' his guide responded. 'What happened was the collapse of Lehman Brothers. Three days afterwards the contractors gathered up their workers and their equipment and left the site. The American funds had dried up. They're still owed a load of money. Around here, people blame George W. Bush!'

It was dusk and getting cold, but having arrived back outside the manor, Marcus continued to stand at the security fence, gazing up at the house. Their guide had offered to take the two men inside, or as near as he could get to it. 'Are you interested in the apartments?' he asked. 'There are seventy-two of them.' He indicated them, running along the back of the manor proper. 'I can get you into them but maybe not right now. Will you be around tomorrow?'

Marcus didn't answer and, tactfully, the guide moved away a little to give him space as he continued to stand at the ugly fence. The sun had set and he was now watching the rooks, chatting busily as they flocked across the roof of the manor to roost in the trees between it and the castle.

He was thinking of the history as outlined, not just of Chieftain Donal Cam O'Sullivan but of the Puxleys, a Welsh family who had built the place with such style, of the IRA men who had burned it down in 1921, and about Daphne du Maurier, who had based her novel *Hungry Hill* on the house and the family who had lived there.

He was thinking, too, of the American investors who had bought into Dunboy before abandoning it to its interior silence and the rooks.

He'd already rummaged through websites, including social media where visitors had posted how they'd been affected by their visits to Dunboy: 'spooky' was the most commonly used adjective.

Marcus still didn't, couldn't, move. Spooky this building was not. Ruined or restored, it was a magnificent and aristocratic presence in a chieftain's landscape.

Their guide had expressed his hope, even confidence, that the place could rise again, that workers could swarm in once more, but as he stood there, Marcus began to worry that doing what he'd *like* to do with the place was so gargantuan a task that he probably couldn't be the one to open its doors to the world – although, he thought, stranger things do happen.

As the light faded further, three singleton rooks, the final stragglers, crossed silently in single file to get home before dark, and the manor seemed to close in on itself, to resign itself to its abandonment.

Maybe, Marcus thought, having worn its finery to attract him through the sunlight, it felt it had failed. Again.

What had happened to him? Since when had he become so fanciful?

Eventually he turned away and went to join Ben in the car.

43

When she closed the front door behind her next morning, Grace's mood was buoyant. And as she slid behind the wheel of her car, she even felt as though she'd lost several kilos.

That she'd slept well helped, but the real reason for the lift in her spirits was that for the next three hours or so she would be warm, in a comfortable seat, with music, podcasts or news programmes at her fingertips, and a good motorway to take her all the way to her destination. Peace, freedom, her own space. The trinity for which she'd wished during more years than she cared to quantify.

She wasn't planning to stay the night in Galway, but to have a couple of hours with Maxine before heading home.

She'd brought her lists and a digital voice recorder, should she think of something to add to her agenda while she was driving.

For instance, as she passed through the village and headed towards the motorway, it occurred to her that she would have to find out somehow whether Leonie's passport was fully in date and for how long. How easy would it be to open a US bank account and set up standing orders to transfer the regular fees to Gould Farm? How much would she need to set aside for petty cash, emergencies, visits from the family? The lease on nearby accommodation? There was a lot to think about.

Some people get ideas when they're in the shower. Grace had always found that her brain was at its most fertile when she was at the wheel of her car.

One of the truly significant hurdles would be to figure out when and how to broach the subject of Gould Farm with Leonie, but that brought her back to the crucial subject of diagnosis. Before she made even a first call to Gould Farm, it had to be in place, along with a referral. There was work to be done in finding someone who'd furnish both. And as for those financial concerns, would Harry have any US contacts from his banking days?

Then the thought occurred: the Bradys were American. Marcus was a businessman. If he was still around, she could pick his brain.

She flipped a Beach Boys CD into the player on the

dashboard. It was a grey day outside but a person's soul would have to be half dead if the Beach Boys didn't work as a reviver.

She remembered Marcus telling her about his own marriage break-up. It still hurt, he'd said, although he didn't miss his ex. What upset him most was that he hadn't seen any sign that she was unhappy. On the contrary, she was always onside when he considered expanding the business, very happy with their Chicago duplex, which was close to the city's Magnificent Mile and fabulous shops. 'I was full-on with work and plans and travelling up and down to Gary,' he'd said quietly to Grace while sitting at the Shelbourne's Horseshoe Bar during their exchange of alcohol-oiled confidences. 'Doing deals with developers and suppliers, being the big businessman. I guess I just wasn't paying attention and she slipped out through my fingers. She was gone before I knew it.

'I was told that this relationship with the other guy had been a flash in the pan, a means to get away from boring old me and Chicago to the sunshine of Florida and like-minded people. Flash in the pan or not, she didn't come back and, after the initial shock, I felt humiliated, and that has stuck to this day.' He'd grimaced. 'For nearly a year, I'd probably have taken her back if she'd asked.'

'Would you still?'

'No. Water under the bridge now. Sorry, sorry, Grace.' He'd put both hands over his mouth. 'Don't know where all that came from. You must forgive me, please. Men and their miseries, eh?' He'd smiled wryly. 'You're a good listener.'

She'd smiled back, then looked at her watch. 'I've very much enjoyed the afternoon, Marcus, the meal, the couple of drinks here, your company too. It's a pity Ben missed the lunch but he's probably having far more fun with people his own age.'

'It was very rude of him. But, hey, silver lining and all that! It allowed you and me to get to know each other a bit better. Ben and I have been strangers in this town and now I, for one, feel we're not. Thank you for your company,' he'd added, shrugging on his jacket. 'We could go back and forth like this all day! Come on.' He helped her off her seat and into her own coat.

As they walked into the lobby, he stopped dead. 'What the— Would you look who's coming in through the doors with two others? I'll kill him!'

'Of course you won't. He's lovely, and he's yours!' Had it been her guilty conscience – or had he then given her a rather strange look?

In her car, the Beach Boys clicked off and, except for the considerable tyre noise emanating from the road surface, she enjoyed the silence. She saw she was coming up to the services area at Enfield and, checking the petrol gauge, decided to call in for fuel and a takeaway black coffee.

The motorways had been of huge benefit to Ireland but driving on them for hours was problematic if you were tired to begin with. She'd been on this one for just an hour and, despite the music, in the last few minutes her eyelids had grown heavy.

It was still only eleven in the morning but, as usual, the service area was hopping. Already some customers were having lunch, hamburgers and battered fish being the most popular choices, augmented with heaps of chips. The smell was irresistible.

Grace rarely ate chips but these, freshly made, glistened alluringly as the cook tipped them into a stainless-steel container.

While queuing at the coffee counter, she'd remembered it was her day for the *Irish Independent,* and had taken a copy from a stand nearby. Carrying her coffee and the paper, she moved along the counter to order the chips. She was out for the day. Might as well make the most of it. Maxine wouldn't be expecting her to arrive much before half past one.

Simple pleasures, she told herself, a few moments later, the salty, vinegary aroma of hot chips tickling her nostrils as she walked across to a window table. Black coffee, chips and a crossword. What else would you want?

Extra salt.

She got some, poured a little pyramid on to a napkin beside her plate, folded the newspaper so the crossword was uppermost, and sat down, dipping her first chip into the pyramid. She solved 1 Across at the first try. She was feeling as privileged as the queen of England.

*

She'd turned off her phone in the service area and, back in

the car, turned it on again to see there'd been a missed call from Harry. He'd left a voice message.

She hesitated. Selfishly, she did *not* want to become embroiled in another crisis with Leonie. Today she didn't even want to hear about one.

She turned off the phone and drove towards the exit, but just before the roundabout, she changed her mind, drove around it and parked again. She couldn't make decisions like that without considering Leonie.

'I've just heard there's been a crash on the Athlone bypass,' the message said. 'You might be as well going through the town. All fine here. Drive safely.'

Good grief! she thought. That call had had nothing to do with a crash on the Athlone bypass. It was Harry not knowing what to do with himself.

Or, more worryingly, letting her know what a good husband he could be, minding their child while at the same time caring for his ex-wife, advising her on how to avoid the wolves who haunted the awfully treacherous road to Galway.

She turned off the phone again and entered the motorway, not knowing whether she was sad or amused.

*

Maxine was delighted to see Grace. She was sitting in an armchair beside her bed and attempted to get up to give her a hug, but one of her legs gave way and she fell sideways, colliding with her bed. She would have slid to the floor if

Grace hadn't managed to catch her, gently placing her back in the chair.

Maxine was dreadfully embarrassed. 'I don't know what happened there. That was the first time since I got here. I'm not really that bad, honest, Grace!'

'Of course you're not, darling,' but in handling her, Grace had been quite upset to feel how bony she was. When at school, while others quickly acclimatised to the cool, damp climate of north Mayo, Maxine had always felt the cold. Even in summer she'd worn a sweater, which had disguised her thin frame. But this was different. Those bones, close to the surface, had been fragile.

But the hospice room was toasty, and all she had on today was a pretty cambric nightgown with white lace across the bodice, under an angora shrug. 'No harm done,' Grace said, as they settled themselves. 'You look well.'

'Liar! Nice try, lady, but I know what I look like and "well" it's not. You know how they say you can lose the will to live? That hasn't happened to me but the will to live has lost me today!' She tried to laugh, but couldn't and winced in pain, reactively clutching her diaphragm. 'Could you find a little red bell somewhere around here, please, Grace? It's never to hand when you need it!'

Grace found it under the bed and gave it to her. Maxine pressed the button. 'Time for the dope!'

'You're in pain?'

'Nothing too bad. They're generous here with the painkillers and I'm not bad enough yet for morphine. Can't wait! Everyone tells me you feel like you're floating happily on fluffy clouds.' Privately, Grace worried. Three to six months? The signs were not auspicious.

'Good afternoon, lovely Maxine!' A nurse came in, wheeling a blood-pressure machine with one hand and carrying a kidney dish, containing pills, in the other. She asked Grace to leave for about five minutes – 'There's a little sitting room just down the corridor, with coffee and tea. Help yourself. We won't be long here, right, Maxine?' She smiled at her patient, then addressed Grace: 'Pretty name, isn't it? I think if I ever have a little girl that's what I'll call her.'

In that sitting room, Grace poured coffee for the sake of something to do, but couldn't stomach it. She moved to the window, which faced onto a large patio, sheltered on all sides by glass awnings. There was nobody about.

The whole place was devoid of the usual hospital sounds, staff chatter, trolleys rolling and rattling, the slamming of heavy doors in the distance. Absent, too, were the smells: of disinfectant, and meat cooked earlier. With its soft colours, the tone offered comfort and calm. It resembled a boutique hotel rather than a medical facility.

Unbidden, an image of her mother's last days rose to haunt her: the small, shrunken body trapped in an open eight-bed ward in a general hospital.

Even well into Grace's adulthood they hadn't got on and Grace truly regretted that but had always felt helpless to remedy the situation.

On the morning her mother died, she had found it exceptionally difficult to stand beside the bed, conscious of the chatter, the swish of buckets and mops up and down the ward as cleaners worked, while she watched her mother's breaths become shallower and shallower, more widely spaced.

A nurse had approached the bed and told her kindly that, instead of standing there, she should take her mother's hand and sit in the chair near her head. 'She'll like that,' the nurse had said. 'It gives them great comfort and helps them on their way. You'll be delighted afterwards that you did it. Here, I'll give you both a bit of privacy.' She pulled the curtains around the bed. 'I'll be just outside if you want to call me.'

Grace tried to obey the well-meant advice. She sat by her mother's head, but could not force her hand to move off her lap. Her mother's, claw-like on the coverlet, had been the one that had placed money on the counter at the hardware shop in exchange for a bamboo cane.

On her thighs, Grace still bore two narrow parallel marks from that beating, pale now and almost insignificant, except to herself. As an inculcated Christian, she had tried very hard to forgive her mother, but had never been able to make the final leap.

That morning, when it was clear that her mother was gone, when the gaps between the breaths had closed, she'd stooped dutifully over the withered face and whispered, 'I forgive you, Mammy.' But nothing happened in her heart: the words had felt flat and meaningless. But as the kind nurse had forecast, as she'd left the hospital that morning, she had been glad she'd done it, but only briefly: the reality was that she'd simply practised the closing ritual expected of a daughter.

But being here in this hospice today, the memory of those clanking buckets loomed again and she wished with positive but redundant intent that her mother had spent her last days here or in its equivalent. Maybe that wish, of no use to her mother, might represent a kind of post-life reconciliation. She turned from the window as she heard the nurse who'd been with Maxine come in to fetch her. 'You found it. Good.'

'How do you think she is?' Grace thought she detected the answer when the nurse hesitated before responding. 'No point in lying,' she'd said. 'It's a very aggressive cancer she has, and she has refused treatment so . . . She trailed off.

'Is there any way of telling how long she has?'

'Only God knows that but in my experience when it comes to the point that she's falling – she told me one of her legs gave way when you came in – that's not a good sign.'

'You mean it's gone to the bones?'

'Oh, Grace – it is Grace, isn't it? – I'm not a doctor and I can't say that one way or the other, even if it was appropriate or allowable for me to comment. She's accepted it, I think. She's certainly not fighting or unhappy, and it's a privilege to be able to make her as comfortable as we can and to see her accept our help. Some people fight to the death, others stay in denial until the very last minute. She's a lovely woman, and if she was my relative, I'd be thinking she has made the right choice.'

Grace went back to Maxine's room, and they spent the rest of their time together chatting quietly. Grace asked after Dieter.

'Good but sad. What can I do except stay positive for him, Grace?' Then Maxine, now a little dreamy but pleasantly so, asked how Leonie was after her ordeal. Grace was able to say truthfully that she didn't know but that she was in the hands of family.

That fired Maxine. 'You mean you're letting Harry get his feet under the table again? *Grace!* How could you?'

Grace laughed. 'No such thing. And I don't reckon that's what he thinks either. He couldn't! But apparently all is not well in the love nest.'

They talked a little about Grace's lists and Gould Farm, how the money for that should be accessed and so on. The tone of the conversation was all so normal that, having been very worried before, Grace now felt, while accepting Maxine wouldn't pull through, her pal might have quite a bit of time left after all. When she was leaving, she promised to visit again within the week. 'Maybe even before that, if Harry can be persuaded to put his feet under the table another day! I know you'll give out to me, Max, but I'm genuinely afraid to leave Leonie alone in the house after what she did.'

'Am I giving out? I am not. I am mild-mannered St Thérèse of Lisieux, the Little Flower!'

As she walked back to the car, Grace was wondering if Maxine had had a point about Harry. What about that phone call? When she sat into the driver's seat she turned on her phone to see if he'd called again. He hadn't. But Marcus Brady had – and hadn't left a message.

She rang him. 'Sorry for missing your call, Marcus. Nice to hear from you. Where are you now?'

'As it happens, I've just arrived back at the Westin in Dublin and wondered if you were around. We might have a coffee or something? There's something I want to discuss with you.'

'That sounds ominous!' She laughed. 'Unfortunately I'm in Galway and only leaving now to drive back.'

'I still have the rental car. Is there anywhere we could meet that would be convenient for you? Some local hotel, maybe. I wouldn't want you to have to drive out of your way or come into Dublin specially. And don't be alarmed, it's not urgent! Just hard to explain on the phone.'

Grace thought quickly. 'I'll have to make a phone call to confirm, but I'll be passing Dublin on the M50 on my way home. I'm sure I can think of somewhere convenient to both of us. I'll text you in the next few minutes. Will Ben be with you?'

'I delivered Ben to Shannon airport this morning. He had to get back. He doesn't have all that many vacation days from his library. But he sends his warmest wishes and said to tell you he's sorry again about not showing up for that lunch date. I'll watch for your text, Grace.'

She was going to ring Harry but decided against it. Instead she texted:

Harry, Max isn't great. I'm still in Galway and probably

won't get back until late this evening. Would you mind staying a little longer, please? Or as long as you can? Thanks, Grace.

There'd been nothing in that text that hadn't been the literal truth. But, for some reason, she felt a tiny bit sleazy.

44

Christmas Eve 2018

Grace was again in her car, this time heading south.

If someone had told her two months ago that on Christmas Eve she'd be leaving Dublin to spend the holiday somewhere other than the city, she'd have laughed like a drain. How? What about Leonie?

To categorise events since the beginning of November as tumultuous would be to understate the case. For years she'd been accustomed to existing on the edge, never knowing from day to day how Leonie would behave. But since that ill-fated (if surprising!) cruise, the waters, not to labour the metaphor, had been rough, not just deep but completely unpredictable as to which direction they would next flow.

The most recent black spot had been Dieter's call early that morning. He had rung to wish her and her family a happy Christmas because, he'd said, Maxine couldn't. In the last three days she had been mostly sleeping and there were times, even when she woke, that she seemed unaware he was there.

'But it's only five days since I was down there, and she was no different from the previous few times I'd seen her!'

'I know,' he said sadly, 'and she was very grateful you took the trouble to come all that way, Grace. She and I are so glad that you buried your differences.'

'I am too, Dieter, truly. She's comfortable? No pain?' The last time she'd seen her pal, Maxine's voice had been significantly weaker and she had nodded off from time to time in mid-sentence, but her mood had been upbeat.

'No pain, definitely,' Dieter replied. 'It was a good decision she made to go into the hospice. I was against it, as you know,' he added, 'but as always she was right.'

She reassured him she'd be back in Galway very soon. 'I hope this Christmas will be peaceful for you both. It will be for her, I'm sure, but for you too, dear Dieter. I'll try ringing her again tomorrow but if she doesn't answer, I'll ring you. Would that be all right? In the meantime, please know that I'm thinking of you both. I won't say "Happy Christmas" but, as I said before, my wish is that it will be as tranquil and as gentle as possible for both of you.'

She'd had mixed feelings as she'd locked up the house this morning, hoping Leonie would behave, afraid Max would go before she could get to Galway again, but as she negotiated her way with thousands of others on to the N7 in the equivalent of a slow-bicycle race, her spirits had lifted.

Leonie had been safely ensconced at her dad's home in Ranelagh since yesterday, and was due to stay there while Cherry and Jasmine were away. The pair weren't due home until 2 January. For Grace, that meant more than a week of freedom.

She detested the annual battle about where Leonie would go for Christmas but because she, Grace, had suffered through those three major episodes in such short order, the two on the cruise and the suicide staging, she had girded herself for the fray this year and had entered it with clear, firm purpose. She was not going to offer a venue for Leonie's Christmas dinner, even if she had to leave Ireland and go abroad, to London or the Canaries. That made her feel mean, even treacherous, but she continued to remind herself of all the advice she'd had about looking after herself too.

Come January, she would no doubt be back in harness.

After the preliminary skirmishes about where Leonie would go, Harry's wife had blinked first – perhaps, Grace speculated, due to a guilty conscience as Cherry had been the one who'd fired the starting gun, setting off all the recent dramas. Or certainly two of them.

Harry had reported that he'd persuaded Cherry that he should, alone, take Leonie to Ranelagh, adding that when she had accepted his proposition, he was 'hopeful' it indicated that the 'break' they had entered at Cherry's request wasn't permanent. 'She'd hardly be offering it, would she, not just Leonie but me being in her house, if it was? This is a sign, wouldn't you say, Grace?'

'I don't know, Harry,' she said, 'and I'm not the one to ask, am I?'

'S'pose not. Sorry. She said it made no difference to her and Jasmine because they'll be away.'

Almost an hour after she had entered the N7, and not yet at Naas, Grace and her fellow travellers had still not cleared a set of monumental roadworks and there was still a distance to go. She was fighting anger now. She had heard chat about the situation on radio news bulletins and traffic-watch services but it was her first experience of it. To keep herself calm she turned on the radio, tuning it to the classical-music channel, Lyric FM, but it was broadcasting an early-music piece from a string quartet. She would have preferred something symphonic, maybe with a lot of brass and drums, something to compensate for the slow pace and the dreary drizzle misting her windscreen.

She turned it off.

Mentally she again reviewed the list concerning Gould Farm. Although little had been achieved, she did have her appointment with the American Embassy on 2 January, a little more than a week away now. She'd found a solicitor whose advice was not to seek an adjournment of Leonie's upcoming court case – for petty shoplifting and resisting arrest – because, he said, as these were Leonie's first ever offences, it was very unlikely that she would be convicted.

And she had telephoned Gould Farm where she spoke

to a woman who'd been very obliging indeed, explaining how to go about securing a medical visa for her daughter. Although cautious about Homeland Security in the present circumstances of the administration, she had assured Grace that nothing was impossible.

She had also said that, all hurdles crossed, they would be happy to take Leonie. Which was the best news of all, but piled the onus for progress on Grace. In the New Year she'd get down to it seriously.

As they all inched along, she thought then about where she was going and, more importantly, why.

After Marcus had called her from the Westin following his return from his first visit to the Beara Peninsula, instead of going straight home from Galway she had left the motorway and driven to the Clayton Hotel close to Dublin airport where they'd arranged to meet. He hadn't needed directions because his hired car had come with fitted satnav.

He'd been waiting for her, just outside the bustling lobby, where people festooned with duty-free were arriving and departing every few seconds, dragging wheelies and backpacks. Many looked as though they'd got out of bed in their pyjamas or T-shirts and hadn't bothered to get dressed, much less had showers, completing their ensembles with sports shoes or flip-flops. With her Aer Lingus heritage, she couldn't help but mourn the era when people had dressed up to fly.

On meeting, she and Marcus had performed the kiss-on-both-cheeks thing. He'd then brought them into the body of the hotel lobby, which was pumping with pop music, but when he asked, a helpful manager gave them sanctuary in a room set up as a library, and refused the five-euro note he had offered her in gratitude. 'No! Thank you, that's not necessary!' She'd hurried off.

Marcus was enchanted. 'If this was the States and I hadn't offered a tip, they'd have been chasing me down to the highway! God, I love Ireland!'

They sat opposite one another and she asked why they were meeting. 'I know you said it wasn't urgent but . . .'

'I'm nervous about putting this to you but I'll ask anyway. I was wondering if you'd come down to Beara sometime soon? There's only one way to say this but I've fallen in love with the place and I want to buy something there. Ben's not interested. He's closed up on me. At heart he's a city kid and I would have thought I was too, but I was wrong.

'I don't know why, but I want to settle down there, certainly for the next few years. I tend not to plan too far in advance. Anyway, Ben will be working at Christmas – that library closes only for the day itself.

'But my point is, Grace, it's hard to house-hunt without back-up, or someone you'd trust to say, "Don't touch that. It would be insane!" I know about buildings and plans and architecture but, for instance, nothing about something called a septic tank. It was explained to me but it still sounds appalling. Apparently a lot of the houses down there don't have town water. The septic-tank thing is just one aspect of stuff I don't know about here – there has to be a lot more I need to learn.'

'I'd love to help you, Marcus! But when?'

This response, from a woman whose habit was to analyse and weigh things up, had been unusually fast. But she had instantly remembered that Leonie would be with her dad for nine days and, having been wrangling with family recently before everyone had accepted Cherry's offer, the prospect of taking time away for a few days without drama or complications sounded almost too good to be true.

Any doubts – how well did she know this man? – could be dealt with later. She smiled. 'It's a great offer, Marcus. Unexpected, but the timing is perfect. I'll be free immediately after Christmas.' She explained the situation with Leonie. Then: 'So you see I won't have to be back until after New Year's Day – so going down after Christmas, that should give us six days, plenty of time. But you have to remember that Ireland is likely to shut down for up to a fortnight over the holidays. We tend to take full advantage of our time off – it's called Irish thinking. So you and I have to organise ourselves before Christmas to have a few places in prospect for when I get down there.'

She was already making mental lists. Grace loved planning a project, but she'd been tied up in Leonie for so long, she had forgone opportunities like this. And now she'd grabbed two! Gould Farm *and* Find a House for Marcus Brady on the Beara Peninsula!

She beamed at him. 'This is terrific, Marcus. I love it!'

'Have you any plans for Christmas yourself, Grace?' he asked.

She had a quick and instinctive answer for that too:

'To watch the telly *all* day. I'm invited to go to my middle daughter's house but I think I'll just stay put, drink wine and eat banana sandwiches!' She'd almost added that she'd had enough of family for a while but managed to restrain herself.

He hesitated and, then, reticently, asked, 'Would you consider coming to Beara *for* Christmas before we start the search? As it happens, I've rented a house down there for the Christmas period. It's a big place and I have it for three weeks while the owners visit family in Vancouver. I certainly don't need something that big and fancy – it's too big for one person. I'll probably hear my own echo. But it was the only house available at such short notice. A bit old-fashioned but very comfortable. It has Wi-Fi and it's right on the sea, with a little jetty. Pity it's not for sale.'

She could already picture the house, its face covered with Virginia creeper, an Irish wolfhound and a Border collie sleeping between the pillars on both sides of the front door. 'It sounds lovely, Marcus. I'd be delighted. Thank you.'

Dear God, she thought . . . *What are you doing? You hardly know this man and now you're going to lock yourself into a big old house with him for Christmas, five hours from home? And what would the family think?* Resolutely, she slapped herself back down. 'Thank you, I'd love to come! I'd be delighted.' She smiled, something of a habit when in the presence of Marcus Brady.

'Thank *you,* Grace, he said quietly. 'I'm delighted too.'

He went on to tell her about Dunboy, and as she watched his face glow with enthusiasm for the place, she decided

347

that her decision to join him had been right on both counts: Christmas and his project. He wasn't someone about whom she needed to be watchful or nervous. He was a nice, decent man, and he obviously had a heart. She'd love to help him. It might be the fun she'd sorely missed in her life for many years.

And here she was now, driving to Beara for Christmas with about a million others and 400 kilometres still to go. But she had cheered up.

She couldn't wait to get there.

*

Nearly five long hours later, her hands fixed to the steering wheel as though with superglue, Grace was approaching the town of Castletownbere. As she came to what was clearly the main street, narrow and with no visible parking spaces, she turned on to the pier. There, in varying degrees of festive dress – bunting, Christmas trees, flashing Santas and reindeer tied to masts – the trawler fleet was tied up for the holiday, vessels large and small snuggling up, like a huge family in one bed.

She knew she'd missed the turning for the house, although he'd said he'd turn on the lights on the gate pillars. What he hadn't anticipated, obviously, was that every set of gates on the whole peninsula had lights in or around it. She got out to stretch her legs and her frozen fingers and rang him.

He was horrified it had taken her so long to get there

but, rather than come and fetch her, he told her that, as she wasn't far away, maybe only three miles, she should turn around and drive back the way she'd come. He'd be out on the road wearing a hi-vis jacket and waving a large torch: she couldn't miss him.

His plan worked and, greetings and car-emptying over, they were soon in the house. All of the windows were ablaze with candles, apparently a Beara Christmas Eve tradition, but other than that there wasn't anything particularly Christmassy on show.

'You brought a tree!' he exclaimed.

'I'm glad I did now. The candles idea is lovely but you'd have to have a tree. It's only a little one. I was sure you'd have something twenty feet tall that was cut down in your honour with a silver axe from some primeval forest! Meantime, I'm willing to bet that word has already spread like wildfire that there's a rich American in town looking at property!'

'People are being very helpful.'

'I'll bet they are.'

'Let's leave all this stuff here in the hall, and go into the sitting room. I've lit a fire. The owners very kindly said I could use their log-pile while I was here . . . You must be starving, Grace! It's Christmas Eve' – he chatted happily – 'I didn't book us anywhere for dinner and the pubs are all packed. I did a little recce around the town earlier and I doubt if we'd get food. I could cook you a steak? I'm so used to eating out in the States that my culinary skills are under-developed, but I can cook steaks and chop onions, and I have a nice apple pie that I got from the grocery store in town. They have their own bakery,' he announced proudly, as though he was the shop's proprietor. He really was smitten with this place, she thought.

'We've been invited to Christmas dinner tomorrow by the woman who owns MacCarthys Bar. There are great pubs here and that's one of them. It's like a kind of hub because it's so central, and she takes in waifs and strays tomorrow, apparently. Strangers like me who don't know how to cook.

'Or we could just hang around here, if you'd trust me to cook a turkey. I've never done it but I gathered from the butcher that you just shove it in the oven and wait until it goes dark brown. Here we are.' He opened a heavy oak door, and they were met with a draught of warm air. 'This is the main sitting room, and I think it's lovely. Who needs central heating when you can have this? I feel I'm at Scout camp!'

The fireplace was massive, the biggest Grace had ever seen, except in movies set in Viennese palaces. Its surround, of blackened wood, was probably oak, and the mantelpiece sported a gargoyle on both corners. The grate was at least four feet long and took massive logs: a cross-hatched pile of seven or eight was flaming high into the open chimney, sparking and fizzing onto the stone hearth.

'I do like a good fire.' Marcus, watching for Grace's reaction, had attempted to emulate the fast, singing west Cork accent but he sounded like Donald Duck, and Grace, laughing, threw herself into one of the big armchairs in front of the blaze.

For the first time that day, she relaxed completely. 'This is gorgeous.' She gazed around the room, with its Tiffany table lamps, breakfront mahogany bookcases, chesterfields, pouffes, faded rugs on the parquet floor, the paintings on the walls having been darkened over the years by smoke.

She'd have a good look around in daylight. 'I brought sandwiches,' she said now. 'They're in the hall in a Tupperware box.'

'Whatever that is.' He went out to search and came back with the right container. 'What'll you have?'

'I figured something like this could happen,' she said, 'that I'd have to feed myself! But I can't face going out in a wheeled vehicle any time soon. Maybe never again. The sandwiches will be grand. But I'd love either a cup of tea or a glass of red wine, please, Marcus.'

'Certainly. Just let me attend to the fire, Your Highness.' He picked two logs from a huge open basket on the floor, but before he threw them into the flames, he stood still for a moment and said, with his back to her, 'I'm so glad you're here, Grace.'

'I am too.' She meant it.

After he refreshed the fire and brought in the drinks, wine for both, they sat for a few minutes, happy to stare into the fire's eager, crackling consumption of new provisions. Grace had often heard that an open fire was great company and now she could understand what that meant. 'Let's stay here tomorrow,' she said. 'You be in charge of an all-day fire and I'll do the turkey. You implied you had one?'

'If you insist. I'll open cans and we can have something called marrowfats, and I have Cork spiced beef – you eat that cold. Sorry about this, Grace. You see, at first I had a mother and then a sister, Ben's mother, and then I had chefs and cooks on call, always happy to throw something into a pan or a wok for me.' He stood up and took a package, wrapped in foil, from the mantelpiece. 'In case I forget, here's Ben's gift. There's a card with it.'

'I'll keep it until tomorrow.' Grace took it. 'That's a tradition we have in our family. We never opened the presents until the dinner was done. It was very good of Ben. You must give me his address so I can thank him.'

'Hold off for a while! You don't know what's in there! It mightn't be worth the cost of a stamp. I can tell you authoritatively what it isn't. It's not chocolates because I smelt it, and it's solid. But it doesn't rattle.'

'Now you've spoiled it!'

'I didn't want you to think it was a diamond necklace and get disappointed!' He left the room, closing the door behind him to keep the heat from escaping.

As relaxed now as a rag doll, still holding the package, she was just dozing off when a sudden squall of wind and rain attacked the house, rattling slates and the old sash windows, drawing the flames higher into the chimney breast, and sending raindrops into the fire where they sizzled. She cosied further into the comfort of the armchair, with its frayed chintz upholstery, and couldn't remember when last her entire body had felt so loose-limbed.

Marcus came back bearing a tarnished silver tray with her sandwiches arranged on a plate alongside two further glasses of red wine, a deep ruby by the light of the lamps. 'It's raining,' he announced unnecessarily, as another squall caused a flurry in the fireplace, further rattling the windows and even the door frames, which had loosened a little over their years of service.

Grace yawned. 'I feel like a character in a Dickens story.'

'And I feel great,' he said quietly, not meeting her eyes while he placed the tray on a side table beside her chair. Then he crossed to the basket to put more logs on the fire. 'Stay well back,' he ordered, hunkering down. 'These logs can get vicious. They spit!'

Although he had his back to her and she couldn't see his face, she realised that again she was smiling. She thought, *I could get to love this man.*

Epilogue

It was late afternoon on Christmas Day.

After their Christmas dinner of burned turkey, marrowfat peas, the sprouts Grace had brought with her – neither had thought of potatoes – apple pie, After Eight chocolates and wine, Grace and Marcus were sitting quietly in the drawing room of his rented house beside the sea, both lost in private thought.

It was dark, and again stormy outside, the wind drawing the log fire, roaring, up the chimney. The noise, augmented by the rattling of slates, window frames and even the draught from the door to their backs, served only to make the room feel cosier.

Grace had made her phone calls in late morning – first to

all three of her daughters. Starting from the top, she rang Adeline, to whom her present had been a weekend of her choosing to a (very fancy) spa in County Wicklow. Adeline, already at Jackie's, thanked her (while hoping she could find the time to use the voucher) but, typically, hadn't been able to resist a little dig: 'Look after yourself, now, Mum, don't do anything stupid, OK?'

Jackie, on the other hand, had seemed genuinely pleased that her mother was looking after her own interests and was delighted with her gift, a voucher for a family holiday, for herself, Mick and Tommy, to Lanzarote. 'And Tommy's made you his own present, Mum. It's a crayon picture of you. I'm afraid you look a little bit like a hedgehog but it has lots of colours. We've had it framed and we're keeping it for you! Happy Christmas, we miss you. Stay warm!'

Next was Leonie. Having chatted a bit more to Marcus, Grace had now accepted that the process of getting her into Gould Farm could take months, if not a whole year. As yet her daughter hadn't a clue about what was afoot and Grace wanted to keep it that way. Even so she was a little apprehensive in case she let something slip. Her daughter spent her life on full alert.

But after an aloof start to the call, Leonie had greatly softened when Grace had asked if she'd liked her Christmas present: a pair of beautifully soft leather boots and a matching handbag in the Ralph Lauren range. 'Thanks a million,' she'd said happily, and although Grace had been listening for undertones, she could discern nothing negative. 'I love them, Mum,' she had chattered on. 'I *really*

Deirdre Purcell

love them. I'm wearing the boots. Hope you have a great day, Mum, wherever you are. Happy Christmas! Here's Dad!'

As she waited for her ex to come to the phone, it would have been an understatement to say she'd taken heart from the call to Leonie. Their daughter had used the word 'love' twice and, despite their history, Grace was happy to read that as love between them. So when Harry came on the line to wish her a Happy Christmas, she'd returned the wish with a full heart.

He had refrained from asking her where she was, simply saying, 'I hope you're having a good time, Grace, down the country I presume.'

'Good guess, Harry!' Grace had actually laughed, a rare occurrence when talking to her ex-husband.

She left greetings on text to both Harriet and Jenny. The latter was in the Canaries because she still couldn't bear to be in Dublin during this time – it having been at Christmastime when her daughter died. She left messages for a couple of her neighbours, and her final call had been to Maxine who, once again, seemed to have regained some strength.

Grace had decided that where Maxine was concerned, she, too, would live day by individual day and wouldn't conduct all conversations in the shadows of death. Her pal didn't want that. Grace couldn't deal with it.

They wished each other a happy Christmas and Grace had to hang up quickly for fear of lapsing into her fears. Day to day she'd been on emotional standby for Dieter's call, but she was giving herself a break today. Everything was going to be okay on this one day, she'd decided.

And, so far, it sure was. After their dinner, she and Marcus sat, again without speaking, in front of the fire, cocooned from the outside world, the light from the Tiffany table lamps pooling on white lace table runners, and the fire burnishing the red wine in their glasses.

Marcus got up and, rather than collecting the TV remote as she'd expected, instead slipped a Bing Crosby *Greatest Christmas Hits* CD into a CD player beside the set.

Bing swung immediately into 'White Christmas', and although it didn't reflect the weather outside right now, it didn't feel like a sentimental cliché, not in this house, not with this fire, not with Marcus, who was, Grace now believed, an emotional man despite his businessman's armour and casual chat.

Seeing him return to his chair, she remembered one last thing she had to do that day. With some trepidation, hoping it didn't show, she opened Ben's Christmas present.

'It's a book!' they exclaimed simultaneously.

Beautifully bound in soft white leather, its pages had been gilded at the edges and its title, *Grace in Winter*, had been embossed in silver. There was no author named.

Puzzled, she cracked it open, saw that, while it had been presented as a book, the pages were blank.

Marcus got it before she did. 'It's a journal, Grace. You're supposed to write in it, chronicling your life, your memories, thoughts, observations. Even your hopes and dreams for the future.' From his chair, he was gazing at her with an expression she might have described as 'inscrutable' and she remembered that look from one evening in the Koselig Bar: *like uncle, like nephew...*

That entry would go in no journal: A ship had taken it away and would sail with it for ever.

'But why, Marcus?' she asked now, puzzled. 'Most of my life doesn't bear thinking about, much less commenting on.'

'He obviously thinks it does. And so do I, Grace. So here's a thought. Maybe don't write about what happened in the past? Start from this day on.' He met her gaze and held it.

'I think I'll start from this day on,' she said softly. 'Happy Christmas, Marcus.'

'Happy Christmas, Grace.'

Acknowledgements

This book is dedicated to my brother and sister-in-law, Declan Purcell and Mary Quinn – Declan for being brotherly but also for extricating me from the quick-sands of technology when it seemed all might be lost; Mary because she is a staunch ally and backup in all circumstances. And thanks to both for helping greatly with contiguous information about Gould Farm – along with my great and dear friend and colleague Rose Doyle.

I am grateful to the team at Hachette Ireland for all the customary reasons, not least for sticking with me (see above) when all did seem lost. So thank you so much to publishing MD Breda Purdue, publisher and editor Ciara Considine (without whom there wouldn't be a book), the doughty Joanna Smyth for whom no request is too small or overlooked. To sales manager Ruth Shern and all the great team there.

Deep gratitude to Brian Finnegan who helped hugely, including during his workshop *Free With Words*. The man is a whizz. Thanks also to the workshop participants: Salli Jane Hepworth-Smith, Teresa Carmody O'Shea, Janelle Pennachio, Bill Hughes, Michelle Scowcroft, Maureen Rhoda and Adele Dahlin. Watch out for those names, along with those of the tutors, Brian, above, and Paul McVeigh, author of *The Good Son*. These people fuel souls.

Thanks too to the following who came up trumps with research details: Larry Quinn, who is a mine of information about all things marine and who briefed me about lifeboats. Donal Kelly, who talked to me about Dunboy Castle and Puxley Manor, and his sister Margaret Cronin, who made that crucial introduction, along with Adrienne and Niki MacCarthy of MacCarthy's Bar in Castletownbere. Sue Booth Forbes who briefed me about her writers' retreat at Anam Cara. Professor Brendan Kelly of Tallaght Hospital and Trinity College, Dublin, for checking an aspect of my own psychiatric research; Ita Hannon and Catherine Meighan likewise. Mary Sheehy, the most reliable and generous person on the planet, who knows much about the game of bridge. Anne O'Connor who helped me stay focused, and Trish Gavin for being a friend in all circumstances.

Dara, formerly on the concierge desk of the Westin Hotel, and Peadar Ó Lamhna of the Revenue Commissioners' communications office, both of whom went to a lot of trouble to answer tricky questions, and Valerie Cox, who seems to know the answer to anything you ask!

And there are people who don't realise how much they helped or in what way: social worker Jacqueline Ryan, and my always staunch and faithful group of friends and colleagues, including Patricia Scanlan and Dermot Bolger, along with past colleagues in RTÉ.

Thanks to my family – sons Adrian and Simon Weckler, Adrian's wife, Catherine O'Mahony, and her daughter, Eve. Stepson and stepdaughter, Justin Healy and Zoe Healy-Jensen with their partners, Ciara O'Callaghan and Claus; Poppy and India Carr-Healy.

Niece and nephews Gillian Lake, Paul and John Purcell, Gillian's husband Ian, Paul and John's wives Juliana and Karla; sister in-law Rosemary Connolly, her husband Frank, brothers-in-law Brendan and John Healy with the latter's wife Deirdre; cousins Barbara, Laura, Philip and Stephen with their spouses, Aidan, Trudi and Penny.

And then there's Kevin.

Kevin Healy, my husband, has no idea how much he has helped with all aspects of creating and sustaining this book. If you're reading this, my gratitude for your unstinting support, in ways that only I know, has been immeasurable throughout the past twelve months, and that's still the case now. Thank you from (what's left of!) my heart.